Dust on a Bowl of Roses

ADELE VINCENT

Order this book online at www.trafford.com
or email orders@trafford.com

Most Trafford titles are also available at major online book retailers.

Print information available on the last page.

ISBN: 978-1-4907-6620-1 (sc)
ISBN: 978-1-4907-6622-5 (hc)
ISBN: 978-1-4907-6621-8 (e)

Library of Congress Control Number: 2015916864

Trafford rev. 10/20/2015

www.trafford.com
North America & international
toll-free: 1 888 232 4444 (USA & Canada)
fax: 812 355 4082

PREFACE

The garden of Hestercombe, a few miles outside Taunton in southwest England, was created by the Lutyens/Jekyll partnership in the early twentieth century. In the 1980s, the period in which this novel is set, the property was owned by the Somerset County Council. The house was used as the administrative headquarters of the county fire brigade, but the gardens were open to the public. Today it is an English Heritage site and a popular tourist center. That much is reality; the rest is fiction. Blymton and all the characters and events of this novel are figments of my imagination. Any resemblance to existing people, places, and events is purely coincidental.

ONE

"You haven't been to Hestercombe!"

"Not yet. I—"

"But you must go. It's a Gertrude Jekyll garden, one of her best. You know who Gertrude Jekyll is, of course?"

"Of course. And I—"

"Then go and see Hestercombe, soon. No excuses. It's open to the public."

On the train from London down to Somerset, Julia Dobson recalled this exchange with the elderly distant cousin who had been her hostess for an extended visit to the Chelsea Flower Show. It did seem odd that she had never been to Hestercombe, only a short drive from Flora Cottage.

She knew that it was reckoned one of the finest Edwin Lutyens-Gertrude Jekyll gardens, a marvelous congruence of design and nature set in the Somerset countryside. It was a curious collaboration. Sir Edwin Lutyens was a dapper young architect who, beginning in the 1890s, was commissioned by wealthy Englishmen to create houses and gardens that drew their inspiration from the Tudor period. Many of his most successful creations were renovations of existing houses, and the redesigned gardens were the crowning glory. Gertrude Jekyll, a stout woman of stern appearance, was old enough to be Lutyens's mother. Her role was to provide the flesh for Sir Edwin's architectural skeletons. His graceful terraces and steps, walls, and paths were a framework that she filled with sweeps of harmonious color, making lavish use of the humble flowers of cottage gardens and bringing her artist's eye and gardener's knowledge of plants to the task.

As the train sped toward Somerset that May afternoon, Julia knew that she would go to Hestercombe at the first opportunity. What she did not know was that she would make several visits to Hestercombe in the next few weeks and that she would find a body in the garden.

The first thing that she noticed on arrival at Flora Cottage was the clematis in bloom over the front door. It was a small-flowered variety, delicately colored, a scattering of fragile pink stars across the gray stone wall. *I've never seen it in bloom before*, she realized. *I must not have been home before in May.*

Is "home" the appropriate word? she asked herself as she fumbled for her key. Yet the gray stone cottage was beginning to seem like home. She walked up the short flagstone path with a proprietorial step, casting a disapproving glance at the crumpling red tulips lined up on either side. The white front door with its gleaming brass handle and slit for letters appeared to be welcoming her as resident, not visitor. *After all*, she reflected, *I have learned to put down roots quickly. That was essential in the kind of life we lived. We couldn't let life slip by while we waited for a permanent home.*

She pushed the door open to find four days' worth of post and newspapers on the mat. She put down her suitcase and picked up the post: a bill and an air letter from America addressed to her and several circulars and a catalogue all addressed to her parents. *How long does it take before that stops?* she wondered.

This was the reality of Flora Cottage despite the starry clematis and the welcoming front door. It was still strange to come into this house as her own, not theirs, to hear not their warm greeting but only the ticking of the grandfather clock in the hall and the hum of the refrigerator from the kitchen. *I should get a dog or a cat*, she said to herself half seriously, forcing herself to cope as people expected. "Julia is such a strong person," she had overheard someone say at the memorial service. "She is badly hurt, but she will survive."

I suppose I must be a survivor, she thought. Frank had helped her through the terrible weeks last winter after her parents were killed in a car accident. But there had been no one to play that role when Frank's plane had slammed into an Andean mountainside. Emma had tried, but Emma had to cope with her own grief at the loss of her father. She was also beginning to shape an independent life for herself, embarking on a career in the north of England. It wouldn't have been fair to lean on her. And Emma wouldn't understand that Julia's keenest pain came from the guilt of her own survival, that she should still be alive, still delighting in the daffodils, while Frank would never see another spring.

It would be so easy to give in, to sink down on the stairs and cry, and perhaps she'd feel better afterward if she allowed herself to succumb. But she had acquired self-discipline along with other diplomatic traits. The steel core that others had observed took control, forced her to move on into the kitchen to put the kettle on for tea.

While waiting for the kettle to boil, she went back into the hall to hang up her coat. She paused for a moment in front of the hall mirror, scrutinizing the figure reflected there. The last few months had taken their toll on her face. The fine mesh of wrinkles under her eyes and the gray hairs now sprouting on her dark curly head undoubtedly owed something to her age. You couldn't escape these signs of maturity once you reached the midforties. But the weight she had lost under the strain showed in her face as much as elsewhere on her small frame. The clear brown eyes that stared back at her uncompromisingly were etched with pain. *And yet*, she told herself, *I have not let myself go. I look after myself.*

The whistling kettle recalled her to the kitchen. A few minutes later, Julia was sitting in the small conservatory at the back of the cottage, a tray beside her with teapot and milk jug and a plate of chocolate biscuits, the newspapers and post in a pile at her feet. She sniffed the milk suspiciously, but it was still fresh.

Through the windows of the conservatory, she could see that the blossom had finally fallen from the huge apple tree that dominated the lawn. Two pots of geraniums in the corner provided a splash of color in what was basically a monochrome room defined by the gray stone wall of the cottage, the white painted doors and framework of the conservatory, and the black and white tiled floor. Julia had often chided her parents for not adding more plants. *This could be used as a greenhouse*, she decided, sipping the hot tea. *I shall buy some tomato plants. Dare I try a grape vine?*

It was time to start making some decisions. Everyone had warned her not to move too quickly, not to make hasty decisions. But it was now six months since her parents' fatal car crash, three months since Frank's plane went down. There were practical decisions she could make, small steps, not major moves, things like planting, rearranging, redecorating, anything that reinforced for her that life was going on without necessarily determining her whole future.

She drank a whole cup of tea before facing the letter. It was from Anne Sheldon. Dear Anne, she had been so anxious to help this past winter, even from thousands of miles away. "Do come over and stay with us for a while," she had pleaded over the phone. "It will help you get over the worst." Tempting as it was, Julia had resisted. Not surprisingly, this letter was a renewal of the invitation. But it continued with reminiscences about years gone by. "I still find it incredible that the circle has been broken. Even though we saw each other so rarely, we kept in touch, and I had visions of someday planning a marvelous reunion for the five of us— have you seen Nigel since you've been back in England? Next year, it will be twenty-five years since we went down, and I had thought that if you and Frank had some home leave, then we would come over, and the five of us might have made an occasion of it."

The letter continued with news that Anne's daughter, Diana, and her new husband were about to arrive in London, where Chip would spend the summer doing research. But Julia, having absorbed this bulletin, went back to reread the first part of the letter. Was it twenty-five years since they had left Oxford?

She tried to recapture the memory of those golden years. She knew Anne from the beginning because they had adjoining rooms in college in their first year. Both were reading for a history degree. In their second year, they met Frank and Nigel, friends from childhood who had gone to the same schools and were now together at the same college. Bob Sheldon had just arrived, a Rhodes scholar from Princeton. Anne and Bob and Frank and she quickly paired off. Nigel had a succession of girlfriends, seemingly unable to find one he could commit to. Usually, the current girlfriend would join whatever jaunt they were undertaking, but sometimes Nigel would come along unaccompanied, and one of the delightful aspects of this group friendship was that it didn't matter whether they were five or six.

For two glorious years they studied together, punted on the river together, cycled out to pubs at Witney and Abingdon, sat in each other's rooms, drinking coffee or wine, listening to music, talking, arguing, growing up together. Then suddenly, it was over, and they were scattered across the world—Bob back to America taking Anne with him, Frank off to serve Her Majesty in the Foreign Service with Julia in tow, and Nigel . . .

Yes, she had seen Nigel. Nigel had come to Frank's memorial service. It had been a fleeting exchange, a warm hug, an awkward fumbling for the right words to say, and then he had yielded to the next sympathizer in line. *But of course he didn't know what to say,* Julia thought now. How could he? He never married, never did make that commitment. Whenever she and Frank were back on home leave, they would have dinner with him, and without fail, the question of Nigel's bachelor status would come up.

"No," he would say, "I haven't found her yet. It's hard to ask a woman to be a policeman's wife. I work long hours, and it's sometimes dangerous. She'd have to make sacrifices."

"But look at Julia," Frank would reply. "She abandoned any hope of a career of her own when she married me. There are women who will make sacrifices for a good, loving partnership."

But Nigel would just shake his head and repeat that he hadn't found one. Even in later years, as he rose to the upper ranks at Scotland Yard and his work became less dangerous, even if more time-consuming, he repeated the same arguments. "The man is married to his job" was Frank's conclusion.

Recalling all this now, Julia wondered about her acquiescence in sacrificing her own career prospects for Frank's. She had enjoyed the opportunity to live in many different countries, meeting so many different people, experiencing vicariously Frank's steady acquisition of power and status. But where did this leave her now, a widow, their one child grown and launched, and years of life yawning ahead? She was comfortably provided for, but she couldn't just sit in this pretty cottage and vegetate. Yet who would employ a middle-aged woman with no work experience? And how was she to face all this alone?

The ringing of the phone checked this dangerous descent into self-pity. It was Emma, confirming that her mother was safely home from London. How was the flower show? How was Cousin Jane? What a shame there were tenants in the flat. It would have been so much closer to Chelsea, and she wouldn't have had to put up with Cousin Jane.

"But I only went because Jane had tickets for the flower show and invited me," Julia protested. "She's not really difficult, just a lonely old woman."

Julia knew that she couldn't have gone to the flat anyway, not yet. This country cottage was neutral territory compared with the London flat, her only true home with Frank, the place to which they had returned on home leaves and to which one day they planned to retire. She couldn't face the flat just yet.

The phone call, however, had snapped the self-indulgent reverie provoked by Anne's letter. Julia went back to the conservatory, poured out one last cup of tea, little better than lukewarm by now, and resolutely turned her attention to the newspapers. Reading the local newspaper faithfully each week was helping her learn more about this part of Somerset, which she knew so slightly. Her father had bought the cottage in Blymton on his retirement just five years ago. The family had no prior connection with the village.

It was a comfortable cottage. Like most houses in the village, it was built with local stone and roofed with red tile. The oldest part went back to the sixteenth century, but previous owners had remodeled and modernized it to meet modern standards of comfort without seriously impinging on its charm. The garden was the right size, a small area in front between the cottage and the road and a larger piece at the back, big enough to challenge her horticultural skills yet not so big as to be daunting.

But before she could decide whether to keep the cottage, she must find out more about the area. The village of Blymton was the usual mixture of quaint and modern. It had a focal point where three roads met in the Market Cross, an open stone structure dating to the fourteenth century. Here local farmers once marketed their produce; now it harbored gatherings of boisterous teenagers. The parish church adjacent to the Market Cross also dated from the fourteenth century, and one or two other buildings were equally ancient. But many of the houses and shops, though old, had been modernized beginning in the 1960s, and later there was a frenzy of new development on the fringes of the village. The new houses had been built with local stone so as to blend in as much as possible with the older buildings, but Julia had the impression that the character of the village had changed somehow with this influx of newcomers. She suspected that beneath the picture-postcard prettiness, there lurked a plethora of demons.

Some of this was reflected in the front page of the local paper—a medley of wife batterings, youngsters racing their motorbikes through the village, multicar accidents on the nearby M5. That was the reality. The coziness was only skin-deep. It was like the garden. Surveying it now from the conservatory, she saw only beauty and serenity. But if she went outside and bent down to examine the plants, she would see signs of borers in the iris, aphids sucking the life out of rosebuds, grubs burrowing in the soil.

But, she told herself resolutely, *it's not only in Blymton. And I have to live somewhere.* She continued turning the pages slowly, scanning both news and advertisements. She even ran her eye over the small print announcing births, engagements, marriages, and deaths and there, for the first time, spotted a name that meant something to her: the announcement of the engagement of Hilary Worthington, daughter of Mr. Ernest Worthington, DVM, and the late Mrs. Ernest Worthington, to Brian Dixon, son of Mrs. Myra Dixon and the late Mr. William Dixon.

The Worthingtons were her next-door neighbors. *He was a portly, choleric man, not the vet I would choose if I had a sick cat,* Julia thought, *though I believe his practice is mainly farm animals.* He had a shingle on the gate of his house, but he worked from a surgery at the other end of the village. According to village gossip, his elderly mother, who lived with him and helped him bring up his two teenage children, was a Bible-quoting teetotaler. As old Mrs. Worthington was something of a recluse, Julia had not seen her in the couple of months she had been living in the cottage. Nor had she seen much of the younger child, a sullen boy of about fourteen who was said to be as disagreeable as his father.

But Hilary was different. Hilary would knock at the door to see if Julia needed anything from the shops in the village. Hilary helped her identify some of the plants that began to shoot up in the garden with the advent of spring. She was a very pleasant, open, trusting child—yes, still very much a child, still at school, couldn't be more than seventeen, so why was she getting engaged? And who was Brian Dixon? The name sounded familiar, but Julia couldn't place it. Was this one of those situations where the young people have to get married because there's a baby on the way? Or did Hilary just want to get away from home?

I'll have to ask Mrs. Mudge, she decided. Mrs. Mudge, the cleaning woman she had inherited along with the cottage, was a wonderful source of village news. Every Friday morning, after Mrs. Mudge had finished the upstairs cleaning, the two of them would sit down with a cup of coffee and have a half-hour's chat about the latest local scandal and where the best bargains were. Mrs. Mudge had advised her on where to get the car serviced, who sold the freshest fish, and what was the quickest back lanes route to Taunton. When the washing machine broke down, Mrs. Mudge knew whom to call. Julia sometimes wondered how on earth she would have got along without her.

She turned back to the newspaper. She was amused by a letter to the editor complaining about litter around the Market Cross from Miss Edith

Baxter, a querulous old lady who often spoke testily to the rector about his sermon on the way out of church. Then, among the announcements of forthcoming events—the annual Blymton fete, a bell-ringing peal—was one that caught Julia's eye. A large boxed advertisement proclaimed that on July 8, 9, and 10, the Blymton Players would present *A Midsummer Night's Dream*.

It was Hilary Worthington who had recruited Julia to join the Players. "You'll enjoy it, and it's a good way to meet people," she had urged. The summer play was the group's principal activity. Hilary had a walk-on part as an attendant at the Athenian court. Julia, volunteering to help the woman in charge of costumes, had spent the last few weeks sewing long silky garments for the Athenian ladies. And now the name of Brian Dixon came back to her. She recalled him as a quiet young man who was working on the scenery. She had noticed him talking to Hilary from time to time, and searching her memory, she could now picture them sitting together in the pub to which the troupe usually adjourned after rehearsal. But this togetherness had seemed part of the general group activity, and Julia had not considered it as anything more than such a friendship. Apparently, it had been more, and now they wanted to get married. She resolved to ask Mrs. Mudge about Brian Dixon.

She found one more item of interest in the newspaper: an announcement that on the first Saturday of June, there would be a garden party at Hestercombe in aid of the volunteer fire units to be opened by a local duchess. *That's what I'll do*, she promised herself. Planning little treats for herself was one of her survival techniques, things she had always wanted to do but, as a vagrant Foreign Service wife, never had the opportunity to do. The Chelsea Flower Show had been one such treat. Hestercombe would be the next.

TWO

The Coach and Horses tried to pass itself off as an olde-worlde pub, but despite the fake beamed ceiling, dark wooden benches, and old prints on the walls, it was quite obviously a late twentieth-century establishment. A few regulars haunted the place, but they were, for the most part, gray, unobtrusive types, indistinguishable from the transient customers, company reps who lived restless lives on the road and, in summer, busloads of old-age pensioners on day trips.

"Why did you want to meet in this dump?" Brian Dixon asked his companion as they took their beers to a corner table.

"Convenience" was the reply. "And privacy. We're not likely to meet anyone we know who might want to butt in on us."

"So what's it all about then?"

"I have a proposition to make."

Brian shifted uneasily on the wooden bench. Mike Hatfield seemed a decent bloke, was usually good company for a beer or a football match. But you were never quite sure what he was up to.

"You want to come back to the brigade?" he asked.

Mike laughed.

"Not on your life. Best thing I ever did was to leave the bloody brigade. I tell you, Brian, there's nothing like running your own business, being your own boss. But that's what I wanted to talk about. I could use a partner."

Mike pulled out a pack of cigarettes and offered one to Brian, who shook his head. Mike lit one for himself and, after looking around to make sure no one was within earshot, explained in some detail how well his business was doing. He was a broad-shouldered, barrel-chested man with a shock of dark curly hair. He had always been a natty dresser, and on this occasion, his smooth navy blazer, gray flannel trousers, and striped tie made Brian, in his worn corduroy pants and hand-knitted pullover, feel decidedly shabby. Mike gesticulated as he talked, a gold and diamond ring flashing on his little finger. His voice, deep and confident, exuded success. Two years ago, he had left the Somerset Fire Brigade, where he had worked as a fireman alongside Brian to start his own business selling fire extinguishers. His start-up capital had been a legacy from a great-aunt, or so he said.

"I hadn't thought of her in ages when I suddenly heard she'd died and left me all this money," he had said at the time. "Apparently, she saw me once when I was two and thought I was a sweet little kid. She'd been in a nursing home for years."

It was a plausible story. And Mike had certainly worked long and hard to build up his business. Brian, watching from the sidelines, had been impressed by Mike's success, or at least by the outward manifestations of success—Mike living in a modern flat in a posh section of Taunton, driving a new sports car, always seeming to have plenty of cash in his wallet.

"After all," Mike finished up, "you don't want to spend the rest of your life on brigade wages and living in some crummy digs in the country, still driving that banged-up Ford. What do you do with yourself these days anyway?"

"I've got friends. We go to the pub, all the usual things." Brian was feeling defensive, as he always did around Mike, yet annoyed with himself for reacting this way. "It's not as quiet and dull as you think. For instance, I belong to a very lively amateur dramatics group in Blymton. No, I don't act," he added, noting the look of surprise on Mike's face. "I'm one of what we call the crew. We build scenery, make props. You should join us. It's a good group of blokes. We have a good time while we're doing the work, and then we go over to the pub afterward. It's a better pub than this place too."

"The beer's not bad here. I'll buy you another."

The pub was filling up now. The air was heavy with the smell of beer and cigarette smoke. Brian watched Mike confidently pushing his way through the crowd at the bar and tried to remember what else he knew about Mike. "Poor boy makes good" was how the story usually went. According to one version, his parents had thrown him out when he left school at sixteen. But on another occasion, Mike insisted he left of his own accord. "Got fed up with being told what to do," he had said. "I knew what I wanted to do with my life—get rich. And I didn't want them getting in my way."

At the next table, a solitary drinker of indeterminate age gazed with rheumy eyes into the middle distance and muttered under his breath.

Odd words floated through the hubbub—"Government, bastards, election, bastards." To the other side, a couple of young men were arguing about football pools. They were a scruffy pair, frayed cuffs, greasy hair, nicotine-stained fingers. Brian ran his hand uneasily through his own hair. He was almost pleased to see Mike's cheerful grin as he put the brimming mugs on the table and lit another cigarette.

"So what about my idea? Any interest?"

"I suppose you'd want me to put some money into the business?"

"It would help."

"I do have a bit in the bank, though I doubt if it would be enough. And I'm not sure I could take the risk of leaving a steady job."

"I didn't think you were a chicken."

"I'm not. I'd take the risk for myself. But I may be getting married soon."

"Married!" Mike was genuinely surprised. "Why, for God's sake? Do you have to?"

"No, no, nothing like that. Her name's Hilary Worthington. She's a member of this dramatics group I was talking about. Her father's the vet in Blymton."

"My, we are moving up in the world. A fireman marrying a vet's daughter. She should make you comfortable."

Brian shook his head.

"I'm not so sure about that. He doesn't approve of me. We'll be on our own."

"Now I remember, I saw you with a girl going into a cinema in Taunton a few weeks ago. If that's the one, she's too young for you. She looks like a silly schoolgirl."

"She is still at school, but she's not silly, and she's not too young."

Brian spoke angrily but defensively, and Mike caught the note of uncertainty in his voice.

"Oh, come on, Brian, you can't be serious. Let her grow up a bit more while you strike out and make your mark on the world. If Daddy's upset at his daughter marrying a fireman, he'll come around all right when fireman reappears as a successful businessman."

"Damn it, I'm not a fireman anymore, and Hilary doesn't need to grow up."

"OK, I know you now have a desk job at headquarters, but I bet you can't afford to get married unless your Hilary gets herself a job. So why not wait a while and come in with me? I'm the best there is at marketing the stuff, but I need someone back at the office keeping track of things while I'm away. I really need you."

Brian hesitated. He was already having second thoughts about a hasty marriage, but for some unfathomable reason, he was reluctant to show too much interest in Mike's proposition. He was also stung by Mike's taunts and inclined to respond in kind.

"Don't you have another great-aunt to pull out of the hat?" he asked testily.

Mike slammed his beer mug down on the table.

"What kind of remark is that?"

"Well, the first one died conveniently, didn't she? I just wondered if you had others lurking around somewhere."

"Hell no! And I don't need that kind of smart remark from you. Who do you think you are?"

It was now Brian's turn to slam down his mug.

"You were asking me to be your partner, Mike. That's some way to go about it, insulting my wife-to-be, making nasty comments about my job. Did you think I would just fall gratefully at your feet? Well, think again."

With that, he got up and walked out of the pub. Mike called after him, "Think it over, Brian," but made no attempt to follow. *That would be the drawback with Brian*, he told himself as he drained his beer. Such an impulsive chap. Still, he couldn't do much harm in the office.

Brian didn't even look back. He drove off through the Somerset lanes at a furious pace. He stopped at a Chinese takeaway in the village next to Blymton to get something for supper and bought a can of beer at the off-license next door.

By the time he reached Blymton, he had calmed down. *I shouldn't fly off the handle like that*, he told himself. It was what Hilary called his Napoleon complex, being quick-tempered to make up for his small stature. But Mike always seemed to provoke him that way. He wouldn't be an easy person to work with. Yet it could be an opportunity. He wasn't sure that he wanted to spend the rest of his life working for the county, possibly ending up as another gray-faced patron of The Coach and Horses.

He did have some money in the bank. Saving at least a few pounds every week had been a habit he had acquired early in life. His mother always grumbled about his father's total inability to save. His father had been a typical English working man who, on payday, gave his wife just enough money for the week's housekeeping expenses and considered the rest his "spending money." Much of this disappeared at the pub on Friday night, and the rest was blown at the betting shop on Saturday morning. On those few occasions when he had significant winnings, the family went to the seaside for the weekend.

Then Brian's father sickened suddenly and died, leaving his mother almost destitute. She quickly found a job that paid enough to cover the rent and put food on the table, but when Brian was old enough to work after school, she demanded not only that he pay something toward the household expenses but also that he put at least a token amount in the bank every week. "That's the only way to guarantee that you'll end up better than your dad," she told him. Hilary, hearing this anecdote, had remarked that she might have done better to encourage Brian to get more education. But Brian knew that his mother, barely literate herself, had never placed much value on schooling, and he was quite happy to aim for upward mobility by saving a couple of pounds every week. Over the years he had managed, by frugal living, to accumulate a few hundred pounds.

However, if he and Hilary were to get married they'd need that money to get started in a flat. Why were they rushing to get married? It was her fault. She wouldn't have sex with him, said she was "saving it for marriage." He wasn't sure whether he admired her belief in the virgin bride, so rare these days, or was irritated by her obstinacy. Perhaps both. Anyway, it had made him propose, and she had accepted, and now she was forcing the issue by putting that announcement in the newspaper. He didn't think her father had seen it yet, but eventually he'd find out, and then all hell would break loose.

He parked the car at the curb on Berry Lane, a quiet cul-de-sac off the main road where he had a room in the house of a middle-aged widow. It was one of a row of dingy red brick houses built by the local council in the 1920s. They had not been well-maintained, and their weather-beaten facades and unkempt gardens contrasted sharply with the smartly renovated private houses along the main road. Whatever his prior mood, Brian's spirits always sank when he returned to this street.

As he pushed through the garden gate and walked up the front path, supper in hand, he noticed fingers twitching the lace curtain in the window. Mrs. Beldington was in the hall when he opened the door.

She was a short, stout woman whose face appeared to be permanently encrusted with makeup and whose hands and neck were always festooned with large and ugly costume jewelry.

"Hello, Brian," she said. "Bringing in your supper, are you? You should let me cook something for you instead of spending your money on that muck. Yes, you got a letter today."

Brian picked up the letter from the hall stand and made his escape upstairs as quickly as he could. The last thing he wanted was Mrs. Beldington mothering him. One advantage of marriage would be escaping her clutches.

He glanced uncertainly at the letter as he climbed the stairs. He didn't get many letters. The handwriting looked vaguely familiar. The Wolverhampton postmark was disturbing. Somehow he knew this letter did not bring good news.

He put the box of Chinese food and the can of beer on the table by the window and rummaged for a fork in the table drawer. The room felt chilly, so he switched on the electric fire. It was a small room, shabbily furnished: a single bed with faded blue counterpane, a large chest of drawers and a bulky wardrobe for his clothes, the wooden table and a couple of wooden chairs. If he wanted to be comfortable while he watched the small television perched on the chest of drawers, he propped himself up on the bed. But he didn't do that very often. He spent as little time as possible in these mean surroundings with a nosy landlady watching every move. *Why do I stay here?* he asked himself every time he came back. It was inertia mainly, that and the inbred thrift that discouraged him from looking for more comfortable but more expensive lodgings.

He laid the letter unopened on the table while he slowly forked up the noodles and pork and sipped the beer, putting off the moment when he had to read it. He was sure it wasn't anything concerning his mother. If something had happened to her, he'd hear about it by phone, not by letter. And this was a thick one. It felt as though there was something inside. The handwriting on the envelope looked vaguely familiar. Eventually, apprehension gave way to curiosity, and he slit open the envelope.

He pulled out a small photograph, a snapshot of a little boy, probably about four years old. He seemed to be a happy little fellow, brandishing a toy truck and grinning into the camera. It looked almost like a photo of himself as a small child, except that to his knowledge he had never worn dungarees at such a young age. In his childhood, little boys were expected to have bare knees. Puzzled now, he turned to the letter and looked first at the signature.

"With love from Ruth."

Brian didn't need to read the letter. The photograph told the whole story. The boy who looked so like himself must be his son. Ruth Matthews, the first love of his life, whom he abandoned five years ago because she was pregnant but insisting on aborting the child, hadn't had the abortion after all. He sat staring at the photograph for a long time.

THREE

With a heavy heart, Brian turned to the letter. It was a rambling account of how, after they had parted five years ago at Ruth's insistence, she came to realize that she had made the wrong decision.

"When I found out I was pregnant," she wrote, "you wanted to get married, but I said no. I didn't want to get married under those circumstances. It was all wrong. I didn't want you to wake up one morning angry at being trapped in a marriage. So I said I should have an abortion and we should separate because after that, things could never be the same again. You argued and pleaded, but I wouldn't give in, so in the end you gave me some money for the abortion, and then you disappeared. I didn't mind. I wanted you out of my life completely. And I did at first want an abortion. But when it came down to actually arranging it, I couldn't. It seemed like murder. So I went ahead and had him. I named him Adam."

Adam, Brian repeated. *That's a good name. I'd like to have a son called Adam. But Ruth is right. I did run away. When I realized our relationship was ruined, I packed up and came down to Somerset, and now, until this very minute, I'd put her out of my mind.*

He gazed out of the window where a gray sky promised an early dusk. His mind drifted back to those carefree years when he and Ruth lived life to the full. She had a delightful sense of humor that could lift him out of the black moods that occasionally descended on him. She was a good-looking girl, probably would beat Hilary in any beauty contest. He tried to conjure up her face and found how difficult it is to visualize clearly the features of someone familiar but long absent. But he could see her hair. It was a rich brown color, thick and lustrous. He would run his fingers through it when she lay with her head on his bare chest. They felt themselves to be invulnerable, exempt from the normal rules of life.

How long ago that now seemed. He remembered the desperation that gripped him when it all fell apart. He had vowed he would never fall in love again. *I did learn from the experience*, he told himself. *If Hilary would have sex with me, I'd make sure she wouldn't get pregnant. To think I've had a son the last four years and didn't know it.* He felt a momentary surge of anger. Why had she waited so long to tell him? Had she married someone else?

He turned back to the letter.

"He's a lovely little boy, the one thing that gives life meaning for me. It's not been easy, bringing him up by myself. Mum and Dad wouldn't have anything more to do with me when they knew I was going to have the baby. I've never been out with anyone else. I have to work, and I spend all my spare time with Adam. As he got older, I felt sure I could see you in his face, and I've begun to wonder whether I did the right thing in sending you away. I thought I didn't love you anymore because you got me pregnant, but now I'm not so sure. I think I was just upset. I think really, deep down, I still love you."

Do I still love her, deep down? Brian wondered. He thought not, but the possibility disturbed him. How on earth did she find out where he lived? The last page of the letter provided the answer. She had bumped into his mother while out shopping in Wolverhampton. His mother had said Brian ought to know and given Ruth his address. *I might have guessed,* thought Brian. *Mum's punishing me again. She thinks there's something wrong with a man who's twenty-six and not married. She thinks that when I find out about Adam, I'll rush home and marry Ruth. She doesn't know about Hilary.*

He drained the beer and wished he'd bought more than one can. He'd reached the point where he didn't want to think. It was all too much to take in. Was Ruth looking for money from him to support the child? He glanced through the letter again. No, she didn't specifically mention money, but the question would surely come up. How could he support both a wife and Ruth's child? And if he had to pay Ruth, there would be no possibility of going into partnership with Mike. But perhaps this could also be an opportunity. Perhaps if he told Hilary about Ruth, she would break the engagement, and then he could afford to take the chance with Mike. And if Ruth needed help, perhaps he could marry her, and she could continue to work, and he could still go in with Mike and . . .

The phone rang downstairs. *Damn,* thought Brian, *that's probably Hilary, and the last thing I want to do now is talk to her.* He waited, tensing himself for the moment when Mrs. Beldington would shout up to him. But when a minute or two had passed without that raucous summons, he realized it couldn't be Hilary. *Right*, he thought, *I'll go out for the rest of the evening.*

He put the photo of Adam in his wallet and stuffed Ruth's letter in his pocket. No sense leaving that for snooping Mrs. B. to read. As he went downstairs, she was in the hall, talking furiously into the phone, but he was out of the door before she could stop the flow of gossip to comment on his departure.

He drove to a village several miles away where he was unlikely to run into anyone he knew. He found a pub where a lively impromptu darts game was under way and let the revelry drown his cares. But driving home, his thoughts drifted inexorably to his problems, more to Mike's offer than to the dilemma of his two women. The offer was tempting, and yet Brian wasn't sure he could trust Mike. He didn't believe the story about the aunt dying and leaving him the money to start up. But where did the money come from? And was Mike being honest with him when he said the business was sound and all set to expand. Why didn't he go to a bank for a loan? *He needs to answer a lot more questions before I can make a decision*, Brian concluded.

The wall of Blymton Manor appeared in his headlights, off to the right of the road as he came into the village. He was close to the Manor gates when a dog raced across his headlight beam, followed by a boy in hot pursuit. He braked sharply, narrowly missing the youth.

"What the hell do you think you are doing?"

Brian was shaking as he got out of the car. He could have killed the kid. The boy looked old enough to know better than to chase a dog into the road, especially at night. Screwing up his eyes to adjust to the darkness beyond the car headlights, Brian recognized the boy as Tim Worthington, Hilary's young brother. As the boy stepped forward, his cropped blond head gleamed in the band of light, and his eyes glittered. Other boys were now materializing, creeping out of the Manor drive or scrambling over the wall. In the wood behind the wall, another dog was making a noise, yapping rather than barking as though it were in pain.

"What's going on here? What's the matter with that dog?"

"None of your bloody business." This came from a youth who seemed older than the others and who now advanced to where Tim was standing. "Why did you let it get away?" he snapped at Tim.

Tim shrugged his shoulders.

"We've still got the other one."

Brian noticed for the first time that Tim was carrying a long whip.

"You ought to be at home now in bed." His anger was rising. He didn't know what these young punks were up to, but he knew it was something bad. And he felt responsible somehow, given Hilary's brother's involvement, though he didn't know what he should do about it. From his slight acquaintance, Tim Worthington was an unpleasant character. Hilary seemed afraid of him, though, with a sisterly solicitude, she would rush to his defense whenever Brian ventured to criticize him.

Tim appeared to be totally fearless. He laughed now at Brian's admonition and cracked his whip. The other youth taunted Brian.

"Why aren't you in bed—with Hilary Worthington?"

The remark offended Brian, but it had an electrifying effect on Tim.

"Leave my sister out of this!" he screamed. "As for you," turning to Brian, "you leave my sister alone—and I mean leave her alone, get out of her life, or else . . . !"

Brian was tempted to box the youth's ears, but the whip and the menacing manner of the other youngsters, now drawing closer, suggested that it might be wiser to withdraw. He leapt into the car and accelerated down the road.

The encounter had disturbed him. He accepted the old cliché about boys being boys. He had perpetrated a few pranks in his own adolescence. But Tim and his cohort seemed to go beyond mere mischief-making. Except for Hilary, the Worthington family were a rum lot. Did he want to be connected with a family that included a vicious son, a rampaging father, and a dour grandmother?

It was almost midnight when he reached home, still shaking slightly. He opened and closed the front door as quietly as he could, hoping that Mrs. B. would be fast asleep, but she appeared in dressing-gown and curlers, watching him suspiciously as he climbed the stairs.

"Your girlfriend phoned you," she said accusingly. "About nine o'clock. Thought you ought to be in. Wanted you to ring if you were home by ten."

Brian retreated to his room without a word. He was glad he had missed Hilary. He had other things to worry about. And he wanted to remind himself of something.

From the bottom of his wardrobe, he pulled a shoe box from under a couple of empty haversacks. Inside was a collection of odds and ends, and on top of them lay a revolver, a gun that his father had kept as a World

War II souvenir. Brian slid the revolver into the table drawer. *I should clean that up and see if it still works*, he thought as he turned his attention to the papers.

He quickly found what he was looking for—a couple of newspaper clippings, yellowing now and crumpled at the edges. He read them through carefully and pulled out his pen to underline some of the paragraphs. *I don't know*, he said to himself. *I just don't know.*

He pushed the clippings aside and examined the other contents of the box, mostly souvenirs of his life with Ruth, snapshots that recalled happy memories, cards she had sent him when they were apart.

One photo evoked a particularly poignant memory. It was just after he had bought a car, a castoff from his employer who gave him a break on the price. He took Ruth out for the day one balmy Sunday in October. They drove over to Ludlow Castle, where they wandered hand in hand among the ruins. Ruth posed for the photograph against the castle wall, warmed by the afternoon sun. She had a quizzical expression on her face, the same look she turned on him later that afternoon when they were sitting in the garden of a village pub and she suddenly asked, "Do you suppose we will ever get married?"

"Why, have you got someone in mind?" Brian parried, unwilling to face the hint. The sunlight shone through the leaves above her head, their red and gold tints reflected on her face. *She's the one when I'm ready*, he thought, *but I'm not ready for marriage yet. Not yet.*

"Don't tease me. You know what I mean. Us, to each other?"

Brian laughed nervously, still trying to keep the conversation from becoming serious. "Oh, I don't know, it would probably spoil everything. You may not love me anymore a few years from now."

She didn't answer, and the topic lapsed as the barmaid came out with their food. It was a month or so later that Ruth told him she was pregnant.

After a while, Brian put the mementos back in the box and added Ruth's letter to the collection. Then he buried the box at the bottom of the wardrobe, undressed, turned out the light, and got into bed. For another hour, he lay there staring into the night and thinking.

FOUR

Mrs. Mudge proved as reliable as ever on the subject of Brian Dixon. Her thin face glistened with excitement as she indulged in her favorite pastime of gossip. She was a lean, muscular woman who did the cleaning with gusto and a surprising competence and who absorbed trivial and useful information with equal enthusiasm. Accordingly, she was able to tell Julia where the young Dixon worked, where he lodged, and how long he had been in Blymton. Village gossip seemed to have been taken by surprise with the engagement announcement, and opinion was divided on the prospects for a successful marriage.

"There's those who say that Hilary Worthington is a lot smarter than he is and that sooner or later she'll find that out and walk out on him," said Mrs. Mudge as she sat with her elbows on the kitchen table, her hands wrapped round a mug of coffee. "And then there's those who say that what Brian Dixon needs is someone smart like Hilary Worthington to whip him into shape, and then he'll surprise us all and be something. I'm sure I don't know. Mrs. Beldington, that's his landlady, says he's off to the pub every night."

"I still don't understand why Hilary would want to get married, at least so soon. She's awfully young, isn't she?"

Mrs. Mudge sniffed and patted her hair. "I don't know about that. I was only seventeen when Mr. Mudge and I got married, and we've done all right. It's making it legal, not like some of these young people today. Our Jack lived with his girlfriend for a year before they got married. His dad was very angry, but Jack didn't pay any attention, just did what he wanted. They only got married in the end because she was having a baby."

"Is that why Hilary's getting married, do you suppose?" Julia felt a little ashamed to be gossiping like this, but that wasn't a question she wanted to ask Hilary and it could be helpful to know the facts. For once, Mrs. Mudge had no reliable information.

"Some people hint at that, but I don't know for sure. I expect she wants to get away from that father of hers. He's a real tyrant, he is. As for that old woman . . ." Mrs. Mudge was for once at a loss for words to convey her opinion of Mrs. Worthington. Her mouth pursed in distaste. She pushed herself up from the table and wiped her hands on her large denim apron as if to rid herself of the Worthington family. "Well, if you want me to clean the silver today, I'd better get back to work."

Julia wondered how Dr. Worthington had reacted to his daughter's engagement. She found out the following morning, during an unexpected encounter as she was working in the front garden.

It was a mild May morning. The sky was cloudy, but it didn't feel like rain. A slight breeze ruffled the branches of the large horse chestnut tree across the street, now heavy with stately white blossoms. It was amazing how fast the weeds grew in the spring. Julia had been away in London only four days, and yet flower beds she had weeded before going away now sprouted grass and groundsel again.

It was a small garden bisected by the flagstone path to the front door. On either side of the path was a narrow flower bed, bare now that Julia had ruthlessly dug up the faded tulips. The garden was enclosed by low stone walls, at the foot of which nestled delicate yellow columbines, an iris or two, bleeding hearts, and many young green plants, several of them unfamiliar to Julia. Small squares of lawn were sandwiched in between the skimpy flower beds and the path, and a tiny circular rose bed sat in the middle of each patch of lawn.

The spring bulbs had been a surprise and a delight. The early ones were over when she first took up residence at the cottage, but daffodils were nodding in the March winds under the shrubs behind the house. *Perhaps I should grow wallflowers here next year,* she thought, leaning over to pull up yet another clump of wayward grass. The prospect of velvety yellow and orange wallflowers every spring was among the things she had most missed in her years abroad. Father had sometimes planted clumps of them around the back lawn. But neither he nor mother had done much with the garden. They were too busy with golf, bridge, and the other social entertainments that affluent retired couples pursue to fill up their lives.

That's all right, Julia reassured herself. *I can now enjoy remaking the garden. Perhaps I should attempt a Lutyens-Jekyll treatment, dig up the lawns and pave this whole front area with flagstone, with drifts of lavender and aromatic thymes here and there. If only Frank were here to share this . . .*

She jabbed at the black stony soil with her hand fork and was wondering how to provide more humus when Dr. Worthington came out of his house and began to walk down the street. Julia hailed him as he passed the gate, and somewhat to her surprise, he stopped. He wore a rough tweed jacket that years ago had adjusted itself to the excess of flesh where his waist should be. His skin had been coarsened by age and the weather, but Julia could see that he must have been a handsome man in his youth. Even now his hair had receded just enough and was flecked with just the right amount of gray to give him an air of distinction. There was authority in his face, and yet Julia sensed also a lurking insecurity. She was sure she would not like to cross him.

"Nice day for working in the garden," he remarked.

"Yes, I enjoy gardening," Julia replied. "I'm beginning to make plans for changing it a bit, though I expect I'll wait until everything has bloomed and I can see exactly what's here."

Dr. Worthington grunted and scratched his nose with his walking stick.

"I've been meaning to ask you, but I didn't want to bother you before." He paused, shuffling his feet and looking as though he wasn't sure he wanted to ask her now. Julia suspected he probably didn't enjoy dealing with people and tried to put him at his ease.

"That's all right. What can I do for you?"

It turned out to be the old apple tree in the back garden, which had been heavy with blossom this year. A couple of branches were hanging over the wall into the Worthingtons' garden, and Dr. Worthington didn't welcome the free apples they presented to him.

"They attract wasps, and then they fall off and rot in the grass, and it's a mess when I mow the lawn," he explained. "Your father had agreed to cut them off when he pruned the tree this spring, but"—he coughed, embarrassed again—"it's getting a bit late for pruning now," he added uncomfortably.

"But I don't suppose it would hurt to trim it back in that one part. It's a mature tree. Of course I'd be glad to do it. I may need some help. Do you think that your son . . . ?"

"Yes, yes. Tim can do it. I just needed your permission. Thank you very much. I'm much obliged."

"Not at all. And by the way, congratulations on your daughter's engagement."

The words came out before she realized what she was saying. The effect on Dr. Worthington was electric. His face turned puce, his eyeballs bulged alarmingly, his jowl trembled, and for one startled moment, Julia thought he was actually going to foam at the mouth.

"She is not engaged!" he shouted, banging his walking stick on the gate to emphasize each word. "She is not going to marry that man. I'll kill him first!"

With that, he turned on his heel and marched on down the street, his anger still visible in his shaking shoulders and brandished stick.

Julia watched him go with some concern. If his response to a neighbor could be so violent, what had he said to Hilary when he first heard the news? A reawakening maternal instinct told her that the girl must need someone to talk to, someone other than an angry father or a grandmother who was likely to be unsympathetic. Perhaps this was an occasion when she could be useful.

She brushed the dirt off her hands and went over to the Worthingtons' house. It was larger than Flora Cottage, though built of the same gray stone. The heavy oak door was unpainted. The mullioned windows arched to a point at the top, giving the house an ecclesiastical appearance. The severity of the gaunt, unadorned facade was reinforced by a front garden bare of flowers or shrubs. Two slim pointed yews at the gate and a matching pair flanking the door completed the funereal effect.

A sulky young teenager opened the door in answer to Julia's knock. He wore very tight faded blue jeans and a heavy black leather jacket. His blond hair was close-cropped. Behind him, the hall stretched dark and cold.

"You must be Tim," said Julia, determined to be bright and cheery amid all this gloom. "I don't think we have actually been introduced, although I have seen you now and again. I'm Julia Dobson from next door."

"Hi," said Tim, the expression on his face registering no recognition or interest.

"Your father and I were just talking about my apple tree at the back that hangs over the wall into your garden. I agreed that the overhanging limbs should be cut off, but I don't feel up to doing it myself. Your father said you might be able to do it for me."

"I can't do it now. I was just going out. Perhaps tomorrow."

"That's wonderful. Why don't you have a go right after lunch? If you think it would be better to do it from my side of the wall, don't hesitate to come round. Thank you very much. Oh," she added, hoping it would sound like an afterthought and not the purpose of her call, "is Hilary in?"

"No, she's at work."

"I didn't realize she was working," said Julia, trying not to sound too surprised. "I thought she was still at school. Where does she work?"

"It's a Saturday job. At the fire brigade headquarters."

"At Hestercombe?" Now she could not conceal the surprise.

"In the garden. She weeds and stuff. Just Saturdays."

Tim was getting fidgety. Either he was eager to go wherever he was going or he found prolonged conversation with adults exhausting. Julia decided it was both. She thanked him and took her leave.

The decision to go to Hestercombe at once was immediate. She felt impelled to talk to Hilary as soon as possible. And there was another good reason, if she wanted one, to go there now. Anne's daughter Diana had phoned the previous evening to ask if she and Chip might come for a visit the following weekend. That would coincide with the Hestercombe garden party, and though she thought it might be fun to take them to that event, Julia preferred to have her first visit to Hestercombe be a quieter occasion when she could observe the garden in relative peace.

It took her some time to find the house and garden hidden in a tangle of lanes a few miles outside Taunton, but after stopping a couple of times to ask directions, she finally found the gates of Hestercombe. She turned her back on the house, stepping onto the great terrace along the south side from where there was a splendid view over the Somerset countryside.

Nothing she had seen in photographs prepared her for this moment. The clouds of the morning were now breaking up and patches of sunlight were illuminating the broad meadows and scattered trees of Taunton Vale. The low rise of the Blackdown Hills shimmered on the horizon. Black and white cows grazed contentedly in a meadow beyond the garden. At her feet, below the stone balustrade, was a second, narrower terrace; and below that lay the Great Plat, a large square divided diagonally by wide swaths of finely trimmed grass, making four triangular flower beds each divided again by paths of pink-gray stone. She was struck by the simplicity of the design, the cool formality of the stone softened by grass and plants and contrasting with the gentle contours of the landscape beyond.

At the far side of the Plat stretched a stone pergola, separating the formal garden from the meadowland below. The pillars of the pergola, covered with climbing plants, echoed the few surviving elm trees rising from the hedgerows of the vale. The flower beds had yet to reach their full summer prime but still shone with the fresh green of spring. Blowsy peonies nodded in the slight breeze, and the first roses were coming out, little flecks of pink among the green.

Julia longed to go down into the Plat and begin a closer examination of the planting. But knowing that her first priority should be to find Hilary and seeing no one except an elderly couple strolling through the pergola, she turned to explore the other main section of the garden that went off at an angle to her left.

From the terrace she went through a gateway to The Rotunda, a stone-walled circular enclosure protecting a lily pool; and from the opposite side, a magnificent flight of broad shallow steps led her down to the Orangery terrace. There she found Hilary, sitting with her back against the sun-warmed wall of the Orangery, eating a sandwich. She seemed genuinely pleased to see Julia.

"Isn't this a lovely garden?"

"It's beautiful. And what a fine place for a picnic."

"I'm not really having a picnic. I was just finishing my lunch. I have a Saturday job here, doing weeding and other odd jobs."

"So that's why you have been so helpful to me in the garden. You're an expert."

"Oh no. But I am learning a lot here. I've always enjoyed flowers but never had much chance to work with them. Father doesn't like them. Brian found this job for me a few weeks ago. He's my boyfriend. He often comes to work on Saturdays—he works up at the house for the county fire brigade—so he drives me here and back."

"That must be very convenient." Julia hesitated a moment and then ventured, "I thought he was rather more than a boyfriend. Didn't I see an engagement announcement in last week's newspaper?"

Hilary blushed. To hide her discomfort, she scrambled to her feet and began gathering up her sandwich papers, pushing them and a lemonade bottle into a voluminous wicker basket. She was a large girl, taller and heavier than Julia. The rolled-up sleeves of her striped shirt revealed strong arms, and her long blonde hair was tied back in a businesslike way. Her features were very English, Julia decided, cheeks still rosy even though the blush was fading, a dimpled chin, and a shy smile. It was the kind of face that was most attractive now and probably into her twenties after which it would mature into a chubby, less appealing one.

"Well, yes," Hilary said eventually. "We are sort of engaged. But I suppose I shouldn't have put the announcement in the paper just yet."

"Your father doesn't seem too pleased about it. I made the mistake of congratulating him when I saw him in the street this morning."

"That would be a mistake! He was furious when he first heard. He never reads the paper, so I thought he wouldn't find out for a while. But of course that dreadful woman in Blundell's told him the very next day."

Julia nodded her head in sympathy. She couldn't remember the woman's name but had seen her behind the newsagent's counter, a gossiping, not-so-young woman who, thinking that she had more than her fair share of frustration and failure in life, tried to spread around as much of it as she could.

"I'm sorry. You don't want to hear all this. And anyway, I should go back to work."

"Is it work that you can do while we continue talking? I would like to hear more. And I suspect it would be good for you to talk."

Hilary brightened immediately.

"I'd love to. I'm weeding the beds in the Dutch garden. Let me see if I can find something for you to sit on."

She took her basket into the Orangery and emerged with a folding metal chair. She led the way up another flight of steps to the Dutch garden. This was a small formal garden of stone paths and flower beds laid out in an intricate pattern. Pink roses were opening up, but the predominant mood was set by the silver-gray foliage of lavender, rosemary, and nepeta. The beds were edged with stachys whose furry leaves were already spilling over onto the paths. *Are they really like lamb's ears*, wondered Julia, remembering the popular name for stachys. *I don't think I've ever been that close to a lamb.*

Hilary, expertly working her small fork around the plants, talked hesitantly at first but gradually opened herself up.

"I'm not desperate to get married. I don't have to, if you know what I mean. But it would be nice to get away from home. Father doesn't have much to say unless he's angry, and then he shouts a lot. Granny thinks the world is going to hell, though I don't know how she knows that when she never goes anywhere, except to chapel on Sundays. Tim was fun when we were children, but now he's just a sulky teenager, all wrapped up in . . . Oh, he's just impossible! Getting to know Brian was one of the nicest things that's happened to me."

"Is Brian ready to get married?" asked Julia, wondering whether the first nice thing to happen to a seventeen-year-old was a sound basis for marriage.

Hilary tucked some loose tendrils of hair behind her ears, stood up, and moved to the next small flower bed before answering. Julia watched her carefully.

"He is and he isn't. He has only a small bedsit at Mrs. Beldington's, and she's a real nosey parker. I'm sure the two of us could manage something better than that. Also"—and here Hilary stuck her head down among the lavender so that Julia couldn't see her face as she spoke—"I've told him I won't go to bed with him unless we're married, and that's another reason for him. Even so," she added hastily, "I'm not sure that he's as thrilled about getting married as I am. He wasn't pleased when he found out I'd put the announcement in the paper, accused me of trying to twist his arm. But he didn't get angry like Father did."

"Why did you put the announcement in the paper?"

"I don't know. I have an unfortunate tendency to do stupid things like that, to act impulsively without thinking of the consequences. I suppose it was to force the issue, get things into the open. I knew Father would be difficult. I just didn't think he'd explode as he did. I thought an early announcement would give him time to get used to it. Brian too. I don't expect we'll actually get married for another year when I leave school."

"But what about university?" asked Julia, deliberately probing. "You seem to be an intelligent girl. Wouldn't you like to get a degree, have a career?"

Hilary hesitated before answering.

"I think I would like it, but I don't know what I'd do—except perhaps horticulture. I love working with plants. They have such uncomplicated lives."

Then a shadow crossed her face. "But Father would never let me do it. He's terribly old-fashioned, doesn't believe in women getting degrees or having careers. He thinks I should already have left school and taken a secretarial job in a nice office, joined the Young Conservatives, and generally made a career of finding the right kind of young man to be my husband. That's what girls are supposed to do."

Hilary jabbed viciously at a clump of stray grass as she spoke. *It's incredible*, thought Julia, *that there are still fathers who think this way twenty years after the youth revolution of the 1960s.* Yet she had an uneasy feeling that Hilary connived at her own misfortune, that rather than stand up to her father, she was seeking the protective arms of a husband.

"Perhaps I could talk to your father sometime."

Hilary looked grateful.

"That would be wonderful. But I warn you, he has an awful temper. He said terrible things to Mrs. Parkinson—that's my biology teacher—when she told him I should think about a real career."

"I think I can handle him," said Julia. "Is that Molly Parkinson who's in the play?"

"Yes, she's Titania. She helped when Father's reaction to the engagement was to insist I give up my outside activities, both the play and this job. She told him I was vital to the play, which isn't true because I have only a walk-on part, but she made him relent."

"And the job? Did he relent on that too?"

"We haven't talked about it since his first ultimatum. I just sneaked out of the house and went to Brian's, and he drove me here."

They talked a little more about the play until Julia, feeling that she'd accomplished her mission, left Hilary and wandered down to the Great Plat.

Hilary watched her walk gracefully down the shallow flight of stairs and disappear beyond the Orangery with a growing sense of admiration. She remembered a remark Brian had made once about an attractive older woman, a phrase that, to Hilary, with her youthful belief that aging must be a disaster, seemed a contradiction in terms. Yet there was no doubt that Julia Dobson, though clearly on the wrong side of forty, was a handsome woman and, despite her bereavements, a woman who seemed to have her life under control.

Hilary had a clear sense of her own inadequacies, not least of which was her inability to assert herself against the stronger wills of the Worthington household, except in such foolish gestures as the public announcement of her engagement. But part of the problem was her own uncertainty of what she wanted out of life. It was beginning to feel as though she was caught up in a rip tide, swept along by events no longer under her own control. *Why must everything be so complicated?* she asked herself as she moved on to the next flower bed in need of weeding.

FIVE

Tim arrived after lunch the next day with a saw and removed the offending branches from the apple tree. He was very competent at the task, working silently, his cropped head glistening in the afternoon sun, undeterred by the breeze that brushed the leaves against his face. Julia tried hard to engage him in conversation but found it hard to produce anything more than monosyllabic answers or shrugs. Only when she touched on Hilary's engagement did she generate any animation.

"Hilary's stupid if she marries that man," he said with disgust.

"What's the matter with him?"

"She can do better than that. He's just a fireman."

"There's nothing wrong with being a fireman," Julia protested. "It's a vital job and often a dangerous one too. Besides, he's now in an administrative position at headquarters, so technically he's no longer a fireman."

"So he sits at a desk and fills out forms. That's not a man's job."

There was no consistency in Tim's argument, but Julia chose to ignore that and instead countered with a defense of Brian as a solid, upright citizen, good husband material, making much of it up since she didn't even know the man but hoping to learn more about Tim from his answers.

"He's just scum!" was Tim's response. "My sister shouldn't be marrying a man like that. Dad should put his foot down and get rid of him. And if he won't, I will!"

Julia was disturbed by the strength of his passion. If Tim talked like that at home, it was no wonder that Hilary was anxious to get away. She watched him as he finished picking up stray twigs and prepared to leave. He had the same strong features as his father. If his expression were friendlier, he could be described as good-looking. Her first assessment of him had been that he was just a surly teenager, but now she wondered if it was more than churlishness. It was easy to imagine this adolescent spite maturing into the rage that Dr. Worthington had manifested.

The subject of Tim came up that evening at the Players rehearsal. Rehearsals were held in the Village Hall, an enormous barnlike structure with a stage at one end. People not actively engaged in rehearsing would sit at the back and chat quietly or drift downstairs to the basement where they could be more lively. In the large basement affectionately known as the Green Room, men were building scenery, and women were working on costumes, while small children helped or hindered both groups. When empty, it was a drab room with dirty cream walls and a low ceiling where cigarette smoke used to hang in the air until the play's director decreed that there would be no more smoking in the Green Room. "This place would be a fire trap with all this paint and flammable material. We daren't risk a fire," he declared. The crew sulked but, for the most part, remembered to go upstairs for their cigarettes. So the scenery was assembled and costumes fabricated without any danger from fire or smoke, and when work stopped, it was all stored in a smaller room at the far end of the basement that could be locked when everyone went home.

Julia did much of her sewing for the costumes at home but often brought it to the Green Room because the company was more congenial than her lonely sitting room. This evening, she also had a specific purpose. She wanted to talk to Molly Parkinson about Hilary. Molly had a major part in the play, her husband Dick was the director, and they had a child with them, a small boy of about three, so she seemed to be in a constant swirl of activity. But eventually, Julia was able to draw her aside and ask her what she thought about Hilary's engagement.

"You probably know more about Brian Dixon than I do," she added.

"Not much. I would expect her to outgrow him in time. Having met her father, I can understand her eagerness to get away from home, but she's not looking at the long-term consequences."

"I've had my own encounters with her father," said Julia. "Her brother too. Hilary seems to be the only normal member of the family."

"Her brother is dangerous. I don't teach him, but I've talked to people who do. He's fascinated by the Nazis, defends Hitler, and says nasty things about Jews and blacks in class discussions. It's a good thing Brian appears to be a full-blooded Anglo-Saxon, or I'd expect real trouble in that quarter. Even so, if I were Hilary, I'd be wary of Tim. I'm told he's unpredictable and can be quite irrational at times."

At this point, Dick Parkinson came up in search of his wife for a quick run-through of the final scene.

"I'm ready," said Molly. "Julia and I were just talking about Tim Worthington."

Dick shook his head. "That young man is a menace."

"But is he any worse than the average teenage boy today?" Julia asked.

"Probably. I'm told he's obsessed with guns."

"He did some tree-pruning for me today and did it very competently," Julia countered.

"Yes, he can be self-disciplined when it suits him. That's what so infuriating. If he'd only get over this Nazi kick, he has the makings of a reasonable man. Now who's going to watch this little rascal while we work? Is Hilary around?"

But Hilary had left. She had sensed all evening that Brian was preoccupied with something and wanted to talk with him in private. With a lover's egotism, she assumed it had to do with their relationship. Once her scenes were over, she prevailed on him to leave, though he went reluctantly. There were too many things on his mind that he wasn't yet ready to share with her.

They went first for a quick beer at The Feathers, across the road from the Village Hall. It was a comfortable pub, small and cozy with warm red carpeting and genuine oak beams across the low ceiling. In winter, a log fire often blazed in a massive open fireplace that on this spring evening was filled with a huge vase of dried flowers. Hilary was always happy here even though she rarely drank anything stronger than cider. Its coziness contrasted so sharply with the cold austerity of her own home and the shabbiness of Brian's room.

"What's the matter, Brian?" Hilary asked as soon as they were settled with their drinks at a corner table.

"Nothing's the matter. Why are you asking?"

"You're distracted. You're bothered about something, but you're not telling me."

Brian shrugged. "Work has been difficult recently, too much to do."

"That's not it. Your mood changed almost overnight. Something happened to change it."

When Brian did not respond, Hilary took a deep breath and ventured the suggestion that it was the engagement notice in the paper that had precipitated his mood swing. "Because if that's what it is, if you're having second thoughts, then we ought to talk about it."

She spoke boldly but awaited Brian's response with some trepidation. She knew she was having her own doubts. The conversation with Julia Dobson had unsettled her. But if the engagement were to be broken, it should be her decision, not Brian's.

Brian was quick to deny any second thoughts but decided that the time had come to tell Hilary about Mike's proposition. There was no way that he was going to say anything about Ruth, let alone Adam, even though Adam's picture was burning a hole in his wallet. But if he told her about the business prospect, that at least should satisfy her curiosity. It would be useful too to know her reaction to Mike's offer. A strong opinion either way might help him in reaching his decision.

Not in the pub, though. This was not a good place for that kind of discussion. He didn't want anyone else to know about it yet. The pub was filling up now as, with the rehearsal drawing to an end, many of the Players wandered across the road for a drink and a chat before dispersing.

"There's something I should tell you about, but not here," he said, draining his glass. "Let's go back to my room. No, it's nothing for you to worry about," he added, noting a look of panic that momentarily flashed across Hilary's face. "It's a business matter."

Nothing was said as they walked arm in arm to the narrow side street where Brian lodged. Mrs. Beldington twitched the lace curtain at the front window as they walked up the path but didn't accost them as they climbed the stairs to Brian's room.

"It's probably no more private here with that woman listening outside the door," said Hilary.

"It's no joke. I'll make some tea."

While Brian went out to the bathroom to fill the kettle with water, Hilary put teabags into a couple of mugs. As Brian came back into the room, she turned to the table drawer for a spoon. But when she opened it, she saw the gun.

"Why have you got a gun?" she asked, her face registering a combination of horror and disbelief.

Brian shut the drawer quickly.

"It's just a souvenir. It was my dad's leftover from the war."

"But why do you keep it? Does it still work?"

"I don't know. I've cleaned it up. It has a couple of bullets in it, but I haven't tried firing it yet."

"Well, don't. I think it's awful. Guns scare me. Why are men so obsessed with them? Tim's even worse. He has a rifle hanging on his bedroom wall. Father gave it to him when he started to take Tim shooting, though Tim treats it as part of his Nazi collection rather than as a gun for sport. I was hoping to get away from guns when I left home. You'd better get rid of it before we get married. Or at least get rid of the bullets."

"Maybe. I expect I'll leave it unloaded after I've tried it out."

"Just keep it somewhere where I can't see it. Now what were you going to tell me?"

Brian explained Mike's offer in barest outline. He didn't mention Mike's name but referred to him merely as "a chap I used to work with." As he talked, he found himself becoming more and more interested in this proposition. The thought of going into business, even on a small scale, was exhilarating. Hilary sensed his enthusiasm.

"It sounds as though you'd like to do it. But why weren't you going to tell me?"

"There are arguments against it. It means putting all my savings into the business, and I was assuming we'd need that money to set us up when we get married—you know, buy some furniture. And I'm not sure how well I'd get along with this chap in a business arrangement."

"We wouldn't need to buy furniture right away. We could get a furnished flat. And I'd be working too. We could wait a few years before we start thinking about children. Or if you wanted, we could delay the wedding for a year or two. I could get a job and save money. I don't think you should refuse the offer just because we're talking about getting married."

"Oh, there's more to it than that. I need to find out more about the business, look at the books, find out why he doesn't go to the bank for a loan if he needs more money. A few hundred from me wouldn't do much for him."

Hilary was preoccupied with her own assessment while she listened to Brian arguing the pros and cons. Perhaps this was the way out of her dilemma. If Brian accepted the offer and they delayed marriage for a few years, she might be able to do some kind of college training. Suddenly and surprisingly cheered by this prospect, she went over and sat at Brian's feet, putting her head on his knees. Brian caressed her hair and was irritated to find himself remembering Ruth's hair, which was glossy and smelled of almonds.

"If you really want to do this and the business details turn out to be all right, then I think you should go ahead and do it. We'll work something out, even if it means waiting."

"There's too much waiting already," said Brian. He lowered himself to the floor, pushing Hilary beneath him. He began to kiss her passionately and ran one hand over her body. Hilary returned his kisses avidly, but as Brian's hand moved more daringly, she pushed him off and jumped to her feet.

"No, Brian. You mustn't. You know I don't want you to do that."

"Why ever not? We're engaged, aren't we? Is this still the way you'd be if we postponed marriage a few years? If so, we might as well call it all off right now."

Hilary didn't know what to say. That was the one flaw in her tidy little plan. Brian would not want to wait so long. Perhaps she should give in. His wandering hand had roused feelings in her that had tempted her to acquiesce. She realized that if he persisted in his attempts to make love to her, she would eventually have to give in. Her body would require it, even if her head told her she should not.

"I'd better go home" was all she said.

"That's a good idea," said Brian brusquely as he got up. "I'll go with you."

Mrs. Beldington peered round her door as they left, but they paid no attention. They walked silently through the village, and at the Worthingtons' front gate, Brian gave Hilary a chaste kiss, said good night, and turned on his heel.

Even before she entered the house, Hilary could hear the rock music coming from Tim's bedroom. She was hoping she could slip up to her room without anyone noticing, but her grandmother appeared before she had reached the stairs. Mrs. Worthington was an impressive woman, tall and more upright than most women her age. Her severe black dress accentuated her bony figure. She was clasping a Bible to her shallow bosom as she confronted her granddaughter. Iron-gray hair pulled tightly back into a bun at the nape of her neck revealed temples throbbing with righteous anger.

"Coming in at this hour, whoring on the Sabbath!" was her greeting.

"Come on, Granny, it isn't even half-past ten."

In response, the old woman brandished her Bible.

"I saw you at the gate. Remember what the Lord said, 'Depart from me, ye that work iniquity.'"

"Oh, Granny!" Hilary was exasperated now and ran upstairs. *Why do all these old women spend their time snooping on us?* she asked herself. *Jealous of youth, I bet that's what it is.* Then she saw Tim standing at the top of the stairs. His skull with its thin covering of hair gleamed in the lamplight of the landing, leaving his face in shadow. Despite the warm spring evening, he was wearing his heavy black leather jacket. On the wall behind him, visible through the open door of his room, was a huge swastika. He held a large whip in his hand.

"I should whip that man! He has no business meddling with my sister. You should stay away from him."

Hilary's irritation turned to anger.

"Get out of my way, Tim Worthington. And stay out of my private life too!"

She pushed him aside and went into her own room, slamming the door behind her. It wasn't just old women who peeped out of windows and listened at doors. Everyone seemed to be persecuting them. She even began to question Julia Dobson's interest in her affairs. It was nice of her to help, but why couldn't she and everyone else just leave her and Brian alone, let them work it out for themselves?

A school textbook lay open on the desk under the window. She still had homework to finish but was not now in the mood for it. It would have to wait until morning. She turned back the alarm clock an extra half hour and quickly got ready for bed. *This can't go on*, she told herself as she lay waiting for the release of sleep. One way or another, it must come to an end.

SIX

"Tomorrow I'll take you to Hestercombe," said Julia, putting the drinks tray down on the little table in the conservatory. The geraniums glowed in a rosy light as the sun lowered itself in the sky beyond the trimmed apple tree.

It was Friday evening. Diana and Chip Walker had arrived about an hour ago. Julia had given them a quick tour of the house and garden and then left them to unpack while she made preparations for dinner. There was plenty of time for a leisurely drink before they sat down to eat. Handing out tall glasses of Pimm's, Julia savored the joy of congenial company that only those who are suddenly and unexpectedly forced to live alone can appreciate.

Diana had her father's coloring, the tawny mane of hair and eyes so light brown they were almost yellow, which made people say Bob was like a big cat. But her features were Anne's. It was like looking at a photograph of Anne of twenty-five years ago that somehow had been given a different coloration. She had the same gentle Southern accent that people at Oxford had found so charming in Bob. Julia had seen Diana only once or twice as a child, when she and Frank had been able to visit America, but the girl had grown into a fine young woman with a sense of style. A crisp yellow shirt and black silk trousers emphasized the trim lines of her body. Unlike Anne, who had always been quiet, even shy, Diana was effusive, enthusing over pictures on the walls, shrubs in the garden, as though she were looking at treasures in one of the stately homes of England rather than the contents of Flora Cottage. Julia suspected that the bluster concealed a certain discomfort at finding herself a guest in the home of someone she hardly knew but who knew her parents well.

Chip was an earnest Midwesterner—from Ohio, he told Julia, making sure she knew that his father was of English stock even though his mother was German. He smiled at her from behind wire-rimmed spectacles in a manner that left Julia uncertain whether he was teasing her.

"What is Hestercombe?" Diana asked, stretching out her long legs as she leaned back in the chair and sipped her drink.

"Hestercombe is an experience. It's one of the most beautiful gardens in England. It's not at its best at the moment. June is a little early. You must come back again in July. But by way of compensation, you'll get a duchess thrown in. There's a garden party at Hestercombe tomorrow afternoon, and the duchess of somewhere or other will be the star attraction. So we can go and drink tea and gaze at Her Excellence, and then we can get down to the real business of the day and wander round the garden. Some of the locals will behave quite outrageously, fussing over her unnecessarily. But I suppose it's a bit of glamor in their otherwise ordinary lives."

"I guess life in a little place like this is rather quiet and dull," said Chip. "Are you going to stay in Blymton?"

"I haven't made up my mind yet," said Julia. "Mind you, it's livelier than you might think. I walk through the village almost every day and everywhere you go, in the shops or stopping to talk to someone on the street, you hear bits of gossip about all sorts of goings on. A couple of days ago, for instance, I was stopped on the street by a young woman with a little boy in tow, a stranger who asked me where Berry Lane was. It's funny, I'm often stopped and asked for directions even when I'm a stranger in the place myself. I don't know why."

"You have a kind face," interposed Chip.

"Thank you. Though I think it may be more likely that I look harmless enough not to threaten anyone. In any event, I gave this young woman directions and thought no more of it until this morning at the post office when I overheard two women gossiping. 'A young woman with a child, it was,' said one. 'Asked if Mr. Dixon was at home. Well, he wasn't, was he, at ten o'clock in the morning. He was at work, and I told her so. She said she'd come back later, but I never saw her again. I told Mr. Dixon, I did, when he came home, and he wasn't half upset. Ran upstairs and slammed his door and then came down a few minutes later and left, and I never saw him again all evening. I don't know what time he came home. But it doesn't look good, does it, a young woman and child inquiring after him.' 'No,' said the other, 'not with him engaged to Hilary Worthington. But then that's young people today. No morals at all, I say.'"

Julia shook her head. She didn't like the sound of it either. Mrs. Mudge this morning had heard the same story, but couldn't add any details. Julia hadn't seen Hilary all week, but this wasn't a piece of information she wanted to share with her.

"So you see, life here can be quite dramatic. In fact, there's more to that story. Hilary Worthington lives next door. The house is a bit Gothic and so are its inhabitants, apart from Hilary. Her father is a local vet, a man who looks like a Colonel Blimp but has a vile temper. Her mother is dead, and the only other woman in the house is her grandmother, her father's mother. By all accounts, the woman is both a puritan and a tyrant who can quote all the bits of the Bible that pertain to hellfire and damnation but knows nothing about joy and love. And Hilary's teenage brother is a skinhead who admires the Nazis and plays awful rock music far too loudly. I can sometimes hear it in the garden."

"It all sounds terrible," agreed Diana. "What's Hilary like? You said she was different."

"Yes, she's very attractive and intelligent with a pleasant personality, totally out of place in that household. And she seems to be desperate to escape. She's just announced her engagement to this Mr. Dixon even though she's still at school, far too young to be getting married. And now there's a strange young woman and child looking for this fiancé, giving rise to all sorts of speculation on the part of his landlady and the other village gossips."

"Wonderful soap opera material," suggested Chip.

"But all this is stuff for you to observe," Diana pointed out. "What exactly do you do apart from walking around the village and shopping— and gardening, of course?"

Ah yes, wondered Julia to herself, *what do I actually do?* But, considering that current dilemma to be too weighty a topic for predinner conversation, she launched into an enthusiastic account of the activities of the Players.

Over dinner—a cassoulet of lamb, sausage, and beans—she permitted the conversation to become more serious, prodding her guests to describe their reaction to life in London. The things they recounted were just what Julia would have predicted. They appreciated the veneer of civility that coated daily encounters but were frustrated by the inefficiencies that Britons accepted with equanimity. They were awed by the history that permeated the fabric of everyday life. They were slightly depressed by the gray damp air that greeted them each morning and often lingered on until dusk.

"But you must know what it's like to take up temporary residence in a foreign city," said Chip as the remains of the cassoulet were replaced with a platter of Camembert and crackers and a bowl of fruit. "You've been doing it for years."

"And every one was different," responded Julia. She poured coffee into tiny gilt-rimmed cups. "I tell you what's even more strange, though, and that's returning to live permanently in England after more than twenty years away. I've been back, of course, every year, and a couple of times we had home postings. And the daily reports from Britain were part of our lives. But I didn't understand how much the country had changed until now. You speak of gentleness, and yet I think we're losing it. I always suspected there was a core of nastiness beneath the British skin, one that we masked successfully by not getting too close to one another, keeping other people at bay with our stiff politeness and our soft voices. But large patches of that cool soft skin have worn away in the last twenty years, and the raw edges are showing through. I see more cruelty and indifference now than I ever did before and more aggressiveness, especially among the young, that makes me fear for the future."

Chip spooned sugar into his coffee and stirred it thoughtfully.

"Could it be that those raw edges were always there but you didn't notice them before?"

"Perhaps," conceded Julia.

"Life seems so much more concentrated, more compressed today," said Chip. "It's not just that television brings the events of thousands of miles away instantly to our attention. It also reports mercilessly on things happening right next door that nobody bothered much about before. And everyone feels obliged to have an opinion about everything."

"It's the decline of morality, public and private," said Diana. "It's happening in America too. I do what I want and if you don't like it, that's too bad. And if you get in my way, I'll punch you."

"We've abolished sin," Chip continued. He was well-launched now. He ran his hands through the long lank hair that was already beginning to recede at the temples. *He will make a good professor*, Julia decided. "No one is held accountable for their behavior anymore. If a teenage girl gets pregnant, it's because she's been exposed to too much sex on television. If a young thug sells dope and shoots anyone who tries to muscle into his territory, it's because there are too many drugs and guns around and not enough jobs, and anyway he was probably abused as a child by a drunken father."

"But do you accept that?" asked Julia. "Don't you believe in Evil Incarnate?"

"You mean that some people are just born bad?"

Julia nodded.

"That's the old controversy about heredity versus environment. I probably come down somewhere in the middle. Most people are a mix of good and bad genes and the environment has some impact on them. So that if our social environment has deteriorated, we could be experiencing a more brutish society. That's particularly true of America where we have much more violence than you do. But the whole Western world is in decline. Spengler was right. Like your flowers out there, Julia, civilization is an organism that flourishes for a while but in the end will die."

"What a grim prospect," Diana said with a shudder.

The conversation continued along these lines for another hour or so, Chip becoming more and more professorial. Julia tried to keep up but gradually subsided and let Chip have the floor. It was wonderful to have guests sitting at her dining room table again. A few sprigs of honeysuckle tucked into the bowl of roses in the center of the table were scenting the air. Candlelight flickered over the pale pink walls and was reflected in the glass-fronted cabinets that still housed her mother's best china and crystal. *This visit is good for me*, she decided. *I must start having dinner parties again.*

She went to bed feeling more relaxed than she had been for many months. Before getting into bed, she opened the casement window and leaned out. Spring had been cool and damp so far, but the last couple of days had been sunny and warmer. The moon was out of sight behind the cottage, but it illuminated the houses across the street and the distant church tower as though they were floodlit. A car roared by, and then, as the sound of its engine faded into the night, she heard the faint but persistent thump, thump, thump of Tim Worthington's music.

Julia pulled the curtains across the open window and retreated to bed. A copy of T. S. Eliot's *Four Quartets* lay on the bedside table. She suspected that it was unorthodox bedtime reading. She didn't fully understand Eliot's metaphysical soliloquizing, but she found his rhythms compelling and his imagery haunting. She lingered now on the first page of Burnt Norton at the line "Disturbing the dust on a bowl of rose-leaves." Ripped from its context—for she was sure that Eliot's meaning was something different—the phrase summarized for her the conversation of the evening, the dust of a crumbling civilization covering the intrinsic beauty of life.

She closed the book and turned out the light. The incessant beat of Tim's music hung on the night air. *Is Tim an example of Evil Incarnate?* she wondered. *The expression on his face when he was trimming the apple tree made me feel he could be capable of deliberate cruelty.* And yet he's little more than a child. Maybe his behavior is no more than an extreme manifestation of adolescent rebellion. He has reason to be angry at the world: his mother dead, his father and grandmother insensitive and incommunicative. Might that anger one day be directed into action? But before she had come to any firm conclusion about Tim's character, Julia was fast asleep.

SEVEN

Brian Dixon's Friday evening was much less relaxing. When it came time to leave work for the day, he found that his car had a flat tire. He threw his jacket to the ground and set to work changing the wheel. It was not a job he found particularly difficult, but he was irritated at this unexpected hitch at the start of the weekend. When he had finished, he wiped his hands on the grass, flung his jacket into the car, and drove off, determined to stop at the first pub he came to for a consoling pint of beer.

He was frustrated there too. When he ordered his beer, he couldn't find his wallet. He had enough change in his pockets to pay for the pint, but no more. And where was the wallet? He tried to remember when he had it last. Not at work. He'd had a few pounds in his pocket to pay for lunch. The wallet must be back in his room. He would have to go and get it before he could buy any supper. Feeling exceedingly irritated by now, Brian drove aggressively home.

The advantage of living in one small room is that a search for missing items doesn't take long. But though he looked in every drawer and pocket and behind and under every piece of furniture, the wallet could not be found. By now, Brian was hungry as well as angry. For the first time, he thought appreciatively about Mrs. Beldington's offer to cook supper for him. But Mrs. B. appeared to have gone out, leaving behind only a strong odor of fried fish. Perhaps he had dropped the wallet back at Hestercombe when he was changing the wheel. He would have to go back there and look for it, but he needed to eat something first. He had nothing better than a can of baked beans. He emptied the can into a saucepan and put it onto the hot plate to warm up. He made some toast and, since he didn't have any beer, brewed himself some tea.

Boring though the food was, it was the least of his present problems. He had to find his wallet, get the tire repaired, perhaps even buy a new one. But these were temporary inconveniences. A more urgent matter was what he was going to do about Ruth. Because Ruth had shown up, literally, on his doorstep.

It was like a bad movie. When Mrs. Beldington told him two days ago, her voice registering both curiosity and malice, that a young lady with a small child had come to the house looking for him, Brian knew immediately that it was Ruth. In a panic, he left at once and stayed out until past midnight. And then yesterday evening, as he arrived home from work, he saw her walking along Berry Lane toward the house.

It was a horrible moment. He didn't want to take her into the house because he knew Mrs. B. would be lurking there, eager to overhear whatever she could and invent the rest. Yet strolling through the village with Ruth and Adam could be equally damaging. Quickly he had ushered Ruth and the child into the car and driven back to Taunton to find an anonymous fish and chip place where he hoped that they could talk without being seen by anyone who knew him.

The two hours he spent there were not the best hours of his life. He was moved by the change in Ruth, a change that was surely attributable to the hard life she now lived. She had clearly done her best to make herself look attractive for him, wearing a jaunty windcheater over an open-necked shirt and full skirt that looked new, if of cheap quality. Her hair still hung loose and lustrous on her shoulders, but he could not miss the strain in the taut muscles of her face, the fatigue in her eyes. The woman across the table was not the relaxed, easygoing Ruth of the past but a creature on the edge, fidgeting, her voice at times verging on the shrill, even smoking a couple of cigarettes, something he had not seen her do before. He wanted to take her into his arms and stroke away the years of pain, but he couldn't even put out his hand to touch hers, though it rested so invitingly on the table beside him.

Ruth did not make any explicit demands, but it was apparent in the way she looked at him and in how she spoke that she was hoping to renew their relationship. Adam was clearly her strong card, but on this evening, he let her down. The child was totally unresponsive to Brian's feeble overtures.

"Why do you keep staring at me?" he asked petulantly.

"You're an interesting little boy." Brian was aware that this was a lame response to a legitimate question. He could have used it as an invitation to a full disclosure of their relationship, but he was not ready to take that step. Adam, being an intelligent child, found no compelling reason to make conversation with this dull stranger. He played with his food and squirmed and fussed in his seat until Ruth let him get down. Then he ran around the tables, crawled under chairs, and generally made a nuisance of himself. Brian found it exhausting and wasn't sure he wanted to be a father.

The conversation was strained. Ruth asked about his work and, rather too casually, whether he had married. Brian could truthfully answer that he had not but did not add that he was engaged. He didn't say anything at all about Hilary, and yet his very silence seemed to hang in the air between them as though both of them knew that someone else was present yet neither would admit it. Brian asked one or two questions about Ruth's present life, but she too was defensive in her replies.

"I manage, if that's what you mean," she said at one point. "I didn't come to ask for money from you."

"Then why did you come?"

Ruth twisted the paper napkin in her fingers for a minute. This wasn't what she had anticipated. She realized now that she had been living a dream. The man sitting across from her might be the father of her child, but he was no longer the Brian who had lived in her heart these last five years. Something had changed him. Clearly there was someone else, even though he wasn't going to admit it. She no longer meant anything to him. He didn't even seem to care about Adam. She looked Brian directly in the eye.

"I wanted you to see Adam," she said.

"You sent his photograph," he pointed out.

"In the flesh. To talk to him. To hold him." She laughed, a laugh that Brian suspected was to divert the tears. "And look at him, behaving like a little brat. Not what I planned."

As if on cue, Adam scrambled onto a chair at the next table and began drumming on the tabletop with his fist.

"Why Adam?" asked Brian as Ruth reached over to restrain the child.

"I like the name. Besides, he was my firstborn, and I thought he was perfection. Not that he's living up to it now," she added as she removed a bottle of malt vinegar from his hands and tried to pull him onto her lap.

Brian looked round at the dingy restaurant with its bare table tops, apathetic waitress, and dispirited customers. *Why did I bring her here?* he asked himself. I shouldn't have done this to her. She deserves something better. He pushed aside his plate as if to dissociate himself from the whole scene.

"I think we'd better go," Ruth said suddenly. "He's tired, that's why he's behaving so badly." After a pause, she added, "I suppose it was a mistake, trying to find you. I don't know what I was expecting. I just felt a need to communicate. But you shouldn't feel obliged to actually do anything."

She was pulling Adam's jacket on as she spoke, her face turned away from him, but Brian could hear the pain in her voice. He deliberately ignored it, and this was what was disturbing him now, twenty-four hours later, as he sat in his room, trying to figure out what, if anything, he should do.

He was uncomfortably aware that he had deliberately made no mention of Hilary to Ruth. It was true that things were a bit tense with Hilary at the moment. He had not spoken with her since their disagreement last weekend; he had deliberately stayed away from the Players' midweek rehearsal. However, his intent was just to give them breathing room, not a prelude to a breakup. But if he was definitely going to marry Hilary, then it was unkind not to break the news at once to Ruth so that she would understand why he was not responding to her overtures. So did not explaining about Hilary mean that he was not going to marry her after all? He wished he knew.

He put his feet up on the table and his hands behind his head and tried to sort out his feelings. There was no doubt that Ruth's reappearance had awakened some of his old love for her. The image of her face floated before his eyes, and he could feel her presence so palpably that he now wanted desperately to reach out to her and say "I'm sorry, Ruth." He tried to combat this urge by focusing on Hilary, but Ruth's image was stronger. She still had the power to attract him despite the ravages to her appearance. He remembered Mike's jibe about Hilary as a "silly schoolgirl" and had to concede to himself that Hilary was a naive teenager when compared with Ruth.

Yet Hilary had such trust in him; he felt that it would hurt her tremendously to break off their engagement. It would be like repeating his error with Ruth years before. Besides, marrying Hilary offered the prospect of a fresh start, a clean break with the past. But in fairness to both, he should make up his mind quickly and send one of them packing.

He rummaged in the table drawer for some paper and began a letter. He wrote, "Dear . . ." and at once realized that he couldn't yet write in a name. Undaunted, he went on. Perhaps the act of writing would yield an answer.

"I'm sorry it has to be this way," he wrote. "I did truly love you, but . . ."

He was interrupted by a persistent knocking on the front door. He was sure that Mrs. Beldington had not returned. He stuffed the letter in the pocket of his jeans and went through to Mrs. Beldington's bedroom at the front of the house to see if he could spot the visitor from the window. The overhanging porch concealed the person still banging the door knocker.

He ran downstairs, calling out, "I'm coming." Whoever it was, he didn't want the whole neighborhood to take note.

"Oh, it's you" was all he said as he opened the door. There was a long pause.

"We still have things to talk about."

Brian shrugged. "I suppose so."

He stood back to let the visitor in and led the way upstairs.

EIGHT

Julia was awakened at dawn on Saturday by a light rain pattering against the open casement. She got up to close the window, annoyed that, after a spell of fine weather, rain should threaten the garden party. But when she rose again a couple of hours later, the rain had stopped, and the clouds were breaking up. She went to the bathroom to brush her teeth, remembering how her father used to console her on damp mornings with a bit of folk wisdom: "Rain before seven, fine before eleven."

From the bathroom window, she could see Hilary in yellow oilskin and green rubber boots trudging through the Worthingtons' garden with a basket of eggs. Dr. Worthington kept hens in a field across the lane from the back garden, hens that laid brown eggs with rich, dark yellow yolks. Hilary waved when she saw Julia at the window.

"Would you like some eggs for your visitors' breakfast?" she called. "I'll come round in a few minutes."

Julia was making coffee when Hilary arrived with six brown eggs in a small bowl. They were still warm. Julia expressed her delight and gratitude.

"And it looks as though we'll have a good day for the Hestercombe garden party," she added. "Sunny but not too warm. I don't think the rain overnight will spoil things."

"Oh no. In fact, it will freshen the garden, make it look better. It had been so dry this past week."

"You'll be there, I expect," asked Julia, handing back the bowl. Hilary leaned over the sink to sniff a jug of lily of the valley on the window sill but could not hide the shadow that passed briefly across her face.

"Yes. I said I'd help with the cakes and jams stall. I'm not sure how I'm going to get over there, but I think I can find someone to give me a lift."

"Isn't Brian going?" asked Julia in surprise.

"He was supposed to. And he may still turn up." Hilary stared at the empty bowl in her hands, almost as if she didn't know where it had come from. "I rang him yesterday evening, but there was no answer.

48

And when I tried again just a few minutes ago, before I went to fetch the eggs, Mrs. Beldington said she hadn't seen him since yesterday morning. She went up to his room to tell him I was on the phone, and he wasn't there. It looked, she said, as though he hadn't slept there last night. The way she said that sounded awfully sinister, as though she was hinting at something horrid. I do hate that woman!"

This had come out in a rapid burst, eyes glistening, shoulders heaving, one hand gripping the back of a chair. But almost as quickly, she calmed down and turned to leave. Julia invited her to drive over with them, but Hilary explained that she ought to be there an hour or two ahead of the opening to help set things up. She insisted that if Brian didn't show up, she could easily call on one of the other helpers to pick her up. She waved a breezy hello to Chip as he came downstairs and, without waiting for a proper introduction, left.

Julia watched her go with some concern. Although Hilary affected to be unperturbed by Brian's apparent disappearance, she was clearly worried. But in the bustle of preparing breakfast and discussing plans for the day with Chip and Diana, Julia soon forgot about Hilary and her troubles.

They spent a leisurely morning wandering around the village. At the newsagent's where Julia went to pay her newspaper bill, the gossipy woman that Hilary had complained about was treating other customers to an account of how Dr. Worthington received the news that his daughter's engagement was announced in the newspaper.

"He was very angry," the woman said, giving the narration as much dramatic expression as she could muster. "He said he'd kill the young man before he'd let him marry his daughter. I don't envy that young woman. She's in for an awful time with that father of hers."

At the village library, where Julia went to exchange her books, they met the rector's wife who also had an opinion to offer. Joan Croft was a sharp-featured and sharp-tongued woman who had no qualms about saying exactly what she thought, even if it offended her husband's parishioners. She possessed neither the patience nor the sensitivity that are supposed to be requisite for a rector's wife, but the people of Blymton didn't seem to mind. They simply took their problems to her husband, who dispensed sympathy much more readily.

On this occasion, Joan Croft shook her head and voiced her disapproval of Hilary Worthington's engagement.

"It's not that I have anything against Brian Dixon. He seems a hardworking, honest young man. But limited. From what I know of Hilary, and admittedly it's not much since her family goes to the Methodist chapel rather than to St. John's, she's an intelligent young woman who could go far and shouldn't have anyone holding her back."

Julia thought this was an ironic assessment from a woman who reputedly gave up a potentially rewarding academic career at Cambridge to marry a clergyman, but she held her tongue.

She drove her friends into Taunton for lunch where they lingered longer than they should. By the time they arrived at Hestercombe, the formalities had already begun. The long drive was packed with cars, but Julia was able to maneuver her car into a small space near the main gate. There were now few clouds in the sky, and it was quite warm as they walked up the drive. *As promised, a perfect June afternoon*, thought Julia.

They could hear the amplified voice of a woman ringing out her appreciation of the valiant work of the Somerset Fire Brigade long before they caught sight of the duchess. She was standing on a small dais on the top terrace, a tall, trim figure in a Laura Ashley blue and white print dress and a floppy pale blue hat. The broad brim shaded her face from the sun, but as she turned her head from one side to another in addressing the crowd, a pretty pink and white face with a border of dark curls appeared.

"She's not what I expected," whispered Diana. "I thought she'd be more regal."

"Ducal," corrected Chip.

"I was expecting an older woman," conceded Julia.

A person standing in front of them turned around on hearing Julia's voice and revealed himself to be the rector of Blymton. In contrast to his wife, Rev. Peter Croft was an amiable man, with a kind face and gentle voice. What brought together two such disparate personalities as the rector and his wife was a favorite topic at Blymton dinner parties. It was generally agreed, however, that he was knowledgeable about a surprising number and variety of topics.

"She's a very modern duchess," he volunteered on this occasion. "I'm her godfather. I was at Cambridge with her father. The family place is on the other side of Taunton, and there was a fire there a few years ago. But the fire brigade came so promptly that the house and most of its valuable contents were saved. So she's very sincere in her appreciation of the fine job they do."

By now the duchess had declared the garden party open, and the ropes confining the visitors to the top terrace were removed. On being introduced to Julia's American friends, the rector launched into an encomium on the virtues of Hestercombe.

"It is simply one of the very best creations of one of England's finest gardeners. Gertrude Jekyll—Julia must have told you about Miss Jekyll?—Gertrude Jekyll excelled herself here. Some people may prefer Orchards or Marsh Court, and of course we all wish that Munstead Wood had survived as it was when she lived there, but the garden at Hestercombe has always been my favorite. It's unfortunate that the view over Taunton Vale from the terrace here has lost some of its splendor with the demise of so many elm trees. A handful remain, but they'll soon be gone. Did you know that American troops were billeted here during the war?"

This was news to Julia, though she had heard that many of the large estates in the West country had been requisitioned for this purpose during the buildup to D-Day.

"That was when the garden began to deteriorate. No money or people to maintain it in wartime. But the county people have done a superb job of restoration. Now I'll leave you to enjoy the garden while I go to look for my wife."

With a hasty handshake, he was gone. Julia couldn't help thinking there was a connection between his sudden departure and the appearance behind them of his nemesis, Miss Baxter, the elderly spinster who was forever complaining about things he had or had not done. She wore a dusty pink toque with a full-blown cabbage rose on one side. Her jowls quivered as she spoke.

"Wasn't that the rector talking to you just then?" she asked fretfully. "I wanted to tell him about vandalism in the church. I saw it this morning when I went in to do the flowers. It's those village lads, I know it is. He should lock the door, and then they couldn't get in, but he won't. He says a church has to be open for prayer, which is all very well, but today's young people have no respect."

She clearly could have said much more, but Julia took advantage of a pause for breath to make her escape.

Chip and Diana were already heading down the short flight of steps to the rose garden where small beds of low shrub roses set in trim panels of grass bordered a narrow stone rill. She let Chip take a couple of photographs then led them off to the left to the narrow terrace overlooking Great Plat. Drifts of blue and gray lined this walk, the pale favorites of cottage gardens—lavender, catmint, lamb's ears, and cerastium. Tiny daisies grew in crevices of the terrace walls. Again, Chip clicked his camera.

"If you don't mind, I'd like to find Hilary first, and then we can explore the garden properly. I expect she'll be at the stalls on the Orangery Terrace."

Julia led the way up two flights of curving Lutyens steps into The Rotunda, where they ran into the Parkinson family. Julia introduced her friends, and Dick, spotting Chip's camera, took him aside for a serious discussion about photography. Diana crouched down to talk to the Parkinson child who was peering into the pond, hoping to see a goldfish. Molly seized the opportunity for a private conversation with Julia.

"I'm very worried about Hilary," she explained. "I drove her over here this morning. Brian Dixon was supposed to bring her, but although his car is parked here, Brian himself seems to have disappeared into thin air. Hilary is putting on a brave front. She says they had a little disagreement after the rehearsal last Sunday, and she hasn't heard from him since, but she's sure it will blow over. And yet I don't think she's so sure underneath. I think she's afraid he's going to break off the engagement. After all, there is the matter of the mysterious young woman with a child who was looking for Brian."

"So you've heard about that. But surely Hilary doesn't know."

"She hasn't mentioned it, but she must have heard. Everyone's been talking about it the last few days. She may well have overheard something. Or Tim may have told her."

"A broken engagement is not the worst misfortune that could happen to her. She might even be relieved."

"I agree. I think the relationship is doomed anyway. But she has to be the one to end it. After all, it was she who put the announcement in the paper that started it. It's very important to her to be in control. There's been so much in her life that she couldn't control, beginning with being born into the Worthington family. Then her mother dies, and her brother turns into a Nazi. The affair with Brian is her first real chance to take charge. That's why she's making light of his non-appearance today. She wants us to think she's pulling the strings, that Brian's the puppet, not her."

"That seems a little harsh," said Julia.

"Perhaps. But I think Hilary is a little more complex than the simple teenage front she presents to the world."

They found Hilary behind the cake stall, looking cheerful enough. Her fair hair was pulled back in businesslike fashion, but she was wearing a pretty flowered dress and delicate pearl earrings.

"No one seems to know where he is," she said in response to a question from Julia. "I shall give him a piece of my mind when he does turn up."

Then, as if anxious to change the subject, she quickly added, "Now I hope you are going to buy something. What about a nice sponge cake? Or one of our homemade jams?"

Julia refused the cake but bought a jar of rhubarb and ginger jam and a jar of Victoria plum chutney. She introduced Diana and Chip, and Diana bought some strawberry jam and, under pressure from Chip, a small but rich-looking fruitcake. After a few minutes of desultory conversation, Julia steered her guests away.

"She's a little uptight, isn't she," commented Chip.

Julia just shook her head. She was determined not to let Hilary's problems spoil their afternoon. She led the way back up the steps to The Rotunda and then down the other side to the east walk above the Great Plat. Water rippled in a stone channel running down the center of the walk. Water-loving plants, forget-me-nots, arum lilies, and water plantains looked happily at home along the channel. Beyond the grass walk and stone paths were broad flower borders ablaze with scarlet poppies, golden iris, and the first red-hot pokers. At the far end, another graceful flight of shallow steps took them down to the Great Plat. Looking back now toward the house, they could see the full splendor of the terraces, walls of warm honey-colored stone softened by the plants spilling over the tops, climbing up from below and even growing out of the walls. Chip clicked away with his camera.

"I can see that it's a beautiful garden," he said. "But what made Gertrude Jekyll so special?"

"It was partly the partnership with Sir Edwin Lutyens. You must admit, the stone walls and stairs and archways are splendid backdrops for her plantings. But as a gardener, she broke away from the bedding arrangements that the Victorians so admired, stiff arrangements of geraniums and dahlias and begonias. Instead, she used perennials and looked for a harmonious blending of color rather than formal patterns. And she brought back into popular favor flowers that had been associated with cottage gardens rather than the gardens of large houses."

"I've seen a lot of unfamiliar flowers," said Diana. "At least, they're unfamiliar to me. What is that, for instance, the plant with the big thick leaves around the roses?"

"That's now called bergenia, though it's had several names over the years. It's a prime example of a plant that Miss Jekyll brought out of obscurity. In fact, it's almost become her signature in a garden. She has been called the queen of the bergenias."

They wandered over the Plat, admiring the roses and the peonies. Most of the visitors were still swarming on the upper terraces or by the food stalls and the tea tent near the Orangery, and only a few had ventured as far as the Plat. When Julia and her companions stepped up to the raised pergola that spanned the south border of the Plat, they had it to themselves.

"How quiet and peaceful it is up here," remarked Diana.

Tall pillars of pinkish stone formed alternately into round or square shapes were smothered in clematis and climbing roses. Oak beams across the top cast shadows onto the stone path and over the clumps of lavender and santolina between the pillars.

"There's got to be a great picture from here," Chip said, positioning himself at the very end of the pergola. He took several pictures, pausing frequently to make adjustments to his lens. Then, intending to take a shot of the Plat through the pillars, he stepped across a mound of lavender to the edge of the retaining wall at the back of the pergola.

"Be careful," warned Diana, watching him balance precariously on the edge of the wall. "And look, you're trampling the lavender."

She pointed to a place by a pillar where the lavender was broken and the soil had been churned up.

"I didn't do that," said Chip indignantly. "It was like that before I stepped across."

"Well, do watch your step. I bet it's a long way down if you fall off the edge."

"I don't plan to fall," Chip replied, laughing as he looked down from the height of the pergola. Then he stiffened and the laugh was cut off.

"Oh my God! There's a body down there!"

Julia and Diana stepped across the lavender and leaned cautiously over the edge. Immediately below the pergola was a narrow flower bed, somewhat overgrown, then a path, and then a stretch of mown grass. Lying prone across the flower bed, half buried in its foliage, was the body of a man clad in jeans and a light gray jacket. He was lying awkwardly, with one arm bent under him. His head was turned to one side. Flowers drooped incongruously over his head and feet. Chip let himself down carefully and leaned over the body for a closer inspection.

"He's dead all right. Can't see how without touching him. Who the hell do you suppose it is?"

Julia couldn't be sure, but she thought she recognized the man.

"I think it's the missing Brian Dixon. I'll go up to the house and call the police. You two stay here in case anyone else comes along. We don't want to raise a general alarm. And I particularly don't want Hilary here. She should be safely behind her stall, but she might have a break and wander over. I'll be as quick as I can."

The house appeared deserted at first, but eventually, Julia came to an open door to a room where a man was poking about in a filing cabinet.

"We've just found a body at the bottom of the garden," she said breathlessly. "Please call the police."

The man looked at her as though he wasn't sure whether this was a hoax or a crazy lady. He slowly sat down at a desk and, pulling a piece of paper toward him, took the cap off his pen.

"Now, ma'am, what's your name?"

"Why do you need my name? Just please call the police!"

"Well, when I tell the police there's a body here, they'll want to know who found the body and where it is, and so I'll have to give them your name since I haven't seen this body."

"If you don't believe me, go and see for yourself. It's lying on the flower bed beyond the pergola."

Julia was almost screaming at this point. The man looked at her for a long minute, then deliberately put the cap back on his pen, took the jacket from the back of his chair, and left the room.

Julia started to follow him, but her legs began to tremble, and she sat down instead, clenching her hands tightly to bring herself under control. A fly was buzzing somewhere in the room. Voices from the terrace floated in through the open window. A clock on the wall ticked loudly, marking each second. She watched it intently, trying hard not to think about what it would mean if the body was indeed Brian Dixon. When the man came running back, his face was white.

"You were right" was all he said. He reached for the phone.

"This is fire brigade headquarters at Hestercombe. There's a body of a young man at the bottom of the garden here. Can you come at once, but come quietly, no sirens. There's a garden party going on here with a couple of hundred people on the premises. We don't want to start a panic."

So ends a perfect afternoon, thought Julia sadly.

NINE

When the man had finished delivering his message, he put down the phone and looked thoughtfully at Julia. For a minute or so, neither of them spoke. The fly settled momentarily on the man's bald head before buzzing away again. Sunlight continued to stream in through the window as though nothing had changed. The clock ticked inexorably on. Julia was the first to break the silence.

"What happens now?"

"We wait for the police." He hesitated a moment then continued, "I think the body may be one of our employees. If so, then we can identify it. But the police will also want a statement from you since you were the one who found the body. You can wait here if you like."

"Oh goodness me, no!" Julia suddenly pulled herself together. "That's kind of you, but I must get Hilary away. I think I recognized the body too, and if we're right, then his fiancée is here at the garden party. This would not be the time or the place for her to learn that he's dead. I shall take her away at once before the police arrive. I'll leave you my name and address, and they can talk to me later at home."

The man didn't seem too sure that this was correct procedure, but Julia left him no choice, departing as precipitately as she had arrived.

Outside the building, she met Chip and Diana coming in search of her. A gardener had relieved them of their vigil by the body. Quickly she outlined a plan for luring Hilary away to have tea somewhere.

"Hilary may resist leaving, particularly since they're serving teas here. I'll tell her that you have been asking what a Devon cream tea is like. I'm taking you to a place in Somerset that serves a cream tea that's better than any in Devon. Back me up, but don't overdo it."

But Hilary was easily persuaded. They found her still selling cakes and jams on the Orangery terrace but eager to leave, a little too eager, Julia decided later, looking back on it. There was a nervous excitement about her, like a young horse before a race.

A police car passed them as they walked down the drive to their car. Another car swung in through the gateway at a rapid pace as they drove out into the lane. *Plainclothes detectives*, Julia surmised, glancing quickly at Hilary to see if she had noticed. But Hilary was deep in conversation with Diana, asking earnest questions about life in America. She remained animated throughout tea, piling clotted cream and raspberry jam on her scones with zest.

Julia, relieved of the need to make conversation, watched Hilary uneasily. It bothered her that the girl should be prattling on, totally unaware that her fiancé was lying dead in a flower bed at Hestercombe. And yet she was reluctant to break the news when she did not know definitely that the body was Brian Dixon. But when would Hilary be told and by whom? And who would be there to comfort her and help her through the grieving?

They sat over tea for a couple of hours. No one was anxious to move. The two Americans were thoroughly enjoying their English afternoon tea, sitting under a tree in a pleasant garden café beside a thatched cottage. Julia merely wanted to delay the moment when Hilary would hear about Brian's death. Hilary apparently had her own reasons for lingering. It was she who eventually brought up Brian's name.

"Brian never showed up at the garden party," she remarked abruptly. "His car was there, but no one seemed to know where he was. I hope he has finally decided to put in an appearance only to discover that I have left. It would serve him right."

Diana began to rummage intently in her handbag. Chip became absorbed in the flight of a butterfly around a nearby flower bed. Julia too was unwilling to look directly at Hilary but dealt with the embarrassment by suggesting that it was time to move on. By the time she had paid the bill and shepherded the group back to the car, the conversation had moved into safer waters. All three were relieved when they dropped Hilary off at her home.

"I think it's time for a drink," said Julia grimly.

They had hardly settled themselves in the conservatory with a supply of gin and tonic before there was a sharp knock at the front door. Waiting as Julia opened the door were two men dressed in plainclothes but readily identifiable as police officers even before they flashed their cards.

They introduced themselves as Detective-Inspector Tom Hughes and Sergeant Jim Nelson. The inspector was a heavyset man, fitted uncomfortably into a somewhat rumpled gray suit. His face was bland and expressionless below rough dark eyebrows and an unruly shock of graying hair. *If I were shown his picture and asked to describe him*, thought Julia, *I would say he's a Russian bureaucrat*. His companion, by contrast, was a young whippersnapper who tapped his toe impatiently on the doorstep and gave the impression he'd rather be spending his Saturday evening somewhere else. Julia took them back to the conservatory and offered them drinks, but they declined.

"You should not have left the scene," the inspector began brusquely. Faced with such obvious hostility, Julia braced herself for a difficult interview. Calmly she explained why she had left and ended by asking, "Was it Brian Dixon?"

The inspector didn't reply immediately but looked at her sternly. *He's deciding how difficult to be*, Julia said to herself, *but I'm not going to offer any further apology. I know I did the right thing*. She stared back at him and waited.

"Yes," he said finally. "Now perhaps you'll tell me exactly how you found the body."

"But how did he die?" she asked when she had finished her account. "I just saw a dead body, no visible signs of death."

"He had been shot in the head," the inspector began.

"In the right temple," the young sergeant added, ignoring the warning look his superior cast in his direction.

"He was lying prone, with his head turned to the left so that he was lying wounded side down. His hand with the gun was also underneath the body."

"You're not saying it was a suicide, are you?" asked Julia in disbelief.

"I'm afraid it looks like that. There was a note too. We're trying to reach his mother, who appears to be his closest relative, but since she lives up in the Midlands somewhere, I doubt if she'll be very helpful about his recent state of mind."

"Young men don't confide in their mothers anyway," interposed Sergeant Nelson.

"Maybe not," said the inspector rather sharply, "but mothers often see much more than sons think they're revealing. However, I think that the young woman who was engaged to the deceased may be most helpful in our inquiries. I understand you can tell us where she lives."

Julia nodded. "She lives next door. You say there was a note. Can you tell me what it said?"

"I'd prefer to wait until I've shared it with the young woman. That's the next step."

"If I may, I'd like to be the one to break the news. The girl's mother is dead, and the rest of her family were not very pleased about her engagement. It's going to be very hard on her."

The inspector raised no objection, though he insisted that he and his colleague would accompany her. They left the Americans enjoying their gin and tonic in the conservatory and went over to the Worthingtons' house.

"Go easy on her," Julia pleaded as they walked up the path to that gaunt front door. "She's little more than a child, and this will be a terrible shock."

"We'll just ask one or two questions and then leave," promised the inspector.

Hilary opened the door. Her face immediately registered alarm, but she said nothing. She led them into a dim parlor furnished with heavy Victorian furniture. Dark red curtains shrouded the tall windows. Julia noted a silver-framed photograph of a young woman bearing a strong resemblance to Hilary displayed prominently on a mahogany sideboard. There were no other ornaments in the room, no plants or flowers. A romantic moorland landscape in a heavy gilt frame above the mantelpiece was the sole wall-hanging.

As they were settling themselves on various uncomfortable chairs and a hard-backed velour sofa, old Mrs. Worthington appeared in the doorway. She remained standing there, grim-faced, while Julia broke the news as gently as she could.

"I have bad news for you Hilary. You must be very brave. It's about Brian. I'm afraid he's—it seems there's been some kind of accident. He's—he's dead."

She paused to allow Hilary to absorb this, expecting a reaction of some kind. But Hilary just sat there, stunned.

"His body was found at Hestercombe this afternoon." This revelation provoked a response.

"At Hestercombe? He was lying dead at Hestercombe while I was there?"

Hilary burst into uncontrollable tears. Julia went over to her and put her arms around the sobbing girl. The two policemen sat looking a little uncomfortable but said nothing. The first person to speak was the old woman in the doorway who muttered darkly, "For these be the days of vengeance, that all things which are written may be fulfilled."

Julia looked at her reproachfully, but Mrs. Worthington glared back unmoved.

"Is Hilary's father here?" Julia asked.

"No. He's away at a meeting. He won't be back until tomorrow evening."

It was no use asking for Tim. He would be no support for Hilary. Julia held on to the girl, waiting for the spasms of grief to abate. When the sobbing subsided a little, she asked Hilary if she felt up to answering a few questions from the policemen. Hilary sat up and faced them.

"I have a question for you first," she said. "When did he—I mean, you say he was found this afternoon, but how long . . . ?"

"We think he died sometime late last night but don't have confirmation of that yet."

"That's strange," interjected Julia. "Why did no one find the—find him until this afternoon?"

"We asked the fire brigade that very question. Apparently, the man who had been detailed to do a last-minute inspection of the grounds before the garden party didn't show up this morning, so it didn't get done."

"And most of the garden was roped off to visitors until after the opening ceremony," added the sergeant.

"And then we all headed for the stalls and the tea tent," said Julia.

The inspector turned to Hilary.

"I don't want to add to your distress," he said kindly, "but I would like to hear from you what kind of mood your fiancé had been in recently. Did he seem depressed at all?"

Hilary looked at him in bewilderment.

"What do you mean? What happened? Was it an accident? Or what?"

She asked the last question fiercely as if anticipating a refusal to answer. Julia looked at the inspector and, taking a cue from him, responded, "He was shot. In the head. The gun was still in his hand."

"That bloody gun!"

"You can confirm then that he owned a gun?" asked the inspector.

"Yes. He inherited it from his father. It was a war souvenir. I only found out about it a week or so ago. He said he was going to try it out and make sure it still worked then he'd put it away somewhere safe. I knew he was asking for trouble, playing around with it. I hate guns."

Julia looked questioningly at Inspector Hughes, who hesitated a moment and then was very blunt.

"It looks as though it was not an accident. We found a note in his pocket. Our inclination is to treat it as a suicide."

Hilary reacted to this suggestion with signs of both horror and fear. Julia watched her carefully as Hilary first gasped in disbelief as she herself had done and then shook her head in denial.

"No, no, no!" she cried. "That can't be! He can't have!"

She was trembling now, clearly frightened as well as distressed. Another dire incantation was heard from the doorway.

"'If thou dost not speak to warn the wicked from his way, that wicked man shall die in his iniquity.'"

This was too much for Julia.

"Mrs. Worthington, if you cannot say something kind and sympathetic to your granddaughter in her grief, you could at least keep quiet."

The old woman turned on her heel, slamming the door behind her.

Inspector Hughes took a paper from his pocket, unfolded it, and handed it to Hilary. She stared at it, not comprehending what it said. Julia looked over and read.

Dear

I'm sorry it has to be this way. I did truly love you but . . .

"That's not necessarily a farewell note to Hilary," she remarked then immediately realized the implication of what she had said. From the scared look in her eyes, Hilary perceived this too.

"Oh," said the inspector. "Who else might it be addressed to?"

Julia hesitated, still uncertain how much Hilary might know about the mysterious young woman and child who had been inquiring about Brian. Hilary, a little calmer now, said softly, "There was a former girlfriend. I'd heard recently some talk in the village about an old affair."

"He told you this?" asked the inspector. "You discussed it?"

Hilary looked very uneasy.

"No. As I said, it was village gossip that I heard. I—well, actually, we hadn't talked since last Sunday."

The inspector examined her quizzically. Julia noticed particularly how his bushy eyebrows rose to meet an especially long lock of hair on his forehead. The sergeant was restlessly tapping his fingers on his knees.

"That seems unusual for an engaged couple living in the same village. Do you often go for a whole week without communicating with each other?"

Hilary fiddled nervously with her skirt. The tears had completely stopped by now, but her eyes remained red and swollen. She sniffed as she quietly answered with just one word, "Sometimes."

"Had you quarreled?"

"No." That was said very emphatically.

Inspector Hughes reached into his pocket again and this time pulled out the photograph of Adam that Ruth had sent to Brian. He handed it to Hilary.

"Do you know who this might be?"

"I don't know," said Hilary. She was puzzled but not visibly upset. "It looks like Brian. It's probably a photo of him as a child."

"It was in his wallet," added Sergeant Nelson gratuitously.

Julia was annoyed. The style of the child's clothes showed that the photo was taken recently. And young men don't normally carry photos of themselves as babies in their wallets. She felt the police were baiting Hilary.

"Well, I don't know. I never saw it before." Hilary thrust the photo away.

A silence hung in the room as heavy as the furnishings while Inspector Hughes studied the photo. Finally, he put it away and resumed his questioning.

"Can you tell us anything about his mood in recent weeks? Was he depressed?"

"No." Hilary's denial sounded sincere.

"Your engagement was not well-accepted by your family, I understand. Was that a problem for him?"

"It wasn't easy for either of us. But it wasn't anything to make us suicidal."

"Did you have any disagreements recently? Any arguments about your engagement? Or marriage plans?"

"No." The denial this time was less sure.

"Any arguments over this other girlfriend?" asked Sergeant Nelson. His role seemed to be to provide the counter punch. Hilary reeled as from a blow.

"I told you we didn't discuss her." She burst into tears again.

Julia was about to protest that they were overdoing it when the inspector rose to his feet.

"I think that will be all for now, though we may need to talk to you again later when you have had some time to recover from the shock."

Julia followed them from the room. Inspector Hughes turned at the front door.

"I'm sorry we had to be a bit rough, but . . ." He shrugged. "I'll have to talk to her again, you too. We'll need statements. There'll have to be an inquest." Then he changed his tone. "If you could stay with her for a little while, I think your presence would be welcome. She's obviously in shock."

Julia closed the door behind them and was returning to the parlor when she noticed Tim standing in the doorway to the kitchen.

"So he's dead," he laughed. "Good riddance."

Julia marched into the kitchen, pushing Tim ahead of her, and kicked the door closed so that Hilary would not hear what she had to say. Mrs. Worthington was sitting straight-backed on a kitchen chair reading her Bible. She looked up as Julia entered but did not speak.

"You two might show a little warmth and affection for Hilary. Whatever your opinion of Brian Dixon, he's now gone out of your lives and Hilary's too. But she loved him, and she's hurting badly. Think about her first, for goodness sake! I'm going to phone the doctor and ask for a sedative to help her sleep tonight. And if you can't say anything comforting to her, then don't say anything at all. Now where's the phone?"

Mrs. Worthington seemed taken aback at this onslaught but said merely, "Out in the hall." Tim glared at her, still grinning maliciously, but said nothing.

Dr. Jessica Woodhouse arrived within five minutes of Julia's call. Jessica had been very sympathetic earlier in the year when Julia was struggling with her double loss, and she had become a good friend as well as medical adviser. She came in now quietly, a tiny woman of uncertain middle age. Her appearance was somewhat Bohemian, long brown hair pulled back into a pony tail that was fastened with a gaily colored scarf. She wore a long denim skirt and sandals and had several ropes of wooden beads round her neck. But her demeanor showed a woman used to command and confident in her ability to deliver.

Julia was finding her role of comforter particularly exacting. Since the departure of the police, Hilary had been weeping on and off, accusing herself of responsibility for Brian's death. Julia countered every accusation, but Hilary refused to be absolved.

"I was always insisting on my own way," she sobbed. "I wouldn't compromise."

"I'm sure that's not true," tried Julia. "You're being selective in what you remember. There must have been occasions when you gave in to him. You're just not remembering them."

"But not the important things," Hilary persisted.

It was with some relief, therefore, that Julia welcomed the doctor's arrival. Jessica quickly took charge, ushering Julia out of the room.

"I'll see Hilary gets to bed and give her a shot to help her sleep. I don't want to leave her with sleeping pills at this juncture. I'll check on her tomorrow. You go back to your visitors."

Reassured by this forthrightness, Julia returned to Flora Cottage, but it was a somber evening. They went to bed soon after ten, feeling very tired. Julia slept fitfully.

She was awakened around midnight by a dream. She was in a garden where the sun was hidden by lines of tall evergreen bushes. She walked along a path between the bushes, a pair of secateurs in her hand. The path was a winding one, and as she approached each bend, she was sure that Frank would be waiting for her around the corner. But each leap of anticipation was followed by disappointment. Frank was never there. At intervals, there were gaps in the ranks of evergreens that were filled with rose-bushes in bloom; and at each one, Julia paused to cut off all the flowers. She awoke with a dreadful sense of desolation that lasted for an hour or two before she finally fell into a deep dreamless sleep.

The somber mood persisted throughout Sunday. Julia called at the Worthingtons' house after church, but Tim said that Hilary was in bed and had declared that she wanted absolutely no visitors. She phoned Jessica, who said that she had seen Hilary earlier in the morning and reassured her that she would be all right. "I think it would be best if she were left alone today," Jessica added.

Nevertheless, Julia gathered a large bunch of flowers from her garden, roses, columbines and a glorious yellow lily that had just come into bloom by the back door. As an afterthought, she tucked a sprig of rosemary into the bouquet. "There's rosemary, that's for remembrance," she muttered to herself as she penned a brief note to accompany the flowers. It was the old woman who answered the door this time. She accepted the bouquet without comment.

Diana and Chip left for London by the late-afternoon train. As Julia stood with them on the platform waiting for the train, she offered an invitation to return.

"Come back next month for the play," she suggested. "This terrible affair should be well behind us by then, and I'll make sure we have an unclouded weekend."

Flora Cottage felt very empty on her return. And she had another troubled night. Again, she dreamed she was in a garden, this time one filled with flowers. She began to cut off their heads, but each time she snipped with her secateurs, a bud elsewhere burst into bloom. Finally, she came to a part of the garden where all the plants were dead. Furiously, she pulled them up and began to plant in their place seedlings from a tray of peat pots that was lying on the grass. But as fast as she planted, the seedlings promptly fell over and died. In great frustration, she threw down the trowel and burst into tears.

She woke up crying, not sure why until the dream flashed back. She was a little unnerved at such vivid and depressing dreams two nights in a row, but a drink of hot chocolate soothed her spirits and helped her back to sleep. She slept well enough the rest of the night and woke much later than usual. The post was already lying on the hall floor as she went downstairs. There was just one letter, but it was a real letter, not bills or advertisements, and she opened it eagerly.

It was from Nigel, a brief letter explaining that the following Saturday he was going down to Cornwall for a sailing holiday and would love to call and see her on the way if that would be convenient. Julia was delighted. She found a postcard and wrote: "Love to see you on Saturday. Come for lunch. It seems ages since we had a chance to talk. There's a lot to catch up. I'll expect you around noon?"

TEN

The police called on Mrs. Beldington first thing Monday morning.

At headquarters, it had been quickly decided that no foul play was involved in the death of Brian Dixon. The coroner would have to determine whether it was an accident or a suicide, and the police should make inquiries to help him in that decision, but there was no urgent need to start that process before Monday morning.

When the inspector, accompanied by Sergeant Nelson, knocked on Mrs. Beldington's door, she greeted them effusively and ushered them into her front parlor, a small room with a slightly musty smell. The stuffiness and the pristine armchairs and sofa covered with a stiff dark green rep suggested a room that saw little use. Heavy crocheted antimacassars and cream lace curtains gave the room an old-fashioned look. Inspector Hughes sat uneasily on the edge of the deep armchair that Mrs. Beldington gestured toward.

"I can make you a cup of tea if you like," she began, but the inspector quickly declined the offer.

"We have just a few questions to ask about Brian Dixon and won't keep you long. When did you last see him?"

"Well. I didn't see him on Friday evening because I'd gone to Taunton for the day to see my sister. I meant to leave right after tea, but we were talking, and so I missed the last bus—they don't run late anymore, you know—and my sister's husband had to drive me home. He wasn't too pleased. He was watching the telly and Peg—that's my sister—she said . . ."

The inspector cut her off.

"So you didn't see him at all on Friday evening?"

"No, that's what I was coming to. I got home late and . . ."

"What time precisely, Mrs. Beldington?" Sergeant Nelson interrupted.

"About ten o'clock, I think. Yes, it was just about ten because I turned on the telly, and they were just starting the ten o'clock news."

"And Mr. Dixon was not home? How did you know?"

"Well, I didn't think so because there was no light in his room. There's a gap under the door so you can tell when he has the light on. There was no light under the door."

"He could have been in bed, asleep," the inspector suggested.

"At ten o'clock on a Friday night!" Mrs. Beldington swayed back on the sofa and, raising her feet slightly, slapped her knees in amusement. "He'd be at the pub, more like it. He was never a one for staying home in the evening."

I can see why, thought the inspector, taking in the prim little room and the garrulous landlady twiddling several ugly rings on her fingers. Large blue veins were protruding on the backs of her hands, and there were brown blotches on the skin. *Nature isn't kind to women as they age*, he thought.

"Did you hear him come in that night?"

"No, and it's usually very late before I drop off. I don't sleep too well, you know, haven't done since my Harry died, and the slightest noise always wakes me up. But I didn't hear a thing."

"And you didn't see him on Saturday morning either?"

"No. Hilary Worthington—and I don't know what she was thinking of, a doctor's daughter, even if he is an animal doctor, planning to marry Brian Dixon. I don't mean to speak ill of the dead, but he wasn't the nicest young man you ever met."

"What was wrong with him?" The inspector was genuinely curious now. "Apart from the fact that he went out in the evenings."

"Did he pay his rent?" interjected the sergeant.

"Oh yes, very particular about that he was. Always paid me in full every time and on time."

"Did he smoke? Play loud music? Forget to wipe his boots?"

"No. He was very quiet and tidy too. His room was always neat when I went in to clean. I really don't know why I didn't like him. I just felt he was, well, sort of secretive."

Sounds like an ideal tenant, thought the inspector. Secretive might mean something, but more likely he was trying to protect himself against a nosy landlady. It wasn't worth pursuing.

"Let's get back to Saturday morning. You started to say something about Hilary Worthington."

"Yes, well, she phoned, didn't she, very early too, and I wasn't even properly awake. Wanted to speak to him. I shouted upstairs like I usually do, then when he didn't answer, I went up and banged on the bedroom door. I thought he was still asleep, you see. It was very early, about eight o'clock, I think. I know I thought it was a bit early for a young woman to be calling her boyfriend."

"And what happened when you banged on his door?"

"Nothing. Not a peep. So I opened the door and looked in. And that's when I saw that his bed was not just empty. It hadn't been slept in! So I knew for certain that he hadn't been home at all. He'd been out all night!"

Mrs. Beldington sat back, her hands folded defiantly on her lap and the expression on her face clearly suggesting that if a person stayed out all night, he could expect bad things to happen to him.

"What did you do then?"

"I went back downstairs and told young Miss Worthington that her fee-on-say, as she called, him was not at home and had been out all night. She wasn't very pleased. In fact, she was rather rude. Slammed down the phone without as much as a 'Thank you for looking.' But then, that's young people today. No manners."

Inspector Hughes shifted the conversation to questions about Brian Dixon's mood in recent weeks. Mrs. Beldington hadn't noticed any strange behavior, any marked changes in mood.

"But there was the letter," she went on. "He got a letter a week or so ago, a big fat letter it was. He hardly ever got letters. That's why I remember it."

"I don't suppose there was a return address on the envelope."

"No, but the postmark was Wolverhampton, if that helps."

"That's where his mother lives," Sergeant Nelson reminded his superior.

"When I gave it to him, Mr. Dixon didn't look as though it was a letter from his mother. He looked at it as though it would bite him. Then he went up and slammed his door, and a bit later, he came running back downstairs and out of the door and stayed out very late. And he wasn't with the Worthington girl because she phoned him while he was out, and he got upset when I gave him her message. Then there was the other young woman."

Mrs. Beldington paused for maximum effect. She was clearly relishing her role as bearer of this important tidbit of information.

"Yes, tell us about this other young woman."

"It was a few days after he got the letter. She came to the door one morning, asking if Brian Dixon lived here and was he at home. I ask, you now, why would he be at home in the morning? She asked me what time he got home from work, and I said about six but that he often went out in the evenings. I asked if she wanted to leave a message, but she said no. She had a child with her, a little boy about three or four. She said she'd come back later, but I never saw her again."

Inspector Hughes handed Mrs. Beldington the photograph of Adam that had been found in Brian's wallet.

"Is this the child?"

"Oh yes. He's a lovely little boy, isn't he?"

"Did you tell Brian Dixon about the visitor?"

"Yes, I did, and wasn't he upset! I told him that very evening when he came home from work, and he went out right away and stayed out all evening again. He knew who she was all right, and he didn't want to see her."

"Did you draw any conclusions from this visit? Did you imagine who she might be?"

"Well, it stands to reason, doesn't it, that when a young woman and child come inquiring for a single young man—I can add up as well as anyone. I think she was an old girlfriend, and I think the child is his. That's only my opinion, but I'll stand by it."

Mrs. Beldington pursed her lips, turning from one policeman to the other, defying them to dispute her conclusion.

Inspector Hughes refused to take up the challenge. Instead, he asked to see Brian's room.

Mrs. Beldington led the way upstairs. The small room looked reasonably tidy, but she apologized for it all the same.

"I ought to have cleaned it up, but when the sergeant phoned me about the accident, he told me to leave the room exactly as it was. Just look at those dirty dishes!"

The remains of Brian's supper still sat on the table where he had left them. The empty bean tin and the dirty pan lay on the hearth by the hot plate. The inspector picked up a saucer that contained ash and a cigarette stub.

"Did Mr. Dixon smoke? I thought you said not?"

"No, he didn't." Mrs. Beldington was genuinely surprised. "When he first came to inquire about the room, he told me he didn't smoke before I even had to ask. I was pleased about that. I didn't want a smoking lodger. I'd be scared of fires. And I never found any sign of smoking before in his room."

"Well, either he was a surreptitious smoker and able to keep his secret until now or he had a visitor last Friday evening. Nelson, let's see if we can track down a person who might have visited him."

The two policemen examined the room carefully, opening drawers, looking under the bed, poking through the contents of the wardrobe. Sergeant Nelson found the shoe box with its collection of photos, postcards, and assorted mementos. Ruth's letter caught his eye. He handed it to his superior with a nudge and a mere "Take a look at this, sir." Mrs. Beldington pricked up her ears, but the inspector read it through quickly then pocketed it without comment. The sergeant glanced at the newspaper clippings that Brian had marked but returned them to the box with the other items without a second look.

"The rest of the stuff in this box seems pretty old. Nothing that could account for suicidal feelings."

"Yes. The accident theory is beginning to look more likely, but let's take the box for a further examination," said the inspector.

"But what about the mysterious young woman and child?" asked Mrs. Beldington, who had been watching the search with fascination. It was like snooping on her lodger herself but being legitimate about it. She kept hoping something much more significant than a cigarette stub would turn up. "Two women in his life. Doesn't that suggest a man up against a terrible decision and deciding instead to take his own life?"

The inspector shook his head.

"Men don't usually go to such extremes over women. He'd have found a way to handle that."

As the two policemen returned to their car, Sergeant Nelson questioned the inspector's apparent shift of opinion.

"No, I'm really still with the suicide theory. There's the note, for one thing. The letter that you found looks significant too. And why on earth would anyone go to the bottom of the garden at Hestercombe for a little target practice? I made that comment to Mrs. Beldington for two reasons. One was that I wanted to cool down her sense of drama. She's got plenty of scope for gossip without adding to the pot. More importantly, as she gossips and relays the information that the police are leaning toward accident rather than suicide, someone with real information about the events of last Friday night and what led up to them may be induced to come forward. It's a slight chance, but it's worth a try."

Inspector Hughes was correct about the gossip. That afternoon, when Julia ran into Mrs. Mudge in the butcher's shop, she heard the full story of Mrs. Beldington's interview with the police.

Julia had given her own formal statement to the police before lunch. It was a very straightforward interview. She described once again finding the body and reporting it. She could not tell them anything significant about Brian's mood or behavior in recent weeks.

"I really didn't know him," she explained to Inspector Hughes. "He was one of the group of young people involved with the play. He'd be there at rehearsals, helping to build scenery and props and part of the crowd that would move over to The Feathers after the rehearsal. But until I learned about Hilary's engagement a couple of weeks ago, I hadn't really distinguished him from the rest of the young men."

"Do you know if he smoked?"

Julia thought hard, trying to conjure up recollections of Brian in the Green Room and the pub.

"I honestly don't know. I don't think so, though most of the young men in the crew do smoke, so it wouldn't surprise me if he did."

And with that, the inspector had to be content.

The police caught up with Hilary again on Wednesday evening. Because Wednesday was rehearsal night, Julia phoned the Worthington house to see if Hilary would like to walk over to the Village Hall with her. She had left Hilary alone, having been assured that both Jessica and, at school, Molly would be keeping an eye on her. Dr. Worthington, who answered the phone, told her rather brusquely that the police had just arrived to take a statement from Hilary, so she wouldn't be going to the rehearsal or anywhere else that evening.

Julia went to the rehearsal anyway. Everyone was very edgy. Some of the young men in the Green Room talked about how they too had been questioned by the police, but to a man they declared that Brian Dixon had not been behaving like someone contemplating suicide.

When Julia felt that enough time had elapsed for the police to have completed their questioning of Hilary, she left the Village Hall and went straight to the Worthingtons' house. She took with her a costume that Hilary was to wear for the last act as an excuse for her late visit if Dr.

Worthington should be the one to open the door. But it was Hilary who responded to her knock. She looked genuinely pleased to see Julia.

"The police have just left, and nobody else is at home, so do come in for a few minutes, if you can spare the time. I'd like a chance to talk."

"You're all alone? I spoke to your father earlier when I called to see if you were coming to the rehearsal," said Julia, wondering how the family could have left Hilary to face the police at home.

"Father had a call to go to a sick cow. And Wednesday is Granny's Bible study night. Tim goes out almost every evening, and in his present mood, I'd rather not have him at home."

They were still standing in the large empty hall. There was an awkward silence, then Hilary said, "Why don't we go and sit in my bedroom, if you don't mind. It's much cozier than the parlor."

Hilary's bedroom was indeed the most congenial room that Julia had seen in the Worthingtons' house. It was fairly large with windows on two sides. Posters of flower drawings covered the walls. There was a white candlewick spread on the bed and a fluffy sheepskin rug by the bedside. A white lily in a pot sat among the books and papers on a large desk under one window. Julia, sinking into an inviting overstuffed armchair, was pleased that Hilary at least had this comfortable refuge.

Once seated, she noticed other things. A photograph of Hilary's mother on the chest of drawers was a companion to the one downstairs. The flowers she had sent were arranged in a vase on a bedside table. Hilary followed her glance.

"Thank you so much for the flowers. They did cheer me up. And I noticed the rosemary—I appreciated that. We did Hamlet at school last year, so I caught the allusion."

"And I see you have a Madonna lily."

"Yes, that's a bit of a puzzle. It was delivered yesterday with an odd note from someone named Mike Hatfield, who says he was a friend of Brian's. But I never heard Brian talk about a friend named Mike. Look, here's the note."

It was handwritten on the kind of notecard florists supply to accompany floral gifts. "Dear Hilary," it ran. "You probably don't know who I am, but I was a good friend of Brian, and I'm very sorry to hear about his untimely death. I expect I would eventually have met you, and maybe our paths will still cross. In the meantime, you have my deepest sympathy. Mike Hatfield."

"That is strange," agreed Julia. "Strange that you had not heard of him and also that he should do this. It almost sounds as though he's a secret admirer."

"I don't need any secret admirers."

"No, you don't. You need a lot of open supporters. I'm glad you went straight back to school. You should also come back to rehearsals as soon as possible."

"School was easy because I had no associations with Brian there. It's the same here. He rarely came to this house because everyone was so nasty to him. I think that's why so far it all seems so unreal. But going to rehearsals or to Hestercombe and finding no Brian there would be very hard."

And yet you have to face up to the fact that Brian has gone, thought Julia, but she hadn't the heart to say this aloud. From her own experience, she knew what the girl was going through, the denial, the refusal to accept that a door had closed forever. The funeral might help. She asked about funeral arrangements.

"I asked the police about that. They said his mother came down from Wolverhampton yesterday and that after the inquest on Friday, she can arrange for his body to go back to Wolverhampton for burial."

"Will you go back with her?"

"I don't think so. I've never met her. I don't know her or any of his family. She didn't even know I existed until the police told her about me. Apparently, Brian hadn't said anything about us to her."

What an unhappy situation, thought Julia. *The child is really isolated.*

"I hope the police weren't too hard on you."

"Not really. They pressed me a lot on Brian's mood recently. I told them that he was not at all depressed. After all, the last time we were together, Brian told me about an offer someone had made to him to go into business. He was quite enthusiastic about it, not at all what you'd expect if he were thinking about suicide. But the police weren't interested. They just kept asking me about that woman and child who've been hanging around."

"Could you tell them anything about her?"

"All I know is what Father said at supper one day last week, some village gossip he'd heard about her showing up on Mrs. Beldington's doorstep asking for Brian. He was really obnoxious about it. And then, Mrs. B. made those nasty insinuations that this was some former girlfriend with his child."

"And I suppose you didn't have a chance to ask Brian about her?"

Hilary didn't answer immediately. She was sitting at the desk, and she stared out of the window for a minute or two. Her lower lip was quivering.

"Actually, I did. I phoned him last Friday evening. He hadn't been at rehearsal on Wednesday. I assumed at first he was still sulking because the previous weekend I'd refused once again to let him make love to me. Later, I thought it might have been the gossip that kept him away. I felt he owed me some explanation and that he should make the first move. But I needed to make arrangements for going to Hestercombe for the garden party on Saturday, so on Friday evening, I phoned him."

She paused, but Julia made no comment, so after a moment or two during which she seemed to making up her mind how much to tell, Hilary went on.

"He said he was busy. He'd have to ring me later. I . . . I was upset. I accused him of having that woman there. He became angry, asked me what I was talking about, said I should know better than to listen to stupid village gossip. But I took this as confirmation that she was there and that was why he didn't want to talk. I said as much to him and slammed down the phone. I thought he might phone back, but he didn't."

"I suppose that's why you were so edgy on Saturday," said Julia, thinking aloud.

"Yes. On Friday evening, I was just angry with him, thinking he was deceiving me. But when I phoned early Saturday and Mrs. B. told me he'd been out all night, I was frightened as well as angry. Had he spent the night with this woman? Was he going to break off our engagement so he could marry her instead? When he still didn't show up at Hestercombe, I was convinced of it."

"Did you tell all this to the police?"

"No, it was none of their business."

"But, Hilary, it could be important."

"Why could it be important? It was only my guess that he was with that woman all night. According to the police, he died about ten o'clock. So maybe she wasn't with him when I telephoned—that was about eight o'clock. Maybe there wasn't anyone with him. Perhaps he had decided this was the evening he wanted to test his bloody stupid gun and didn't want me to know about it"

Hilary was near to tears, but Julia felt compelled to warn her that she was heading down a dangerous path.

"Hilary, you must be careful. You may get away with a small lie with the police. But—"

"I didn't lie to them. They asked me if Brian and I had discussed the woman and her child. The child wasn't even mentioned. I just asked if she was there, and all he said was that I shouldn't listen to silly gossip. I don't call that a discussion. And I still insist it's none of their business. Some things should be kept private."

"But Hilary, if you're asked questions like that at the inquest, you'll have to give direct answers. You'll have to be completely truthful."

Hilary was silent.

"You'll be under oath, you know."

Hilary burst into tears and flung herself headlong on the bed. Julia went over to comfort her. "I know how awful this is for you," she began.

"Oh, Mrs. Dobson, I know you understand. It's everyone else. They couldn't leave us alone while Brian was alive, and now that he's gone, they want to tear everything to pieces that was precious for me."

And for a while, the two woman sat and held each other, each absorbed in her own grief and each deriving some small measure of comfort from the other's presence.

ELEVEN

At the inquest, however, Hilary was not asked specifically about her last conversation with Brian and so did not have to choose between truth and perjury. It was Brian's mother, not his fiancée, whose testimony produced the most dramatic effect.

Hilary had been excused from school for the morning so that she could testify at the inquest. Julia offered to drive her into Taunton and to deliver her to school afterward. This was a great relief to Hilary who had expected, and dreaded, that her father would accompany her. But at the last minute, he was called out to another sick cow. Julia had a passing irreverent thought that Dr. Worthington might have an agreement with a friendly farmer to bail him out of these awkward occasions, but kept it to herself.

Hilary was extremely nervous at the prospect of having to be interrogated in public even without her father present. She fidgeted through the first part of the proceedings, apparently playing no attention to the autopsy report—"Death would have been instantaneous from a gunshot wound to the right temple"—or the police report—"The body was lying facedown, the right arm and hand, with fingers still clasping the gun, lying beneath the body. We found no fingerprints on the gun apart from those of the deceased." She became visibly distressed when Ruth's letter was introduced as evidence of Brian's personal problems.

After the police reports, the first witness to be called was Mrs. Beldington. She readily testified to Brian's discomfort on receiving the letter and on hearing that a woman with a child had been looking for him, but to her manifest disappointment, she was dismissed after she had answered these few specific questions.

Then it was Hilary's turn. Standing in the witness box in her navy school uniform, golden hair neatly brushed back, Hilary looked even younger than her seventeen years. The initial questions were easy, and the coroner spoke gently to her. How long had she known Mr. Dixon? What was their relationship? Was he pleased about their engagement, looking forward to marriage and their future together?

Hilary answered each question as briefly as possible, fidgeting with her fingers as she did so. However, she became animated for a few minutes as she related Brian's excitement at the prospect of going into business with a friend. No, she didn't know who the friend was, Brian didn't mention any names. The coroner showed a little interest in this report but then shifted his questioning to more dangerous ground.

When had she last seen Mr. Dixon? Julia noted with some concern that Hilary seized the verb "see" as her cue and referred to the Sunday before his death. She declared that they had had a slight disagreement that day, and she had not seen him since then. She was waiting for him to apologize, and she presumed that he was waiting for her to make the first move. Yes, she had heard about the woman who was inquiring about him in the village, but she wasn't very worried about it. She assumed he had girlfriends before he met her, but since they were engaged to be married, she believed this woman posed no serious threat. She testified that the note found in his pocket was indeed his handwriting, but she insisted that she had no idea what it signified.

Her most difficult moment came when she was asked about the nature of their disagreement. She blushed and muttered something about it not being anything important, but she was not allowed to get away with that.

"Come, come, Miss Worthington. It was serious enough for you to avoid each other for a whole week. What were you disagreeing about?"

"He wanted me to go to bed with him, and I wouldn't."

Hilary spoke so quietly that she was barely audible, and she was asked to repeat her answer more loudly, which she did with great embarrassment.

"I see. And had you disagreed about this before?"

"Yes."

"And with similar consequences, that is deliberately not seeing each other for several days?"

"Sometimes."

"Did he seem to be more than normally upset on this occasion?"

"He seemed to think it was different now that we were engaged."

"But you didn't."

"No."

This last answer came out as a half-sob. She was clearly on the verge of a breakdown. The coroner tactfully shifted to more routine questions, this time about the gun. Hilary described seeing it in the drawer, warning Brian that it was dangerous to have it lying around and eliciting from him a promise that as soon as he had tested it to assure himself that it still worked, he would put it away, perhaps even consider disposing of it.

Brian's mother followed Hilary into the witness box. Myra Dixon was a shapeless, nondescript woman wearing an ill-fitting gray-brown suit that matched her short, frizzy hair, giving her a sad, monochrome appearance. She clutched a large vinyl handbag against her stomach as she answered the questions put to her. She was clearly intimidated by the court. Her eyes darted nervously from coroner to the police to the public benches, where a handful of spectators watched curiously. From time to time, she took one hand away from her handbag to push her glasses up the bridge of her nose. She licked her lips furiously before she answered each question.

She too was initially brief in her answers. No, her son had never exhibited any unusual behavior in the past. He was not a clumsy person, not accident prone. He had been a lively boy but never one to give her any trouble. Yes, he'd been a good son, especially after his father died. He was her only child, so he'd had to take a lot on his shoulders. He didn't move away until he knew she would be all right on her own. Yes, she knew he had the gun. It had belonged to her husband.

No, he hadn't told her about his engagement, had not even mentioned that he had a girlfriend. But they didn't communicate with each other very often. She wasn't a very good letter writer, and he didn't much like to write either. She didn't much like the telephone. But he would have told her eventually, she was sure of that. She confirmed that the handwriting of the note was definitely his.

She appears curiously detached, thought Julia, watching her with interest. Perhaps she was just numb.

Myra Dixon came to life, however, when the coroner referred to the mysterious young woman in Brian's life and what she had to say provided the meat of the story when the inquest was reported in the local weekly paper.

"Oh yes, I know who that was. That was Ruth Matthews, I'm sure it was. Brian was courting her when he was living at home some years ago. Such a nice girl she was, and she's become a really fine young woman."

"Had you seen her recently?"

"Yes, indeed. I bumped into her in Marks and Spencer a few weeks ago. She had the child with her. I could tell at once that it was Brian's child. He looked just like Brian at that age, except that his hair was a bit darker. But then Ruth's hair is darker too."

"Did she admit that your son was the father of her child?"

"Yes, she did. She said she was, well, expecting, when he left to come down to Somerset, but she didn't tell him because they had fallen out. I said he ought to know, he'd want to know. I thought he'd like to have a son and that if he knew about the boy, he'd most likely marry Ruth."

"Did you tell all this to her?"

"Oh no. I just said he should know about the boy and gave her Brian's address."

"You didn't write to him yourself with the news?"

"No. I didn't think I should do that. It was up to her to write and tell him. Of course, I didn't know anything about this other girl." She gestured toward Hilary but didn't look in her direction.

"Did you know about Miss Matthews's visit to Blymton?"

"No. The first I knew of that was when the police asked me the other day about a young woman and child inquiring for Brian, and then I knew she'd tried to find him."

Inspector Hughes testified that they had tried to track down Miss Matthews but had so far failed to find her. She had left the inn at Blymton on the Friday morning but had not returned to her flat in Wolverhampton. Her employer knew nothing of her whereabouts except that when she had asked for her two weeks' holiday pay, she had mentioned that she was going down to the West Country.

The coroner, summing up, was very puzzled by the whole affair. There was no doubt that Mr. Dixon died from a gunshot wound fired from his own gun and by his own hand. But whether the act was intentional or accidental was not at all clear. The note certainly suggested suicide, but the deceased's behavior prior to his death did not indicate any such intention. He had definitely talked about firing the gun to see if it worked, but Hestercombe was a strange place to go to test a gun. It was a strange place to choose for suicide for that matter. He was tempted to issue an open verdict, but for the sake of the deceased's mother and fiancée, his verdict would be death by misadventure.

Julia heard the verdict with relief, but Hilary seemed stunned. *It's delayed shock*, Julia concluded. *The fact of Brian's death has finally come home to her. Perhaps it would have been better if she had seen the body last weekend. I know how unreal it can seem.*

"What about some lunch before I take you back to school?"

Hilary nodded and let herself be steered toward the courtroom door. Myra Dixon was standing just outside, looking around with a forlorn air as if expecting someone to tell her what to do next. Hilary suddenly came to life. She went up to Brian's mother and held out her hand.

"Hello, Mrs. Dixon. I'm Hilary Worthington. I had hoped to meet you in happier circumstances."

"Yes, well . . . I wish Brian had told me about you. It was one more shock."

Julia stepped forward and introduced herself then, on the spur of the moment, invited the woman to join them for lunch. Myra Dixon made the usual polite demur and then, with a wan smile, acquiesced.

Julia suggested a nearby restaurant, a small quiet place, much frequented by soft-spoken gray-haired ladies carrying large shopping bags. The service was slow, but eventually they were eating—omelet and chips for Hilary and Myra, a slice of quiche and a small salad for Julia.

The food came none too soon. Conversation was slow and stilted. Julia began to think that inviting Myra Dixon had been a mistake. But when the plates had been removed and replaced with cups of coffee and little glass bowls of ice cream, Myra slowly brightened up.

"I'm sorry if I've not talked much. I'm still feeling a bit numb. I can't believe all this is happening. What did he mean, misadventure?"

"He was suggesting it was an accident rather than a suicide," said Julia.

"Of course it wasn't suicide. Brian wasn't the type to want to kill himself. But he wasn't clumsy." She swirled the spoon in the liquid at the bottom of the glass bowl, then looked up at Hilary. "He was a good son to me. When his dad died, he insisted he was now the man of the house, and he got a job after school as soon as he was old enough. He wanted to give me all his earnings, but I made him bank some of it. I thought he should do better out of life than his dad. And all for naught. All for naught."

She bent her head and, pulling a paper tissue from her handbag, blew her nose noisily. Julia put a sympathetic hand on her shoulder.

"I'm sorry, I suppose it's the shock. You see, when I bumped into Ruth Matthews and heard about the child, I really thought that the next news I'd hear would be that he was going to get married and settle down, not this—I'm sorry, Miss Worthington, I—"

"Please call me Hilary. And don't feel any need to apologize. Brian should have told you about our engagement, but it had only just happened, and I think he was not too sure about it himself. I probably pushed him into it before he was ready."

Myra reached over and patted Hilary on the arm.

"They're never ready. You have to push. That was Ruth's fault. She should have made Brian marry her when she found out she was expecting. Oh dear, I hope you don't mind me talking about her like this, but it's just that I know her so well, and I really don't know you at all, do I?"

By now the waitress had brought the bill, which Julia quickly picked up, and Hilary, looking at her watch, said she should get back to school. Julia offered to give Myra a lift to her hotel, but she declined, saying it wasn't far and she would enjoy the walk. But before they left the table, Myra asked Hilary if she would like to go back to Wolverhampton with her for the funeral.

"Thank you," Hilary said after a moment's hesitation. "I'll ask Father if I may go—no, I'll tell Father that I'll be going."

A few minutes later, out on the street and about to go their separate ways, Myra Dixon suddenly said, "You know something's been bothering me about that inquest. They said Brian was found with the gun in his right hand. But Brian was left-handed. Why would he have the gun in his right hand?"

"Yes!" exclaimed Hilary. "Why would he have the gun in his right hand?"

Julia was aghast. "Why didn't you say something to the police?"

"They didn't ask me which hand he used. And until this morning, I didn't even know the gun was still in his hand."

"That piece of evidence could have reinforced the accident theory," said Julia, trying rapidly to think through the implications of what she had just heard. "He might have been just holding the gun and tripped."

"Oh no," Hilary burst out. "Don't you see, Mrs. Dobson? It wasn't accident or suicide. Someone tried to make it look as though he'd shot himself. Someone else shot him. It was murder!"

TWELVE

Nigel's visit could not have been more opportune. Hilary's conjecture gave Brian's death a totally new dimension. Julia had never been comfortable with the options presented by the police. Neither accident nor suicide seemed to fit the man's character or the circumstances. Even so, to go from saying that accident or suicide seemed improbable to saying that it must be murder was making a tremendous leap. Who would have done it? Why at Hestercombe? And what, if anything, should be done about it? Hilary wanted to go straight to the police, but Julia convinced her to wait until she'd had a chance to ask Nigel's advice.

All these questions buzzed around her head as she prepared for his arrival. She had dressed with care that morning, not wanting to look like a bereaved woman. She had also taken great pains to make the table look attractive, laying her mother's best Royal Worcester china over a dainty cloth and arranging marinated vegetables and ham slices on flowered platters. She had been out early to buy the ham and fresh bread and, to her relief, had met no gossips, no one anxious to hear about the inquest or express an opinion on the verdict.

Hilary had appeared at the gate while she was gathering red poppies for the table, a large shopping basket on her arm.

"I've been doing some errands for Gran, then I'm off to help Mrs. Dixon. We're leaving this afternoon. You will ask your policeman friend what we should do, won't you? I'll phone you later."

And with a wave, she was gone. *I'm glad Mrs. Dixon is making use of her*, Julia thought. *It will help both of them get through this awful period.*

Back in the house, as Julia busied herself, dipping the stems in boiling water then arranging them in a low glass bowl with some feathery foliage, she felt a building sense of excitement. It was almost as though she were preparing to entertain a lover. It was ridiculous to think of Nigel in those terms, and yet he had always been important to her. "The rock" was how she and Anne would refer to him at Oxford, the one they could count on for helpful advice or a shoulder to lean on when things went wrong. You could confide in him too and know that he would keep the confidence.

There weren't many people she could talk to. She was an only child, as was Frank. Emma was their only child. Life in the Foreign Service had made it difficult to form and keep close friendships. So it wasn't surprising that she felt a special bond with Nigel, who had known her since college and known Frank even longer. This would be the first opportunity since Frank's death for a prolonged conversation with him. It was perhaps as well that she wanted to ask his advice about Brian's death. It would prevent the occasion from degenerating into a sentimental rehashing of old times.

Nigel drew up just before noon in a navy blue Volvo. He was a tall man with no sign of the belly that many men have developed by their forties. He wore a crisp white open-necked shirt neatly tucked into a pair of khaki twill trousers. Though smart and trim, he was not a handsome man. His nose was too big, and his eyes too close together. His coarse, short hair was still dark, with no trace of the gray that makes older men look distinguished, though it was beginning to recede above each temple. He had a serious aspect, suggesting a man of thought rather than action, yet Julia knew he was both. His early years at Scotland Yard had been full of action and danger, which he had met with great daring and courage. He was slow to smile, but she knew he had a wonderful sense of humor. *Dear old Nigel*, Julia thought as he greeted her at the gate with a solemn hug, *he is like the brother I never had.*

Julia poured two large glasses of lemonade, and they took lawn chairs out into the garden. For a while, they avoided talking about Frank. Julia asked Nigel about his work and later told him about the visit of Diana and Chip, hoping that this would provide a way to introduce the murder question. But before she could broach the issue, Nigel was off in a different direction, speaking of Diana's parents and the lost hope of a reunion of the five Oxford friends.

"Julia, I don't think I was adequate when I spoke to you at the memorial service," he said, "and I don't know that I can do better today, but how cruel life has been to you this past year. You seem to be handling it remarkably well, but I expect that underneath and in private, you have been through hell."

Julia could feel the tears forming at the back of her eyes. She forgot about the suspected Hestercombe murder. For the first time in months, she was with someone she could talk with freely about the nightmare of her loss.

"And I feel so useless," she finished. "What do I do for the next twenty, thirty, or however many years I have left? You don't know how many times I wished I'd gone with Frank to that meeting, been on that plane with him."

"The fact that you weren't suggests that there's still a purpose for you. I think the first step should be to get you back to London, away from this rural hibernation."

"I'm not exactly hibernating here." Julia smiled through her tears, thinking of the events of the past week. She leaned forward and squeezed Nigel's arm.

"Bless you, Nigel. It's been good for me to talk like this. I think I'll work things out eventually, but it will take time. And now I must give you lunch so that you can be on your way."

Briskly she swept up the lemonade glasses and led the way inside to the dining room. As she poured out two glasses of Moselle, she launched into an account of what she had been doing in recent weeks.

"Life in the country hasn't been too boring," she began. "In fact, in the last few days, it's begun to get a little too exciting."

Nigel listened without interruption, while she recounted the whole story, beginning with the engagement announcement in the local paper and ending with the startling disclosure about Brian's left-handedness.

"Hilary is convinced it was murder," she finished, "and I'm inclined to agree with her. But who could have done it, and why? And what, if anything, can we do about it?"

"What catches my attention immediately is the missing young woman and child. It seems ominous that they should have disappeared into thin air."

"Do you think she might have killed him?"

"It's possible. If he had told her he was going to marry someone else, she might have killed him in anger—the If-I can't-have-him-no-one-else-shall syndrome. But it takes a pretty unbalanced person to act that way. Or it may have been unintentional, a threat that went wrong. A person with a firearm who hasn't been trained to use it is particularly dangerous."

"But how did she get his gun? And what were they doing at Hestercombe?"

"Perhaps he wanted to go somewhere away from his lodging and the nosy landlady, a quiet place to talk undisturbed."

"And where was the child when all this was going on?"

"That's a good question. Hardly with them, I would think. Perhaps left behind at the inn."

"Except she had already checked out that morning."

"So the missing-young-woman-as-killer theory has large holes in it. Let's try the reverse. Suppose she was proving a nuisance to him, threatening to disrupt his bright future with young Hilary, demanding money to support his child. He kills both of them to dispose of the problem, again perhaps in anger, perhaps after a few drinks."

"But if he killed them, where are the bodies? And why is he dead?"

"Yes, we'd need bodies. And they may still turn up. As for him, this scenario would assume that he was horrified to realize he'd killed them, and so he killed himself too."

"But not with the gun in his right hand."

"That's true. So her disappearance may be entirely coincidental. All the same, if I had been in charge of this investigation, I think I'd have made more of an effort to find her."

"But the police never considered murder. Not publicly anyway."

"Even so, she might have had useful information about his state of mind in the last few days before his death. It really is odd that they just vanished."

Julia got up to remove the empty plates and bring in a lemon tart.

"So if it's not the former girlfriend, who else might it be?" she asked as she went back into the kitchen to put the coffee on. When she returned, Nigel was staring thoughtfully out of the window.

"He was found in the garden at Hestercombe where he works. Could it have been the result of a quarrel with a fellow worker?"

"Perhaps. But nobody has even hinted that he was on bad terms with anyone at Hestercombe. His supervisor testified at the inquest. He declared that Brian was well liked, a good worker, got on well with everyone. He did say that Brian seemed a bit edgy the week before he died, but there was nothing to suggest that this had anything to do with work or the people there."

"Let's think about motive. Who would want Brian Dixon dead?"

"At least two people next door," said Julia grimly. "Hilary's family was very opposed to her engagement. Both her father and her brother talked to me about it in very violent terms. Dr. Worthington said more than once in public that he would kill Brian before he'd let him marry his daughter. And Hilary's brother told me that his father should get rid of Brian, but if he didn't he, Tim, would."

"Both those threats sound to me like bluster. I've met that kind before, lots of loud talk but no real intent behind it. If Hilary's father had been really determined to kill his prospective son-in-law, he wouldn't have gone around proclaiming his intention to the world. He'd have quietly set to work planning and executing the death."

"Why does this matter to you?" Nigel asked when they had left the table and were settled with their coffee in the conservatory. "You say you hardly knew the young man."

"I think we owe it to his good name to prove that Brian Dixon was neither suicidal nor careless. I also believe in bringing murderers to justice."

"Very high-minded of you. But that's too glib. There are plenty of other causes you could take up, if you really want to right the world's wrongs. Why this particular one?"

Julia didn't answer immediately. *Why am I so obsessed?* she wondered. Nigel sat quietly, content to wait for her to think it through. Eventually, she said, "I feel a natural sympathy with Hilary, losing a loved one suddenly and unexpectedly and in such a cruel way. But you're right, there's no apparent reason why I should be so caught up in this, especially since it reopens the wounds. I've been dreaming about Frank recently, disturbing dreams where he is near to me, palpably near, and yet he eludes me. Perhaps Frank's death has something to do with it. I'm sure there was a bomb on his plane. I know the government suspects it, and there's still some kind of investigation going on. But there's nothing I can do about that. I can't go chasing international terrorists. But if I could help to bring a Somerset killer to justice, perhaps that would be a satisfying, even if vicarious, way of avenging Frank's death."

As he listened, Nigel had slumped in the chair, his elbows resting on its arms, his hands together covering his nose and the lower part of his face in a gesture long familiar to her. His dark eyes watched her intently. She was leaning forward in her chair, staring into the coffee cup cradled in her hands.

"I don't think I'm behaving this way consciously," she said. "In fact, I'm articulating it now for the first time because you're asking me." She looked at him directly. "Do you think the case could be reopened?"

"Possibly. Especially if I put a word in with my old friend Jack Shaw, who's now in charge here in Taunton"

"Would you do that?"

"Do you really want me to? Do you want to stir things up? It could get very unpleasant."

Julia looked puzzled.

"Once the police start asking the kind of questions we've just been asking, there's no knowing where they will end up. One possible suspect we haven't discussed, for instance, is Hilary herself."

"But that's impossible!"

"You say that because you know her or think you know her. A neutral policeman might see her as a jealous young woman, upset by the appearance of not just her fiancé's former girlfriend, but also his child. If the missing woman doesn't turn up soon, they might even wonder if Hilary killed all three of them."

"But it's Hilary who is insisting that it's murder after the coroner had ruled it accidental. Why would she do that if she were the murderer?"

"Guilt. Remorse. You may not know Hilary as well as you think. It's very easy to accept the face that a person chooses to present to the world. But most people are a complex mix of emotions, aspirations, and motives. I've seen plenty of pleasant young women in my time who have turned out to be quite nasty underneath. Hilary seems to be quite good at manipulating people. Announcing her engagement publicly without the knowledge of either her family or her intended fiancé suggests to me a young woman who thinks she can push people around."

"You wouldn't talk like that if you knew her."

"My dear Julia, that's not the point. What I'm trying to make you understand is that if this case is reopened, everyone is suspect, and the police will be thorough to the point of ruthlessness in their investigation. What were you doing that Friday evening, for example?"

"I have an alibi. Diana and Chip were here, and we sat up talking quite late. But I'm willing to take the risk of being suspected. I do feel strongly that there should be a new investigation."

"Then perhaps I could phone Jack now. You might like to meet him anyway. He and his wife are old friends of mine. We arrived at Scotland

Yard about the same time, but he didn't enjoy London life, and he didn't adapt to the pace of the Yard. He left after a few years to come down to Somerset, but we've kept in touch. Let me give him a brief synopsis of what you've told me and suggest that you meet him to fill in the details."

Julia left him at the phone and went into the kitchen to wash the dishes. She closed the door so she couldn't hear what he was telling Jack Shaw. She was quite shaken by what Nigel had been saying. If it did get rough, particularly for Hilary, she would have to help her face it. But Julia remained sure that Hilary was innocent, as sure as of her own innocence. She scrubbed the plates and glasses fiercely as if, by doing so, she could eradicate any lingering doubts.

After what seemed an eternity, Nigel came in to the kitchen.

"Jack has invited you for tea tomorrow. That gives you twenty-four hours to think it over. Jack's a good chap. He'll hear you out. But if you decide after you've slept on it that you want to leave well alone, you can just have tea and a chat and make some new friends."

"Thank you, Nigel. I'm so glad you came today. You've helped me probably more than you know. And now I must let you go, or you won't get down to Cornwall in time for dinner."

"I shan't want much dinner after that splendid lunch. But there's one thing I'd like to do before I head for the motorway. I'd like to take a quick look at Hestercombe. You've piqued my curiosity. Can you direct me there?"

"That would be difficult. It's not easy to find. Let me lead you there."

Hestercombe was basking in the warm June sun when they drove in tandem through the gateway and up the long drive. The Blackdown Hills shimmered in the distance as Julia and Nigel stood on the top terrace overlooking the Great Plat. Large white lilies were in bloom, and the bergenias thrust their thick oval leaves upward toward the sun.

"It is beautiful," said Nigel.

"And so peaceful. It's hard to believe that something violent and ugly happened here."

"But that's life, the good and the ugly side by side."

They went down to the rose garden where the dainty China tea roses were now in full bloom then walked slowly along The Grey Walk. Bees were busy in the catmint. The East Rill was ablaze with scarlet poppies, yellow irises, and red-hot pokers.

"The stonework is magnificent," said Nigel.

"Gertrude Jekyll once compared it to the 'gathered ribbon strap work of ancient needlework.' The patterns are formal, intricate in detail, but the garden isn't as severe as the French or Italian classical gardens because of the informal masses of color and texture."

Finally, they came to the pergola. Julia showed Nigel how Chip had first seen the body as he stood on the edge of the wall. They went through the archway at the end of the pergola, down the steps, and round the corner to the place where the body had lain.

"This is very open," Nigel remarked. "I'm surprised no one spotted the body before you did."

"The main activities of the garden party were up on the top terrace and around the Orangery. And this part is outside the garden proper. Most people wouldn't come down here, and someone on the pergola wouldn't have seen it without stepping over to the edge of the wall as Chip did."

As he got into the Volvo, Nigel's final comment was "Enjoy your tea with Jack and Helen. I just hope you aren't opening Pandora's box."

THIRTEEN

Julia dreamed again about Frank that night. She was walking once more down a path lined with tall evergreen bushes, but this time, it was a straight path. She could hear Frank talking to someone on the other side of the bushes. It was unmistakably his voice, even though she couldn't hear the exact words. The bushes were impenetrable; she couldn't even see through them. She kept on going, wanting to keep up with the voice, looking for a gap, waiting for the end of the path; but there was no gap, no end in sight. She called out Frank's name several times and woke up shouting "Frank!" Her nightdress was dripping with sweat, and her limbs were trembling uncontrollably.

It was very early, but already the first light of day was visible through the curtains, and she could hear the caroling of a thrush somewhere in the garden. She lay in bed for a while, trying to recapture the sound of Frank's voice, but it was irretrievable. She wondered why she was now having these terribly frustrating dreams about Frank when she didn't dream at all after his death. Was it delayed shock, brought on perhaps by Brian's death?

Julia couldn't answer the questions or go back to sleep, so she got up and took a quick bath to refresh her sweaty body. She made coffee and wandered into the conservatory, brooding over Nigel's warnings. Would it be rash to ask for the case to be reopened? She stared out into the garden where the trees and shrubs were now in full leaf. A stand of lupins reared red, pink, and cream spires along one wall. The thrush was still singing away in the apple tree. It was all so peaceful. Why not let things rest? Brian Dixon was dead and would soon be buried. Perhaps the secret of his death should go with him to the grave. And yet . . . She remembered yesterday's conversation with Nigel, her answer to his question about why she was determined to pursue this. Despite what she had said, she wasn't sure that she was subconsciously trying to avenge Frank's death, but some instinct told her that if she didn't act, the negligence would nag her for years, perhaps forever.

Hilary too was keen to press on with an investigation. She had called from the station on her way to Wolverhampton, eager to learn the outcome of Julia's consultation with Nigel. Julia told her about the introduction to the local police chief but added Nigel's advice that they might be better off doing nothing. She relayed the warning about the possibility of unpleasantness, tough questions, everybody being a suspect, Hilary included. Hilary insisted that she was not afraid of questions.

"Hilary, do you realize that you'll have to tell everything to the police, including the phone conversation with Brian that Friday evening? In fact, you'll have to allow me to mention it when I talk to the local police chief about reopening the case. He won't do it on Nigel's word alone. That simply opens the door for me. They may need more evidence than the fact that Brian was left-handed. Your phone conversation with him that evening suggests that there was someone with him, and that too may be critical."

"You can mention it if you must. I want to know the truth, whatever it is."

It was remembrance of Hilary's firm determination that resolved Julia's last doubts. She wasn't due at Jack Shaw's house until four o'clock, but by early afternoon, she was so restless that she had to go somewhere, do something. On the spur of the moment, she decided to go to the afternoon rehearsal of the play.

Now that the first performance was only a month away, Dick had increased the number of rehearsals. Today, he had decreed, would be a full run through on the outdoor stage. The weather was promising. With luck, this would be one of the years when they could actually perform their summer play outdoors.

The location for the outdoor performances was Blymton Manor. Julia had never been there, never met the occupants. All she knew of it was the ancient stone wall that stretched for several hundred yards at one end of the village. Its large iron gates were usually open, but the drive was lined with huge horse chestnut trees, and as it curved off to the right almost immediately, it was impossible to catch a glimpse of the house from the road. The rehearsal gave her the long-awaited excuse to drive through the gates and round the curve for her first look at the manor house.

It turned out to be a handsome stone house of the Elizabethan period. The drive emerged from the trees to an open area. A wood lay to the right and to the left an enormous lawn. It was one of those rare summer days with a cloudless sky, and the grass glowed under the hot sun as Julia drove up to the front of the house. A few cars were lined up on the gravel, and several bicycles were parked on the grass.

All the activity seemed to be taking place behind the house. She set out across the grass, feeling now the full heat of the sun and wishing that she had worn a hat, and came to a broad terrace that stretched across the back of the house. Wings jutting forward at each end of the building, and a smaller projection in the middle—the traditional E shape of fashionable Elizabethan houses—created a natural framework for the terrace stage, where the Athenian lovers were already quarreling.

Molly, awaiting the cue for her first entrance, waved to Julia. She was talking to a woman whom Julia had seen once or twice in the village and who was now introduced as Bridget DeVere, the lady of Blymton Manor. Bridget DeVere was short and slim, with a face that was far from beautiful yet had its good points. A broad and deep forehead rose above finely shaped eyebrows and light hazel eyes that fixed Julia now with a steady but friendly gaze. Her chin was firm, even pugnacious. A light dusting of freckles on her nose, curly reddish-brown hair, and a colorful peasant skirt topped by a plain blue T-shirt, gave her a girlish look. As Molly hurried away for her first scene, Bridget grasped Julia's arm in a strong grip and said how delighted she was to meet her.

"Molly told me that I would find you a kindred spirit. She says you are a keen gardener, for instance. I would love to do more with this place, but it's so huge I don't know where to start."

"You surely have some help?"

"A local farmer sends his son over once a week to cut the grass, but that's about all we can afford. The place eats money. We've been here only two years since my husband's grandfather died. He lived to be ninety and hadn't spent any money on it for years, so we're having to do a lot of renovation. But I expect we'll get round to the garden one day."

"What would you do?" asked Julia, looking around at the vast expanse of grass. "Break up this lawn?"

"Old pictures of the house show formal rose gardens, herb gardens, even a lily pool, with very little open lawn. A nineteenth-century DeVere did away with all of it and put in that awful shrubbery. That would have to go."

"But it's a wonderful setting for *A Midsummer Night's Dream*."

For the woodland scenes, Dick had shifted the action to an area at the end of the terrace where an exuberant Victorian shrubbery shielded the outbuildings from view. Puck and various fairies were flitting in and out of the bushes, then Molly and her fairy king husband made their entrance. Oberon's "Ill met by moonlight" sounded odd under the relentless glare of the sun.

"The shrubbery is useful for this play," admitted Bridget, "but it's a year-round nightmare. It's too dense and too close to the house."

"Too damp?"

"No. It's mischief makers that I worry about. We have trouble with them in the wood beyond the drive. I'm afraid that one day they'll make their way round to the shrubbery, and then they'll be right up to the house."

"Mischief makers?"

"Teenage boys from the village. They must be about fourteen or fifteen years old, too young to be working or driving but bursting with hormones and energy and nothing constructive to absorb it all. There's nothing in the village for young people to do—no disco, no youth club, not even Scouts. So they roam around in packs, entertaining themselves with petty acts of thievery and vandalism. This spring, some of them began roaming through our wood. They light bonfires, usually when we're away, but we came home early once and surprised them. They'd been indulging in some bizarre rite. We found mutilated animals on the ground and a strong smell of marijuana."

"Can't the police help you get rid of them?"

"They claim they're shorthanded and too busy to worry about young boys letting off steam. It's the parents I blame. They shouldn't let their sons go out like that night after night. Some of them come from respectable families, like the local vet's son. But you must know Tim Worthington—doesn't he live next door to you?"

Julia drove out of Blymton Manor in a very different frame of mind from when she turned in through the gates just a short time before. The woods that had seemed so pleasant and inviting now appeared menacing. Bridget's complaint about the delinquent boys brought back the dinner-table conversation with Chip about the decline of Western society. It certainly was a changed country from the one she had left twenty years ago. And if the police were so busy that they couldn't deal with teenage gangs, then they wouldn't be pleased to reopen a case they believed to be over and done with.

The Shaws lived in a quiet neighborhood on the outskirts of Taunton. Their comfortable, unpretentious house was of the 1930s vintage, with a yellow stucco facade, large bay windows, and a frosted-glass front door. Inside were pale fitted carpets, family photographs on top of glass-fronted cabinets, and the faint smell of the Sunday roast lamb lingering on the air. This was the England she remembered from her youth. Some things had not changed.

Jack Shaw grasped her hand firmly, brushed away the large golden retriever that bounded up to greet her and steered her into the sitting room and a commodious chintz-covered chair. Julia decided at once that this was a man she could trust. He was a well-built man, though even if he were to stand up straight, instead of slumping his shoulders, he would not be tall.

He began the conversation with the obvious remarks, commenting on the heat, inquiring about Nigel, offering condolences on her situation, but in a gentle unobtrusive way that didn't demand more than a polite superficial answer. Julia concluded that he was probably very good at putting people at their ease and off their guard before springing the question that would lead to self-betrayal.

His wife was a clear contrast. Where her husband was calm and deliberate, she was bright and brisk, almost impulsive. She burst in from the kitchen with a tray full of tea things and quickly set the agenda.

"We'll have tea—Jack, do move that little table closer to Julia, there's a dear—and then I'll take the dog for her afternoon walk, and you and Jack can discuss murder. How would you like your tea, Julia? Milk? Sugar? Jack, pass the scones and the jam."

The tea was poured and stirred, the scones and jam were passed, and the conversation covered safe and pleasant topics such as gardening. Helen did most of the talking, gesturing as she spoke, leaping up to consult a dictionary of roses at one point, disregarding the wisps of fine, fair hair that escaped from the knot at the back of her neck. Then suddenly she jumped up and said, "Time for walkies!" The dog that had been sleeping peacefully by her chair sprang to life and barked excitedly. There was a flurry while Helen searched for the leash, the dog padding back and forth impatiently, and then they were gone, and the room was still.

"You want to talk about a possible murder?"

It was an abrupt opening, but Julia welcomed Jack's directness.

"I don't know how much you know," she began.

"I know a young man was found dead in the garden at Hestercombe, shot in the head by his own gun, which was in his own hand. You found the body, I believe. The coroner, in his wisdom, declared that it was an accident, although he clearly suspected that it might be suicide. Why do you think it was murder?"

"Because the gun was in his right hand and yet he was left-handed."

"That was not brought out at the inquest."

"No. I believe the first official statement about the body mentioned that the gun was in his right hand, but the point wasn't emphasized. I think everyone assumed that he was right-handed. It wasn't until afterward that Mrs. Dixon—the young man's mother—commented that it was strange that the gun was in his right hand when he was left-handed."

"It's certainly curious. But is it enough to prove murder? If I'm to reopen the investigation, I'll have to have a good case for doing so. There'll be a lot of pressure not to do it."

Julia looked puzzled.

"They won't be too pleased at Hestercombe, for instance. It was bad enough for them having a body turn up in the garden. They're now assuming they can put the whole affair behind them and forget it. Starting to ask questions and drawing attention to their misfortune all over again won't go down well."

"Especially if it turned out to be a fellow worker who killed him."

"Right. And we'd certainly have to look into that possibility. But if we draw a blank there, where else could we look?"

"Perhaps Brian stumbled on a vagrant, hoping to sleep undisturbed under a bush. Or a group of teenagers looking for a quiet place to smoke a little pot. There was a fight, and he was killed. I saw trampled plants on the pergola above where we found the body as though there had been a struggle."

It sounded ludicrous, but Julia was recollecting Bridget DeVere's report of wild youngsters in her wood. If the village boys were behaving like that, then such speculation was not totally absurd.

"If he was killed by strangers, then we have a cold trail, and I wouldn't expect much success in making an arrest. But if it was random,

I wouldn't expect the killer to spend time arranging the body to look like a suicide. No, if we suspect murder, I think we're better off assuming Dixon knew his killer, probably arranged to meet that person at Hestercombe."

"Or they went there together," said Julia. She was thinking of Hilary's phone call and her suspicion that Brian had someone with him that evening. She took a deep breath and related what Hilary had told her.

Jack frowned.

"You say she didn't tell the inspector about that conversation? That was very stupid." He paused then added, "Of course, it also leaves her exposed, unless someone can vouch for her whereabouts that evening. If she thought he was spending time with an old girlfriend, she could have been angry or jealous enough to spy on him, follow them to Hestercombe, and confront him."

"How could she do that? She has no car, can't drive."

"That's a good point. But that's the means. The motive is more important. If someone has the motive, a real, burning motive, they will find the means somehow. Does she have a bicycle, for instance? She's probably not a strong suspect, but she'll have to be checked out. I suppose you realize that if we're talking about reopening the investigation, there will be lots of rough questions. Anyone with the slightest motive or opportunity will have to be investigated."

Julia nodded. Jack went over to the mantelpiece and picked up a pipe. "Mind if I smoke?"

When Julia raised no objection, he proceeded to light it.

"I hear old Nigel finally gave up smoking," he said between puffs. "I know the doctors had been after him for years. He finally paid attention—unlike me." He chuckled. "But Nigel always did have better judgment than me. That's why, if he took you seriously, I'm willing to do the same. So"—he threw away his last match and settled back in a chair—"who had reason to want Brian Dixon dead?"

Julia considered her next words very carefully.

"One or two people were extremely upset by Hilary's engagement to Brian. Her father, for instance. When I congratulated him on his daughter's engagement, he got very angry. He said he would kill Brian before he'd let him marry his daughter. But I didn't take him literally. He's a very irascible man, but I don't think he'd have the guts to kill someone, even in anger. And even if he did, I don't think he'd have the presence of mind to stage it as a suicide."

"That sounds like a reasonable assessment. Determined murderers don't usually go around boasting of what they plan to do. Who else?"

"That also rules out Hilary, doesn't it?" interrupted Julia, who was still one step behind Jack. She had been shaken by his quick suggestion that Hilary could have killed Brian. First Nigel, then this police officer had jumped to that possible conclusion. Would that be the thrust of the inquiry? But it was a preposterous idea. "I mean, if she had killed him and tried to disguise it as suicide, she'd have known to put the gun into his left hand."

"Unless she was really clever and put it in the right hand in the belief that no one would suspect her of making such a mistake. But," he added quickly, noticing Julia's irritation, "I don't really suspect your young friend. I'm just warning you that the inspector may not let her off so lightly. What about the tyrannical old grandmother you said lives in the Worthington household? Should she be suspect?"

"She certainly had motive. She expressed satisfaction at hearing of Brian's death. She might have thought she was carrying out the will of God, removing a sinner. That's the kind of person she is. She's still a muscular woman. I think she'd be physically capable of it. But she's very unsociable, rarely leaves the house. I don't think she would be a credible suspect."

"So we can probably leave her for the moment. Who else do we have?"

"Hilary's younger brother, Tim. I'd say he's about fourteen or fifteen, a surly lad but strong and with a streak of cruelty. He also threatened to kill Brian. And when he heard about his death, he laughed and said it was good riddance."

"That's hardly an indictment for murder."

"I agree. That's the problem. The whole Worthington family seemed to be lined up in implacable opposition to Hilary's engagement, and they are certainly pleased now that he's out of the way. But that doesn't mean they stooped to murder."

Jack puffed thoughtfully on his pipe for a minute or two.

"On the other hand," he said, "it's surprising what seemingly respectable people are capable of when they feel they have their backs against the wall. It's the obverse of the amazing bravery that people often display in a crisis. There is evil in the world, and it's often hidden beneath the surface."

Once again, Julia remembered the dinner-table discussion of evil and depravity, and her spirits drooped. She looked past Jack to the window and the roses she could see outside. There was a bowl of yellow roses on a table. Julia fixed her eyes on them, wondering if they were McGredy's Yellow and willing the flowers to counteract her gloom.

Jack broke into her reverie.

"There's also the question of who was with Dixon that evening when Hilary phoned him, assuming she's correct in suspecting he was not alone. Which leads me to another person we haven't considered, the former girlfriend. We could presume she had a motive too—anger or revenge if she made overtures to him and was rejected."

"Nigel also put forward a variation of that theory—that Brian might have killed her and the child and then killed himself in a fit of remorse."

"I'd say that's a long shot, but her disappearance is puzzling. Finding her would have to be one of the first tasks."

The roar of a motorbike shattered the Sunday quiet and the vibration, slight as it was, caused a few of the yellow petals to drop onto the table. Julia's thoughts now swung back to Tim.

"My first impressions of Tim were that he was just an extremely rebellious adolescent, but I'm beginning to think he's malicious. I've heard other disturbing reports."

She related what Bridget DeVere had told her about the mischief makers in the wood.

"Not very nice. I wish we did have the manpower to investigate incidents like that, but your friend is right. We can't afford to spend time on minor cases of delinquency, even though we know that by not paying attention now, we may one day be dealing with those same boys after they've committed much more serious crimes. And that's why I have to consider the evidence very carefully before reopening a case."

Jack got up to find more matches to relight his pipe. He looked at Julia with a slight frown and then said very deliberately, "I think on balance it's worth taking another look. I'll talk to Inspector Hughes in the morning."

Julia felt herself relax. It was as though a weight had been lifted from her shoulders. Whatever happened next would be out of her hands.

She thanked Jack, but he cut her short.

"You may not thank me when this is over. If we can find someone at Hestercombe who had the motive and the means, it could be a simple matter. But if we have to look for a killer elsewhere, say Blymton, it won't be an easy investigation."

FOURTEEN

"Somerset on the boil" was the headline in the local paper as the hot weather persisted through the week, accompanied by drought, bothersome flies and frayed tempers. Even Julia, who had endured many a tropical summer, found the heat unbearable without air-conditioned rooms. She was watering the parched roses early Tuesday morning when Dr. Worthington appeared from his front door and stormed toward the low gray wall separating his lawn from Flora Cottage.

"What's all this about? Why are you interfering?"

"I don't understand."

"You've been talking to the police, raking up the death of that Dixon fellow. And now they're bothering me with questions, questions they have no business asking."

"I'm sorry if you've been bothered, Dr. Worthington. But I do think it's important to get to the bottom of what happened at Hestercombe."

"But I had nothing to do with that. So why did that infernal policeman spend hours last night interrogating me and my mother and my son? And he threatens to come back again. He says he needs more information about our whereabouts the night that damned fellow killed himself. He wants to talk to Hilary when she gets back home. It's a damned outrage, I tell you! And I'll thank you to stop putting ideas into Hilary's head. Just mind your own business!"

Having delivered his message, Dr. Worthington stalked angrily back to the house, leaving Julia a little disturbed by his vehemence. She hadn't expected the unpleasantness to come so quickly or from that quarter. All the same, she was gratified that Jack had wasted no time in getting the investigation under way.

Inspector Hughes's interview with the Worthington family had been prolonged and contentious. He was not in the best of tempers as he parked at the front gate and walked up the path to the house. He had plenty of misgivings about his chief's decision to reopen the case and, like the chief, had quickly concluded that the swiftest disposition would be to find the murderer within the fire brigade. However, he had spent most of the day interviewing Brian Dixon's fellow workers without finding any promising leads.

He banged the heavy door knocker just as the Worthingtons were finishing supper.

"Not another sick animal, I hope," the doctor growled.

Mrs. Worthington calmly put down her spoon and went to the door. When she returned, however, she was not quite so calm.

"It's that policeman again. He wants to talk to us."

"What policeman?"

"When you were away. He came to tell us about the death of your daughter's paramour."

Tim had risen from the table at the mention of the police and was trying to slip quietly out of the room when his father bellowed to him to stop.

"You're not going anywhere! I expect you and your friends have been up to some mischief again. Mother, take the police officer into the front parlor and tell him we'll be there in a minute when I've finished my pudding."

He spooned down the rest of his pudding, while Tim stared glumly at his plate. Then he wiped his mouth and pushed back his chair.

"Let's see what this is all about."

They walked across the hall to the parlor where the old lady, perched straight-backed on the hard velour sofa, was lecturing a man standing before her.

Inspector Hughes, relieved at the interruption, identified himself.

"Yes, yes. I'm Dr. Worthington, and this is my son, Tim. I see you've met my mother. Don't pay any attention to her moralizing. She cooks well, and that's what counts."

He was trying to be affable, but he didn't deceive the inspector. The man was clearly nervous. His son didn't look very comfortable either. The boy sat down and began picking at a small hole in the knee of his jeans. The old lady, silent now, was glaring at the detective. *If looks could kill*, he thought.

"I'm here to ask you some questions in connection with the death of Brian Dixon."

"I thought that was all settled. Didn't the coroner rule that it was an accident?"

"He did. But new information has come to us, which suggests that it might be murder. At least we have to look at the case again in the light of this new evidence."

Inspector Hughes was not all that convinced the new information was compelling. He had to follow orders, but he would take care not to stretch his credibility too far.

"I don't see how we can help you."

"To start with, he was engaged to your daughter, was he not?"

Dr. Worthington bristled.

"I did not accept that engagement. The marriage would never had taken place."

"Dixon's death certainly made sure of that. Some people might say that his death was the perfect way to make sure he would never marry your daughter."

"That is outrageous! How dare you accuse me of murder! I never heard such—"

"Dr. Worthington! I am not accusing you of murder. But you did have a motive, did you not? You were heard to say that you would kill Brian Dixon before you would let him marry your daughter."

"Who told you that?"

"Several people in the village heard you say it."

"It's a damned slander! I'll—"

"No, Dr. Worthington, I believe you made the threat. But because you made it so often and so publicly, I don't believe you actually intended to kill him and certainly not so furtively. I think the threat was just a bluff, a way to relieve your feelings."

This was too much for the doctor. His face was now dark red, his eyes were bulging, and his temples throbbed. He sputtered, trying to get out words, but was too overwrought to form more than syllables. Mrs. Worthington stared calmly at her hands, totally unperturbed by her son's performance. Tim, however, seemed mildly amused, watching the duel between his father and the policeman as though he were watching two mongrels scrapping.

Finally, the inspector managed to calm Dr. Worthington enough to sit down and listen.

"I repeat. I'm not accusing you of anything, except perhaps overreaction, though it seems you make a habit of that. I merely remarked that you would appear to have a motive. Therefore, before I can stop wasting my time on you and your family, I have to establish where you all were that Friday evening. Once I am assured that you were far from Hestercombe, I can rule you out and move on to more promising suspects."

But if Inspector Hughes thought this reasonable suggestion would help to soothe the enraged doctor, he was mistaken. The man stared at him, his mouth open, but now, the inspector perceived, it was fear rather than rage that choked back his words. He decided to let the man sweat for a minute or two, but surprisingly, Dr. Worthington made a quick recovery.

"Well, that's no problem, no problem at all. Yes, I was away that whole weekend, left Friday afternoon."

"Where did you go?"

"To a conference, a veterinarians' meeting, the other side of Plymouth."

"The conference lasted the whole weekend?"

"No, it was just a one-day affair, but I stayed there for the entire weekend, did a bit of fishing. I don't often have a real holiday, you know. Vets, like doctors, are always on call, so if I can take off for a weekend, I seize the opportunity."

He was smiling now, seemed almost relaxed. Even so, he went over the window and raised the sash, muttering as he did so, "Stuffy room. Women will never open windows."

The inspector was glad of the breath of fresh air that swept into the room. He ran a finger round the inside of his collar and watched the vet walk clumsily back to the circle round the empty fireplace and lower himself into a chair.

"Plymouth. Let's see, that would be less than a three-hour drive. If you left in the afternoon, you'd be there in time for dinner. Where did you stay? We will need to verify that you were there and your time of arrival."

"I don't remember the name of the place. It was one of those awful American-style hotels, Best Quality, or something like that. Artificial greenery and piped music everywhere, soft beds and no decent gin in the bar."

"Perhaps you have a receipt or a notice of the meeting that will give the name of the hotel? We really will have to check up on that. And perhaps you could tell me how you spent the evening. Were you with other people who can vouch for your presence there and so lay to rest any suspicion that you might have been at Hestercombe?"

"Yes, of course. Yes, well, whatever one usually does on those occasions. Had a few drinks in the bar, dinner with some of the chaps, then turned in fairly early."

"How do you define early? Nine o'clock? Ten?"

"I was in bed by ten, I believe."

Ten o'clock. Probably a three-hour drive away from Hestercombe. The pathologist had expressed an opinion that death had taken place about ten o'clock, certainly well before midnight. It was unlikely that the doctor could have driven back in time. All the same, thought the inspector, *I'll have to confirm that with his friends.*

"I'd like the names and addresses of one or two of the people you were with. I don't doubt your word"—noticing the vet beginning to bristle—"but that's standard police procedure. We have to check every statement. Who were you with?"

Dr. Worthington shook his head.

"I really would have to ask their permission first. One can't give people's names to the police just on request. That's not done."

The vet spoke testily, but he didn't seem rattled. All the same, the inspector had a hunch that he wasn't telling the whole truth, that he wasn't just having an innocuous evening out with the boys. Perhaps it was a poker night. Perhaps he lost money. He could insist on the names at once, but it wasn't worth it. And the hotel people might be able to tell him what he needed to know.

"I'd be obliged if you would get permission and then let me know. Two or three names will do. The name of the hotel is more important just now. Perhaps you could start looking for it while I talk to your mother?"

Dr. Worthington went over to a desk in the corner and began to rummage in its interior. The inspector turned his attention to the old lady, now fixing him with a baleful eye.

"May I ask what you were doing that evening, after your son left for the weekend?"

"I was here all evening. I have nothing to hide. I am a respectable, God-fearing Christian. I do not go gallivanting with the wicked worldly sinners out there."

"Were your grandchildren at home with you?"

"No. At least Hilary was at home, but as I remember, she spent the evening in her bedroom. Tim was out. He was consorting with devils, as usual. That boy has not been trained up in the way he should go."

She switched her glare momentarily to her grandson, but he was not at all disconcerted. He grinned maliciously, intently picking away at his jeans.

"Were you here, in this room, all evening?"

"Most of the evening. I was reading the good book for a while, and then I had some mending to do. I went into the kitchen later to make some preparations, after which I went to bed. I invariably go up to bed at ten o'clock. Is there anything else you wish to know?"

"Was Tim still out when you went to bed?"

"Yes. If my word prevailed in this house, he would not be out at that hour. But his father indulges him. I have told him 'Chasten thy son while there is hope,' but he hears me not."

A vigorous rustling from the desk and an impatient snort suggested that while her word might not prevail, it was certainly heard. Inspector Hughes felt a brief pang of sympathy for the vet. He sensed the steel in the old woman's soul. Even on this sultry evening, a chill emanated from her presence.

"Did you lock up the house before retiring?"

"The front door was left unbolted for Tim. He has a key." She saw the look of surprise on the inspector's face and added, "I depend on the Lord for my protection, not on locks and bolts."

"And Hilary? Was she upstairs all evening?"

The old lady nodded.

"You didn't hear her come down to make a phone call?"

"No."

"She didn't come downstairs at all?"

"I did not hear her."

That was the problem, the inspector realized. *The walls of these old houses were so thick you could creep around without even the most acute ear hearing a thing.*

"Are you sure she was in her room when you went to bed?"

"Yes. I called out good night to her as I usually do, and I believe she replied." *Or did she think Hilary replied, if that's what she usually hears?* the inspector wondered. Perhaps Hilary went out after that. Or she could have crept out earlier and been back by ten. I'd better press the pathologist to be more firm about the time of death.

"One last question. Does Hilary also have a key to the front door?"

"She does."

The inspector made a note and turned to Tim.

"And where were you all evening?"

"Out."

"Obviously. But where? What were you doing? And who was with you?"

"I was with the gang, I expect. I dunno where we were. We don't keep records."

"Now there's no need to get cheeky. Surely you can recall something you did."

"But that's two weeks ago, or almost. I don't even remember what I did last Friday, let alone the one before. We don't have any set routine. We do just what we feel like. I do know we weren't at bloody Hestercombe doing any bloody murders."

"Who else is in this gang?"

Tim named several youths. Inspector Hughes recognized one or two as young delinquents who already had a police record and a couple more on their way to that end. He noticed that Dr. Worthington had stopped fumbling in the desk and was now listening intently. Probably this was the first time he'd paid attention to the company his son was keeping.

"Those are not the best companions for a bright young man like yourself."

If the inspector thought the compliment would soften up the youth, he was disappointed. The cold, hard expression didn't change. The boy has inherited the steel of his grandmother and the fire of his father, he surmised. Given the right direction, he could make something of himself. But there didn't seem much point in working on him at this time.

"If you don't remember where you were that evening, I don't suppose you remember what time you came home?"

"No. Late, I expect."

"After midnight?"

"Probably."

"And the front door was unbolted? At least, if that was the usual practice I assume you would remember if the door had not been left unbolted?"

"I don't ever remember the front door being bolted."

"I have the name of the hotel where I stayed." Dr. Worthington came across the room with a piece of paper in his hand. "It was the same place where the meeting was held, the only reason I'd stay at a place like that. Here's the notice I received about the meeting."

Inspector Hughes jotted down the name of the hotel then closed his notebook with a snap.

"Thank you, Dr. Worthington. Please don't forget to get me the other names I requested. As for you, young man, I expect I'll have more questions for you, but that will do for now. In the meantime, put your memory to work and see if you and your pals can remember what you were doing two Fridays ago. I don't think it will be too difficult once you put your mind to it." *I'll bring you down to the station, see if I can't scare you a bit*, he told himself.

As he turned to leave, he said to the boy's father, "You should pay more attention to what he gets up to. If he's involved with that crowd, it's only a matter of time before he gets into serious trouble."

Julia was the next to find Inspector Hughes on the doorstep, notebook in hand. He arrived on Tuesday morning, soon after her encounter with the angry vet. She showed him into her small sitting room and offered him a cool drink, but he declined without even a thank-you. She made some inconsequential remark about the hot weather, but he ignored it and went straight to the point.

"Tell me again about finding the body. What were you doing at Hestercombe that afternoon?"

Julia sighed. Jack had warned her that the inspector would not be pleased at being told to reopen the investigation, but she hadn't expected him to be so hostile. *Two can play at that game*, she decided. *After all, I don't have any pertinent information. I didn't kill Brian Dixon, and I have no idea who did. I just happened to find the body. And if they'd done their job properly the first time, they wouldn't be coming back now, sniffing at a cold trail.*

She answered his questions tersely and managed to stay cool as long as Inspector Hughes was asking her about the body. But when he switched to questions about Hilary, about the girl's mood that afternoon, Julia grew increasingly angry.

"You say Miss Worthington seemed tense, jittery, when you first saw her at the garden party. Did that strike you as odd?"

"No. She had told me earlier that she and Brian had quarreled, and now it seemed that he had disappeared. Any young girl would be upset at that."

"Do you still see it as simply as that?"

"What do you mean?"

"Now that we know her fiancé was actually dead even as you were chatting away at the garden party, don't you think her nervousness might have been due to the fact that she knew his body was laying not far away?"

"Of course not!"

"She let you take her away from the garden party, didn't she? Was she eager to leave?"

"Yes, but—"

"Perhaps she was keen to get away before the body was found, as it surely would be before the end of the afternoon? Would that seem a plausible explanation for her agitated manner?"

"Inspector Hughes! I must protest! You're letting your imagination run away with you. Nobody was thinking about bodies or even crimes. It wasn't death in the air but deception, betrayal, loss of love. Hilary was behaving as any seventeen-year-old girl would behave who fears that she's been jilted. You may not remember, but at that tender age, emotions are very powerful, and one has little experience of how to handle or control them. You really mustn't read into Hilary's nervousness anything more than that."

"Yet I also know, as I'm sure you do too, Mrs. Dobson, that powerful emotions, particularly among immature young people, can lead to rash and even criminal actions."

"But what I keep trying to tell you, Inspector, is that Hilary was not behaving like someone who's done something rash or criminal. You have asked me to describe her behavior, her mood that day. She did not display an ounce of guilt or shame, then or since. She was puzzled by Brian's disappearance and worried—not worried in the sense of being concerned for his welfare, but more for the implications of his disappearance for the future of their relationship. Even though she did not say so explicitly, I was sure she believed that Brian had left her and gone off with the mystery woman."

"Did anyone else have these same observations?"

"Yes, you should talk to the Parkinsons. They were at the garden party. Both Dick and Molly Parkinson teach at the school Hilary goes to, and they are also involved in the summer play that both Hilary and Brian were part of."

The inspector duly noted these facts in his notebook. Then he shifted direction.

"What's your impression of the Worthington family? Good neighbors?"

Julia offered her usual analysis of the Worthingtons: her uncertainty about whether Tim was beyond redemption or just a lonely unloved child trying to attract attention, what she thought was the bad influence of the grandmother, the vile temper she had experienced from the father. The inspector interrupted her at that point.

"And Hilary?"

"She seems to be the misfit in that house—pleasant, friendly, willing to help. I assume her genes came from her mother's side of the family."

"Yet presumably she could also have inherited the vile temper, the fanatical temperament, but manage to keep them under control. All right, all right—" as Julia took breath for another protest—"that's all I'll say for now, and all the questions I have too."

Julia watched his car pull away from the gate, angry at his presumptions yet trying to tell herself he was only doing his job, that there was no malice involved.

She was turning back into the house when another car pulled up at the gate with a blast on the horn. Bridget DeVere waved from the window.

"Can you come for coffee tomorrow morning? About half past ten? Good. I may have to ice the coffee if this awful heat doesn't go away. By the way, did you hear about Miss Baxter's cat? She found it dead, mutilated, and nailed up on her front door! Ghastly business! Must dash, see you tomorrow."

FIFTEEN

"It was nailed to the door, spread-eagled, as though it were a butterfly displayed in a collection. She found it when she went out to spread crumbs for the birds. I know most people think of Miss Baxter as a nuisance, but she's really a very gentle person with a soft spot for animals. I suppose she only talks so much when she's with other people because she's alone most of the time."

I'm beginning to understand that, thought Julia. *I hope it doesn't happen to me.* They were in a cozy sitting room off Bridget DeVere's kitchen. Bridget had not iced the coffee. The sunbaked walls of the outbuildings, visible through the window, basked in the unremitting heat, but the thick stone walls of the house and a light breeze stirring the curtains kept the indoor temperature tolerable.

It was a pleasant room, small but high-ceilinged, with pale yellow walls and glossy white woodwork. A terra-cotta vase filled with dried teasels, reeds, and grasses shielded the empty fireplace. Photographs of children cluttered the mantelpiece. A large white porcelain cat stared down from a shelf over Bridget's desk. Below, stretched out on the desk itself, slept a long-haired Persian cat, also white. It appeared oblivious to the tale of slaughter.

Jessica Woodhouse had provided Julia with information about the family history of Sir Richard and Lady Bridget DeVere. Blymton Manor had been built at the end of the sixteenth century by another Richard DeVere who prospered as a merchant during the trading boom of Elizabeth's reign. DeVeres had lived in the house ever since, almost dying out once or twice, but some distant kinsman had always turned up to claim the inheritance.

The value of the estate declined sharply during the twentieth century, partly because of high taxation but partly because Richard DeVere's grandfather, who was the squire of the manor for most of the century, lived the life of a gentleman of leisure, spending what the estate did produce on London nightlife and sprees on the French Riviera. His only son, John, Richard's father, rebelling against this extravagance, flirted briefly with Communism. Fortunately, by the time he left Cambridge, John had discarded politics in favor of engineering, and he went on to earn a creditable reputation and a good deal of money. The old man affected to disdain his son's eagerness to participate in the world of manufacturing, but he was heartbroken when John died of a stroke at the early age of forty-two. From them on, he lived the life of a recluse in the steadily deteriorating manor house at Blymton. Sir Richard, who had inherited his father's aptitude for engineering and had developed a head for business, took advantage of his father's fortune and the entrepreneurial spirit of the 1970s to build a successful company manufacturing spare parts for airplanes.

Mrs. Mudge added snippets of information about the present occupants. "They have lots of parties," she confided one day. "Dinner parties, lunch parties, garden parties. She often asks me to help out in the kitchen and wait at table. "'You're so reliable, Mrs. Mudge,' she says. And I likes to help her 'cos she always pays me, in cash, on the spot. Not like some of these fancy people around here who say they'll send a check next week, and you still have to remind them. No, Lady DeVere is a good lady. She's no side, does much of the cooking herself and works right alongside you."

Bridget greeted her eagerly when Julia presented herself at Blymton Manor on Wednesday morning.

"I'm so glad you could come," she said after settling Julia in the yellow-walled sitting room with a cup of coffee. "There's such a dearth of intelligent women to talk to in this village. Oh yes"—as she noted Julia was about to protest—"there are several bright young mums, but all they want to talk about is babies. I'm past that stage now. Rachel, my youngest, is ten, quite grown up. And there are women like Jessica Woodhouse and Molly Parkinson, but Molly's at school all day, and Jessica's busy with her patients. The only woman besides me who doesn't have a job is the rector's wife—you must know Joan Croft? And now there's you, though I expect you'll be off to work before too long."

"Not for a while. I don't know what I'd do. And I'm trying not to make major decisions too quickly."

Bridget, sensing that she might have touched a nerve, didn't press the point except to say, "You'll find it's deadly boring living in Blymton when you haven't a job or babies to take care of. I can keep myself occupied since we're still restoring this house, and we do a lot of business entertaining, but mostly it's my hands that are engaged, not my head. That's why Joan and I have coffee together at least once a week so that we can have an intelligent conversation. Of course, "she added, "Joan writes, which keeps her brain functioning."

"Writes? Do you mean books?"

"Mostly articles and reviews for scholarly journals. She has a PhD, you know, could have been a don but chose instead to marry a country parson and have children. She really doesn't have the right temperament for the rectory—too sharp, not sympathetic enough, at least that's what people say. She doesn't have much patience with talkative old ladies like Miss Baxter. It was Joan who told me about the cat. Apparently, Miss Baxter went straight to the rectory to seek consolation, but she got short shrift from Joan, who told her there were plenty of stray cats around so she could easily find a replacement. Some people don't realize that a cat can be like a child for a woman living alone. Or any woman whose children are no longer around for that matter. That's what Lady Selena does for me, don't you puss?" Lady Selena didn't even blink. "I believe the rector ministered more kindly to his bereaved parishioner."

Further discussion of Joan Croft was cut short by her arrival. Julia had a slight acquaintance with Joan from Sunday mornings in church or random encounters in the village, but this was her first opportunity for an extended scrutiny. Joan was a tall, lean woman whose sharp features were softened slightly by short light brown hair that curled in wisps over her high forehead and circled her ears. Her shoulders were very straight, and she held her head back so that her chin appeared to be the dominant feature of her face. But her eyes also compelled attention. Her gaze was penetrating, uncompromising. Julia decided that she would have been a formidable don.

Joan quickly disposed of the cat question.

"I expect the cat was killed and hung on the door by the same obnoxious boys who have been invading your wood. Sooner or later, someone will catch them in the act, and that will be the end of their depredations."

"It can't happen soon enough for me," said Bridget. "I don't feel anything is safe as long as they are on the rampage."

"There are more troublemakers abroad than those boys," Joan observed. "Plenty of adult ne'er-do-wells who are on the lookout for promising houses to break into. To say nothing of young people looking

113

for a squat. Julia, you were lucky they didn't break into Flora Cottage while it was empty last winter."

"Mrs. Mudge was keeping an eye on the cottage for me. And Hilary Worthington was helpful too. I'm told that when the New Year's Day storm littered the garden with branches and other debris, she went in and tidied things up."

"You're still right to recognize that luck played a part," Joan insisted. "But if we're going to discuss crime, I'm much more interested in who killed Brian Dixon. It appears that the police now believe it to be murder rather than accident and are questioning everyone in Blymton about their activities on the night he was killed. We had a supercilious young sergeant on our doorstep this morning, right after breakfast."

"That seems rather a waste of time," protested Bridget. "Surely no one could suspect the rector of murder?"

"Clergymen have been known to kill, even mild-mannered ones. But I think the purpose was not so much to check on us as to pry information out of Peter about some of his parishioners. I'm afraid Peter wasn't very cooperative. He launched into a discursive meditation on the psychology of murder, and after five minutes of that, the young man took his leave."

"I suppose the police will be here eventually," said Bridget. "And when they come, I'll remind them about the boys in our wood. I think there could be a link. Tim Worthington is one of the gang."

"I've wondered about Tim," said Julia. "He did make threats against Brian in my presence. But how would they get over to Hestercombe and back?"

"Bicycles?" suggested Joan.

"It doesn't have to be the whole gang," Bridget pointed out. "I've noticed one or two of them riding motorbikes. Someone could have taken Tim on the pillion."

Julia shook her head. "That suggests it was all planned, and he had an accomplice, and somehow that doesn't fit. Tim likes to create an aura of violence and postures a lot. But I suspect he acts impulsively."

Bridget poured out more coffee all round.

"Perhaps he and others saw Brian driving off and decided to follow him," she suggested. "That would be acting on impulse."

"But why would they trail him all the way to Hestercombe? Why was Brian going to Hestercombe anyway? He'd finished work for the day."

"Perhaps he was aware they were following him and drove to Hestercombe, hoping they'd not follow him inside. Or perhaps it was coincidence that they all converged on Hestercombe on the same evening."

"I think you're both wrong focusing on Tim," Joan interposed. "Ernest Worthington is a much more likely suspect."

"He certainly made enough threats," conceded Julia. "But I believe it was pure bluff."

"Yet he does have a terrible temper," observed Bridget. "I wouldn't be surprised if he turned murderous."

"I think it goes deeper than merely bad temper," said Joan. "People who've lived in Blymton longer than I have say he used to be quite different. That was before his wife died. They were said to be a very lively couple, active socially, part of the county set. Village gossip says he changed overnight when she died, became withdrawn, moody."

Julia couldn't resist asking if his wife's death had been at all suspicious.

"Oh no. It was sudden and unexpected, but it was very definitely caused by God and not man. It was a brain aneurysm."

"How long ago did this happen?"

"About twelve years ago. We came to Blymton ten years ago, and she died a year or two before that. His bad temper was firmly established by the time we arrived. His mother had moved in to take over the housekeeping. I think it's a shame he never remarried." Joan put down her cup and, leaning forward, fixed her steely gray eyes on Julia. "I think a lot of his hostility to Hilary's talk of marriage was the normal reluctance of a father to admit that his daughter may be reaching sexual maturity and be ripe for plucking by a stranger. But I think in his case it was intensified by his own sexual frustration."

Julia thought she glimpsed a flicker of a grin. Even so, she asked, "But could that be a motive for murder?"

"It's odd you should describe him as frustrated," said Bridget. "I had been wondering if he had a secret mistress. I've bumped into him once or twice in places far away from Blymton. One evening, I remember at Paddington when we were catching the train home after a day in London and he was just arriving at seven o'clock in the evening."

"What's wrong with that?" asked Julia.

"Nothing, except that he looked awfully embarrassed. Richard and I were sure he was off to some assignation. Then a couple of months ago, when I was down in Dorchester visiting my sister, I saw him coming out of a shop with a woman on one arm and a full shopping bag on the other. Now perhaps he too has a sister in Dorchester. But when he saw me, he looked very guilty and quickly headed off in the opposite direction. I think he's leading a double life."

"But Julia's probably right," said Joan, who had been staring into her coffee during this narration. "None of this necessarily indicates that the man would resort to murder."

"What about his mother?" asked Julia.

"You mean why didn't he murder her? Now that wouldn't surprise me, though I suppose I shouldn't say things like that. But she is impossible."

"But could she murder someone?" Julia persisted.

"With that Manichean outlook on life, it is not inconceivable" was Joan's verdict.

"She's a strong woman for her age," Julia noted.

"But she hardly ever goes out, doesn't drive," said Bridget. "If Brian had been found dead in the Worthingtons' garden, she might be a prime suspect. But I can't see her hiring a taxi to take her to Hestercombe for the purpose of killing someone."

"Or making a righteous killing—which is how she would characterize it—look like a suicide," added Joan.

For a moment or two, no one spoke. Julia, turning her gaze from the photographs of innocent young faces on the mantelpiece to the deep blue, heat-filled sky outside the window, thought how absurd it was to be speculating about Mrs. Worthington as a murderer.

Bridget, thinking much the same, jumped to her feet and picked up the coffee pot.

"Julia, I promised you intelligent conversation, and we're sitting here gossiping. I shall make more coffee, and we can start again. But," she added over her shoulder as she went into the kitchen, "I still think those boys had something to do with it."

SIXTEEN

"Why aren't the police going after the Worthingtons? That's what I want to know."

That was the general opinion among the young men working on the scenery in the Village Hall. A rehearsal was taking place under the warm evening sun at Blymton Manor, but the crew was in the Green Room, hard at work on the backcloths that would be needed if rain drove the performance indoors. Julia was there too, having been asked to help with the building of the ass's head for Bottom's love scene with the Fairy Queen.

The Green Room, being below ground level and thus without windows, was uncomfortably warm and close. A small electric fan whirred away at one end of the large table, but it failed to stir up more than a faint breath of air. *It would be nice to have a couple of large ceiling fans like we had in the residence*, thought Julia, once again wiping the sweat from her brow. The vehemence of the crew's opinions about the police investigation did nothing to lower the temperature in the room.

"They insisted I tell them exactly where I was and who I was with every minute of that Friday evening," grumbled one young man as he pounded nails into a strut.

"Did they want to know all the juicy details?" teased another.

"They wouldn't get anything very spicy from Joe, would they, my lad?" commented a man who was older than the rest and a member of the parish council, a fact that he reminded them of now and then. "Joe's a man for good clean living, ain't you, Joe?"

"None of their bloody business, and none of yours neither." Joe pounded the nails even harder.

"It's a good job they haven't talked to me. I went to a couple of pubs and then to the cinema, but I didn't see anyone I knew all evening. I didn't know I might be needing an alibi." This came from a hefty young man with dark curly hair whom Julia hadn't seen before, but then the membership of this group seemed to be fluid. He had ingratiated himself into the group by making himself useful, passing tools, stirring paint,

117

cleaning up spills. He helped the older man lift the duke's throne onto the table where they could more easily finish gilding its massive claw feet.

"Thanks, Mike. But I can't see the police coming after you. You've only just started working with the Players. It's people who knew Brian that they're after."

"I don't know why they're bothering with you lot anyway," said Mike. "I'd have thought they'd start with the people he worked with. After all, the body was found at Hestercombe."

"They've been over there, all right" was the answer. "A couple of blokes were complaining in The Feathers last night. Given everyone a real hard time they have and didn't come up with a bloody thing."

"And what about the Worthingtons?" This came from a quiet young man who was methodically painting leaves onto a tree, one leaf at a time. "From what I hear, they didn't like him. I don't think Hilary was all that smitten with him."

"Do you suppose she was the one who clobbered him?"

"Perhaps he wasn't living up to her expectations."

"More likely the other way round. The girl's like a lump of ice."

"Yeah, perhaps he wanted too much too fast."

"Still no reason to kill a man."

"That family was always peculiar."

Julia, listening to this as she diligently built up layers of papier-mâché over a wire frame, grew increasingly uneasy with the direction this conversation was going. It was this concern that led her to call on Jack Shaw the next day.

He looked more formidable at work than he did at home, but his manner was friendly as he greeted her and offered her some refreshment. His office was remarkably cool on this hot day. Open windows on two walls encouraged a light breeze, and so far the sun was not shining through either of them.

She began by thanking Jack for getting the investigation under way so quickly. He shrugged.

"If we were going to do it, there was no point wasting any more time. The trail is cold enough as it is. We haven't made much progress so far. In fact, unless we have a lucky break soon, I fear we may run into a stalemate. We've just about ruled out Dixon's fellow workers at the fire brigade headquarters. It's puzzling that the staff working there that night weren't aware of any comings and goings, didn't hear the shot, but that's what they tell us. Only three people were on duty, and none of them was alone for more than a minute or two. No one was behaving suspiciously. And all those who were off-duty at the time claim to have been with other people all evening, though we haven't finished double-checking those alibis yet. What's just as important is that we've found no hint of a motive there, no one who had any quarrel with young Dixon. He was well-liked, friendly, hadn't upset anyone. So now our only realistic option is to focus on friends and acquaintances outside work and on the Worthington family."

"Yes, I know your inspector has been there. I was accused the next day of interfering by an angry Dr. Worthington."

"Inspector Hughes was there again last night to talk to Hilary." Seeing Julia's surprised reaction to this news, he added, "You didn't know she was back from the funeral? I believe she returned yesterday afternoon. Hughes wanted to get to her at once. I haven't seen his report yet, so I don't know how it went."

"Isn't that a waste of time? Surely she had already told him all she knew?"

"You forget that at the first interview, she didn't mention the phone call to Dixon on the night of the murder. It was important to talk to her before her memory of the conversation began to fade."

Jack took a piece of paper from his desk.

"There is one development you may not know about. The missing former girlfriend and child have turned up alive and well."

"That's good news. At least we know that we're dealing with only one body. Where was she?"

"She showed up at the young man's funeral on Tuesday. I had a man there, and he interviewed her afterward."

"Why did she disappear? Where had she been? Or would you rather not tell me these things?"

Jack glanced at the paper in his hand.

"I can tell you most of what we learned. Her name is Ruth Matthews, and Brian Dixon was the father of her child. You heard that at the inquest, of course. She came to Blymton two weeks ago, hoping for a reconciliation. She had written to him beforehand—we have the letter. She called at his digs—the landlady has confirmed that—but he wasn't in. What we did not know before was that she came back the next day, that was the Thursday, I believe, and this time she met Dixon. He drove her and the child to Taunton, where they had a meal in a café. She says that she didn't tell him she would like to resume their former relationship. She didn't want to push herself onto him. She was just hoping that he would make the first move. She claims that he didn't."

"Did he tell her that he was engaged to someone else?"

"Apparently not. It was a double shock to her, as it was to his mother, to learn first that he was dead and second that he had a fiancée."

"Was there just that one meeting?"

"Yes, according to her. She left Blymton the next morning, took the bus to Taunton and from there a train down to Cornwall. There is a gap in her story at the moment. We've checked with the inn where she stayed in Blymton, and she did leave on the Friday morning after inquiring about buses to Taunton. She says she got off the train at Penzance and stayed on Friday night at a bed and breakfast, but she can't remember either the name of the landlady or the street. The next day, she took a bus out to a small fishing village, found another bed and breakfast, and spent the next few days crying while her little boy played among the rocks. She did have the name of that landlady, and we have confirmation of her stay there. But we're still trying to establish where she was on the Friday night."

"I presume she swears her innocence."

"Of course. And I believe her. I don't think Hughes considers her a prime suspect either, though we'll both feel better when we have proof that she was in Penzance that Friday night."

"Who are the prime suspects?" Julia asked then added quickly, "All right, all right. I shouldn't ask."

"I'm sorry," said Jack and paused for a moment, observing Julia carefully. "It's not that I don't trust you. But you might say something unwittingly that would not be helpful. It could also be dangerous for you to know too much." He paused again, as if uncertain whether to say more, then resumed, "On the other hand, you could be helpful to us. If you see or hear anything that seems pertinent—people often talk more freely among themselves than they do to a policeman. I'm not asking you to betray confidences, of course. But if it's something vital that we seem to be overlooking . . . And I'll keep you as well informed as I properly and safely can."

I'm being asked to be a police informer, Julia said to herself and didn't feel very comfortable. But then she reasoned, *I got myself into this, so I shouldn't resent being asked to do a little snooping.* She thought briefly about relating Bridget DeVere's account of Dr. Worthington's activities but decided it was just gossip that could have no bearing on this investigation.

"I'll keep my eyes and ears open" was all she said.

Hilary presented herself at Flora Cottage that afternoon after school. The girl looked pale and tired. There were dark circles under her eyes.

"Come in and have some tea," suggested Julia. "Or I have lemonade if you'd prefer it."

Hilary gratefully accepted the offer of lemonade.

"This heat is getting me down. It was awful on the train coming back from Wolverhampton yesterday. I almost fainted at one point. I'll be so glad when we get back to our ordinary cool English summer."

Julia laughed. "I'll remind you of that when we have a July with weeks of rain and cool temperatures."

"But this heat is just as bad. Rain may depress people, but heat overexcites them. Two young men got into a fight on the train yesterday, and I know it was the heat that turned their argument into a brawl."

She followed Julia into the conservatory and stretched out happily in a wicker armchair. She loved this room, so different from the gloomy house next door. It was filled now with light, though shaded from the direct sun by a rattan screen rolled down over the roof.

"I'm glad that's over," she said.

"The funeral?"

Hilary nodded. "There weren't many people there. I was the only outsider, except for a man sitting at the back that I think was a policeman. They were after me again last night, you know. I'd barely got home before Inspector Hughes was on the doorstep with his questions."

She paused. Julia was about to ask how the interview went when Hilary reverted to the topic of the funeral. "Brian's old girlfriend was there too."

She paused again, and this time Julia didn't even attempt to say anything. It was better to let her talk at her own pace. Hilary continued slowly, with many hesitations.

"I liked Ruth, that's her name. I didn't talk to her much, but she had a long phone conversation with Mrs. Dixon the day before the funeral. I didn't see the child. Brian should have married her, probably would have anyway. She looked very unhappy when I saw her at the funeral." Very softly and with great difficulty, she added, "I think she may have loved Brian more than I did."

There was a long pause here. Hilary was lying back in the wicker chair, head back, eyes closed. A slackening of her mouth and quiver of her chin made Julia afraid that the girl would start to cry. But Hilary remained remarkably dry-eyed.

Finally, she spoke again. "I think the police are shamefully coldhearted. The plainclothes man went up to Ruth right after the funeral. I almost wish we hadn't started this investigation. No," she quickly added, "that's not true. We have to find out what happened, for Brian's sake. I owe that to him and to Ruth. But I know I'll hate every minute of it."

"Was it very unpleasant yesterday evening?"

"It was awful. But that's partly my fault. Inspector Hughes was furious that I hadn't told them about my phone call to Brian on the Friday evening. I thought Ruth was there and that's why he was being so evasive. But she says she saw him the previous evening, and by Friday night, she was down in Cornwall."

I hope that's true, thought Julia. I hope the police can trace the bed and breakfast where she stayed. Hilary continued, "Inspector Hughes seemed very cross that Granny didn't hear me telephoning Brian or that I don't remember whether Gran called out good night to me on her way to bed. She usually does, and I usually call back, but I don't always hear her, and I can't honestly remember whether or not I heard her that night. I don't know what they think I was up to. I was just in my bedroom, trying to concentrate on my homework and not think about what Brian was up to."

I know what the police are thinking, Julia told herself. They're thinking that if Hilary was able to creep downstairs and use the telephone in the hall without her grandmother hearing, she could have crept out of the house without being heard. Mrs. Worthington might have imagined hearing Hilary respond to her good-night call. And if the door was left unbolted for Tim, Hilary could also have returned undetected. Both Nigel and Jack had warned her that the investigation would probably be unpleasant. Now, for the first time, she realized how disagreeable it could become.

SEVENTEEN

The three-room flat over a shop in suburban Wolverhampton had been shut up all day while Ruth Matthews was at work, so it was like opening an oven door when she returned home on Friday evening. She flung open all the windows and turned on a small electric fan in the kitchen, but it appeared to have little effect on the hot, moist air. Adam was whining, and not only from the heat. There had been a fight at the creche that afternoon, and Adam had been implicated. "It's the weather," the woman in charge had said when Ruth arrived to pick him up.

It's getting to me too, she thought as she poured some Ribena for Adam, automatically responding to his complaints, while half of her mind was rehashing the events of the day and the other half was wondering what she could prepare for supper without doing any cooking. It had been a terrible week. First, to come back from holiday and hear from Mr. Sparks, her boss, that Brian was dead and the police had been inquiring about her. Then the awful experience of the funeral and the brief encounter with Brian's latest girlfriend, who had claimed to be his fiancée. The funeral and the police questioning had taken her away from work, which made Mr. Sparks unhappy. Mr. Sparks didn't like change, and the girl who had filled in while Ruth was on holiday was most unsatisfactory.

Grief, fatigue, the heat, and anxiety about the police inquiries were weighing heavily on her as she boiled a couple of eggs and chopped them up for sandwiches. Anger too was throbbing below the surface. Why hadn't Brian told her he was engaged? Mrs. Dixon had said nothing about it either, when Ruth phoned her on hearing the bad news from Mr. Sparks, still hoping that he might have got it wrong. The girl had been sitting with Brian's mother for the service and rode with her to the cemetery. Ruth had been puzzled but assumed she was a Dixon relative. She was quite unprepared for the awkward moment at the graveside when the girl stepped forward and introduced herself. She looked so young and vulnerable, pretty—despite a face disfigured by tears—yet still not what Ruth thought of as Brian's type. In the last day or two, mingling with the anger at Brian and his mother, was anger directed at herself. Perhaps Brian had said nothing about his engagement because he wasn't sure about it. Perhaps, given time and an expression of interest from herself, he might have made an overture. Perhaps . . .

She persuaded Adam to eat most of his sandwich and tempted him further with some fruit from a tin. He was such a finicky eater. But she too had little appetite. She made herself a cup of coffee, hoping it would give her energy, and lit a cigarette. *I've got to stop this smoking,* she told herself, but cigarettes and coffee had kept her going through these awful last few days. At least she hadn't turned to drinking.

The doorbell downstairs rang as she was flicking the television knob, searching for something that Adam could watch. She pressed the intercom button and asked warily, "Who is it?"

It was Mrs. Dixon. Surprised yet somewhat pleased at the prospect of adult company, Ruth pressed the release button to open the downstairs door. Myra Dixon climbed the stairs heavily, panting by the time she reached the top. Damp wisps of hair clung to her brow, and her cheeks were flushed. She sat down with relief on the chair Ruth proffered.

"I can't take much more of this heat. Yes, thank you, dear, a cup of tea would be very nice. Hello, Adam. I don't suppose you know me."

Adam, who by now had lost interest in television and was playing on the floor with some toy cars, stared hard at her for a minute or two, uncertain whether this strange gray woman posed some kind of threat. But she had a friendly face, and she was smiling at him, waiting patiently for him to respond and not trying to smother him as motherly women often did. He gave her the benefit of the doubt and smiled back. She reached into a large canvas shopping bag.

"Would you like to have this bus to add to your car collection?"

It was a miniature red double-decker bus, a little scratched and worn but still serviceable. Adam seized it happily.

"It belonged to Brian. I thought he might like to have it," she explained as Ruth returned with the tea.

"He'll love it. He spends a lot of time playing with his cars. Did you say thank you, Adam?"

"Thank you," said Adam obediently then jumped up, ran across to where Myra was sitting and, squeezing her arm in a gesture of genuine gratitude, sang, "Thank you, thank you, thank you."

"He plays with cars a lot," repeated Ruth. "It's one of the few things he can do here in the flat."

Myra, who had been surreptitiously surveying the room ever since she arrived, knew what Ruth meant. It was not a large room, hardly big enough for a lively, growing boy. Through the open doorway, she could see what appeared to be a small kitchen. A closed door must lead to the bedroom. There was nowhere outside to play. Impulsively, she invited Ruth to consider moving in with her.

"You know my house, it's not big, but it's roomier than what you have here. And there's the garden for Adam to play in. I wouldn't charge you very much, less I'm sure than you have to pay here. I still have to work, so I couldn't offer to watch Adam during the day, but there's a good child-minder down the street. And I could take care of him in the evening if you wanted to go out."

Ruth's instinctive reaction was one of anger, sensing an implied criticism that the flat was unsuitable. *What right does she have to come here, uninvited, and judge me?* she asked herself. *And could I share a house with Brian's mother after what happened?* Then she remembered that this was Adam's grandmother. Her own parents had given up on her. They hadn't been to see where she lived or to visit their grandson. If Myra Dixon cared about her grandson, that was a plus. Even so, five years of struggling on her own wasn't a habit easily dropped. She declined the offer, but kindly.

Myra nodded, accepting the refusal easily. It was too soon to make that kind of offer. She should have known better. She and Ruth had a good relationship once. She had looked forward to having Ruth as a daughter-in-law. But that was several years ago, and too much had happened in the meantime. They had to rebuild the bond of affection and trust that snapped when Brian took off for Somerset.

She took a shoe box out of her canvas bag and held it out to Ruth.

"This box was found in Brian's room in Blymton with some photographs and letters and cards. The police gave it to me after the inquest. I've kept one or two pictures for myself, but I think you should look through and see if there are any keepsakes you would like to have."

Ruth took the box and began to spread the contents out on the table.

"Fancy him keeping all these old things," she said. "There are several photos here of his new girlfriend. What was her name?"

"Hilary. Yes, I suppose I should send them to her."

Ruth looked at the Hilary pictures with mild curiosity before laying them aside. She picked up a small newspaper cutting and handed it to Myra.

"Here's the announcement of their engagement. I don't want that. What's this?"

She opened up a much larger newspaper clipping. It was a news story about a fire in a Somerset village with a photograph of firemen carrying a woman out of a burning house. Ruth scanned it for any mention of Brian but found none. Several paragraphs were underlined, and Brian had written notes in the margin. There was a second newspaper clipping with a further report on the fire, but no more pictures. "Perhaps you should send these to Hilary too," she said.

Memories came flooding back as Ruth picked up snapshots of herself as a teenager clowning on the grass, herself and Brian huddled together for warmth against a snowy landscape, a photograph he took of her at Ludlow Castle, a formal portrait taken for her eighteenth birthday. There were birthday cards she'd sent to Brian, a Valentine still in its envelope, a postcard she'd sent from York when she went north for a family wedding. It was a struggle to keep back the tears at the sight of a happier, carefree past and the thought of what might have been.

The mementos began to break down the wall that had grown up over the years between the young woman and the mother of her former lover. Ruth began to talk about Brian, about the lost years.

"I shouldn't have been so proud and stubborn. I should have looked for him long ago. We had such a good thing going." She looked again at the Ludlow picture, and her own face smiled back at her, a face from the past, from another lifetime.

"You should never have let him go. You would have made him a better wife than the other girl. Mind you, I like Hilary. She's pleasant, thoughtful, well brought up. But she doesn't suit him like you did. I don't know what it is, but you have something she doesn't. Perhaps it's just that you can stand on your own two feet. Hilary is so—so dependent. I think Brian would have got tired of her."

"He didn't tell me there was someone else when I met him a couple of weeks ago. I've been very angry about that, feeling as though he'd lied to me or was too cowardly to tell me. And yet I also wonder if it was because he was having second thoughts about this other girl, wanted to keep the door open. After all, he'd kept all these photos. I shouldn't have given up so quickly. I tend to be impulsive. I shouldn't have . . ."

Her voice trailed off, and she sat still, gazing at the Ludlow photograph.

EIGHTEEN

Early Saturday afternoon, a squad of daredevils parachuted into the middle of Blymton's playing fields, trailing orange smoke. As soon as they landed, they peeled off their protective suits and mopped their sweaty faces. The crowd, who had cleared a space for them to land, cheered lustily. At the far end of the field, several raucous young men were hustling recalcitrant donkeys in what purported to be a donkey race, an event that no one was taking seriously, least of all the donkeys. Older men, their jackets off and sleeves rolled up, were examining a parade of antique vehicles, nodding knowledgeably as they peered at and stroked a vintage Austin Morris or a gaudily painted steam engine. Their wives lingered in a stuffy tent, surveying tables laden with jars of homemade jam and chutney, fingering delicate baby clothes and sturdy kettle holders, and muttering to one another about the dreadful heat. People of all ages and sizes flocked to the ice cream stands, which were in danger of selling out by midafternoon.

It was the annual Blymton fete, at which villagers more usually complained about cold weather or rain but which this year was held on the eighth day of the heat wave. The previous evening, the weatherman had warned of a chance of thunderstorms that could bring the temperature down; but as late as three o'clock, the remorseless sun beat down from a cloudless sky. People shook their heads and said that the weather forecast was wrong again. But Julia felt the heaviness in the atmosphere and saw that the air was thick with moisture. She felt that a storm was brewing just below the horizon.

She wandered aimlessly around the field, stopping here and there to exchange a few words with people she had come to know. She felt remarkably detached from her surroundings. The Blymton fete was so different from the nostalgic scene of the English at play that she had carried in her head all these years. She hadn't anticipated parachute jumpers or the rock band that played ineptly but loudly or the rowdy youths with green spiky hair and ragged jeans, acting as though they owned the place. She thought she spotted Tim at one point, speeding away on the back of a motorbike. Two policemen, stripped to shirt-sleeves because of the heat, were patrolling the field, their eyes darting restlessly over the throng as they walked solemnly in step. *Are they just keeping an eye on the rowdies?* Julia wondered. *Or are they on the lookout for a potential murderer?*

She drifted toward the tea tent. The tea was weak, but it was hot and refreshing. The tent was crowded, and the only empty seat was a rickety chair near the entrance, almost in the sun. Julia moved it a little further into the shade and sat down cautiously but thankfully. Until that moment, she hadn't realized how tired her feet were.

Close by was the cold drinks table where she now saw Hilary, waving to her from the queue. The girl was with a group of young people, some of whom Julia recognized from the Players. She was pleased to see Hilary out with friends, apparently enjoying herself. It suggested that she was beginning to restore normality to her life.

Earlier that day, Julia had been less sure it would happen so soon. She had been up early, intent on weeding the herbaceous bed in the back garden before it got too hot. It was infuriating how weeds thrived through heat and drought, while more desirable plants wilted and died. The bed by now should be lush with bloom, but the plants had not filled out as they should. They probably needed to be divided and replanted. The flower bed was narrow and contained mostly big shasta daisies and lupins, with a few daylilies now coming into bloom. It should be broader, making room for peonies and delphiniums, and then some stronger colors like rudbeckia, coreopsis, and red-hot poker. And in future, it should be well-mulched to reduce these endless chores of weeding and watering.

She was struggling to remove some grass from the center of a clump of daisies when Hilary hailed her. She came through the back gate, an empty bowl in her hand.

"No eggs again this morning. The hens won't lay in this heat. Granny's threatening to wring their necks if they don't produce soon."

"I don't blame them for slacking off." Julia laughed. "I wish the weeds would do likewise. They seem to flourish in the heat."

"Would you like me to help?"

"That's kind of you. But"—Julia suddenly remembered that this was Saturday—"what's happening about Hestercombe? Do you still have your job there?"

"I don't know. I haven't asked. But I don't think I could go back. It's a lovely garden, and I enjoyed working there. But I couldn't face it yet. It would be awkward too while the police are still investigating the murder."

"Yes, I can see that. But it's a shame for you to lose the experience. You can certainly help me until we find you a better alternative. And I don't mean just help with the drudgery, like weeding. I want to remake the whole garden. I can't start until the autumn, but I have to begin planning now. You could help me with that."

Hilary's face lit up.

"I'd really enjoy that, though I don't know much about garden design."

"Neither do I. We can learn together. I'm not looking for anything drastically different. I just want to make it my garden, not one I've inherited from someone else. I was reading something by Gertrude Jekyll last night that expressed it perfectly. She said a garden should fit its owner and his tastes like his clothes do, neither too big nor too small but just comfortable. That's what I want, a comfortable garden."

Later, Julia wondered whether she had done the right thing enlisting Hilary's help. She believed the girl could be helpful, and she was sure the experience could be useful to Hilary. But she didn't want her to see this as a substitute for a normal social life. Now watching Hilary interact with the group around her, Julia was reassured.

The group had finally worked their way to the front of the queue when a young man came up whom Julia recognized as the curly-haired newcomer to the Players' crew. He said something to Hilary that Julia didn't catch, but she heard Hilary's response.

"So you're Mike Hatfield! The one who sent me the lily."

As Hilary stepped aside, drink in hand, to talk with Mike, Julia couldn't help overhearing some of their conversation.

"How did you know Brian? I don't remember hearing him talk about you."

"We'd known each other a long time. I was in the county fire brigade when he first came to Somerset."

"It's odd he never talked about you."

"There was perhaps no reason. I left the brigade two years ago, and we hadn't seen much of each other since then. Though I did run into him a few weeks ago, and he said something about being engaged."

"Thank you for the plant. It was kind of you to do that, especially since you didn't know me."

"But Brian had talked about you. In fact, you posed a bit of a problem for me. I'm in business for myself now, selling fire extinguishers. He probably didn't tell you, but I wanted Brian to come in with me. He said he didn't think he could afford it because he was going to get married."

"That was you then. Yes, he did tell me, but I don't think he mentioned your name."

Julia, absorbed in watching them, failed to notice that the occupants of an adjacent table had left and their place taken by Miss Baxter. She accidentally jostled Julia's chair as she settled herself in.

"Oh dear, I'm so sorry. I hope I didn't make you spill your tea."

"That's quite all right, Miss Baxter, no harm done."

"This heat is terrible, isn't it? I really don't like to be out when it's so hot, but I wouldn't miss the fete for anything. I always look forward to sampling some of Mrs. Watchett's sponge cake. She makes the lightest sponge cake imaginable. Have you tried it yet?"

Miss Baxter chattered away, not looking for any response, and Julia was content to sit and listen for a few minutes. She drained her tea, noticing with some annoyance that there were tea leaves in the bottom of the cup.

"Just look at that," she said, holding out her cup. "It's not often you see tea leaves these days. I'd have thought they be using tea bags."

"They may be, but you know, those things can burst open. I've had that happen to me once or twice. But let me look at what you've got there." Miss Baxter held out her hand for the cup. "Let me see what the tea leaves say."

Julia handed over her cup, curious to hear what Miss Baxter would predict. Her grandmother, she remembered, had enjoyed reading the tea leaves. *I suppose that's a dying art in this age of the tea bag*, she mused, *even if some do split open.*

Miss Baxter shook her head. "It's not very clear. But I think I see two young men. Yes, two young men, one of whom could be dangerous, could do you harm. You'd better beware."

Julia was puzzled. The only young man she was likely to encounter was Tim.

"You sound serious, Miss Baxter."

"Yes, indeed. And it doesn't surprise me. In this day and age, young men, even boys, are so violent. You'd better hold tight to your handbag and don't go out alone after dark."

Julia smiled to herself but merely said, "I'll certainly keep that in mind. Thank you for the warning."

The arrival of another elderly lady to claim a vacant seat at Miss Baxter's table gave Julia an excuse to slip away. As she left the tea tent, she saw Hilary and Mike walking slowly away, deep in conversation. Mike had his hand under Hilary's elbow and was gently steering her away from the rest of the group. *Well*, thought Julia approvingly, *perhaps this Mike will be a new interest for her. He's certainly better company for her than me.*

Half an hour later, emerging from the flower tent where she had studied prize-winning dahlias and roses, Julia saw the storm building on the horizon. It was a gradual darkening of the sky toward the west rather than an accumulation of distinct clouds. The air was very still and tense, the electricity almost palpable. The fete had long since lost its freshness. Feet had worn the dry grass into ugly bare patches at the thresholds of the tents. Discarded plastic cups and scraps of paper were scattered here and there. Children, exhausted by heat and excitement, fought and cried. *Time to go home*, Julia decided.

She reached Flora Cottage only minutes before the first rain began to fall. Heavy drops beat down on the conservatory roof as she hastened to close windows.

Later that evening, when the wind had subsided though rain was still falling steadily, she stood at the back bedroom window, surveying the damage in the garden below. A limb from the apple tree was splayed across the lawn. There were puddles in the flower bed where she had been weeding. The daisies and the lupins had been beaten down. *Stakes*, she thought. *I should have staked them. More work. It was like caring for a child.*

The patter of rain was the only sound to disturb the evening. No rock music was blaring from the Worthington house tonight. *How much of a menace is Tim?* she wondered, recalling Miss Baxter's odd prediction. *Should I keep an eye on him?*

Over in the Worthingtons' garden, she saw Hilary, a yellow oilskin over her head and shoulders, on her way to shut up the hens for the night. Perhaps the hens would now start laying again.

NINETEEN

Julia was applying the finishing touches to Bottom's ass's head, painting large dark eyes around the holes that would allow the actor to see what he was doing. It was a satisfying task, even though the paint was slow to dry. The hot and sticky humidity of the previous week had now been replaced by the more common cool dampness. The rain that began after the fete was still falling steadily twenty-four hours later.

The rehearsals had returned to the Village Hall, and as predicted, the Players were grumbling as much about the rain as they had about the heat. It wasn't just the weather. It seemed as though a jinx had suddenly fallen on the play. The actor playing Bottom, cavorting a bit too boisterously on stage, fell, twisting his ankle. He complained that Flute had tripped him, a charge Flute denied vigorously. Both Oberon and Titania were developing colds and sniffed unhappily through their scenes. One of the crew members, hurrying to finish off a piece of scenery, hit his thumb with a hammer. The thumb swelled and turned livid, but he heard little sympathy from his mates who chided him for his carelessness and suggested that his aim had been impaired by too much lunchtime beer.

The Parkinson child, entrusted to Hilary's care while his mother was on stage, slipped away, causing great consternation. Hilary came running downstairs to the Green Room in search of the boy. He was discovered in the adjacent storeroom, which someone had left open. The windowless room was dark, but there was enough light from the open door for the child to see a box filled with miscellaneous items—small props from previous plays, a few tools, a ball of string, and a roll of colored paper. He had most of these items on the floor when Hilary found him. She tossed everything back into the box and hustled the child outside, firmly pulling the door to behind her.

"This door is supposed to be locked," she complained. "Does anyone know where the key is?"

"I thought you were planning on getting married" called out the young man with the purple thumb. "You're going to have to polish up your child-minding skills before you try again."

"Aw, come on, Joe, that's not nice," said one of his mates. He turned to Hilary. "There should be a key in the shoe box on the shelf near the door. Two in fact. Dick had a spare one made after the original key went missing for a few days. But you don't really need to lock it now. Just close it, and we'll lock it when we leave."

Joe couldn't resist another jab.

"She's the one who persuaded the police it was murder and set them to asking us all these bloody stupid questions."

"What's the matter with that then?" asked another crew member. "Are they still looking for a blow-by-blow account of your evening?"

But the banter was interrupted by Hilary, pausing on the staircase, to call out.

"You won't have to put up with it much longer, Joe. The police are pretty close to finishing their investigation. We'll soon know who did it."

As she spoke, she scooped up the Parkinson child and ran up the stairs, bumping into Mike Hatfield, who appeared in the doorway at the same moment. He started to say something to her, but she brushed him aside angrily and disappeared into the hall. There was an awkward silence, and then somebody said, "Well, that's good news, isn't it."

Julia, sitting quietly but uneasily at her small table during this episode, finished her work as quickly as she could and hurried upstairs. Hilary, her charge restored to his parents, was standing by the door, already enveloped in her large yellow oilskin. She was in earnest conversation with Mike but reached out to Julia as she passed by.

"May I walk home with you Mrs. Dobson?"

Mike smiled politely at Julia. "I'm trying to persuade her to come to The Feathers. Just for a little while."

"No, I don't want to go to the pub. I . . . I think I'm getting a cold and ought to go home to bed. Besides, I still have to shut up the hens. It's getting dark, and there are so many foxes around."

"Then let me take you home. I have a car. It would only take a couple of minutes."

"Thank you, but I'd rather walk. And I'd like to walk home with Mrs. Dobson. We have some things to talk about."

By now, Julia felt she had no choice but to respond to Hilary's request. The girl's behavior seemed odd, encouraging Mike at the fete yesterday, now putting him off. And why had she made such an outrageous and obviously false statement to the crew downstairs? Far from being about to resolve the case, all indications were that the police were totally baffled.

She put the question to Hilary as soon as they were clear of the hall.

"I don't know" was the initial response. Hilary trudged through the rain, shoulders hunched, refusing the shelter of Julia's umbrella even though water was dripping over the top of her hood and down her face. "I was just so angry with them, constantly making nasty remarks. If it wasn't for the Parkinsons, I'd leave the Players."

"All the same, that was a rash statement to make. If word gets around that the police are closing in, even if that's not true, it could propel the murderer to some act of desperation."

Hilary sneezed.

"Oh dear, you are catching a cold. You should have let that young man drive you home."

"I suppose I should. Mike isn't bad, and he did know Brian. I don't want him to get too keen. I don't want a new boyfriend just yet. It's much too soon."

Julia understood that. She also felt that Hilary, with the resilience of youth, would recover sooner from the loss of a boyfriend of a year or two than she would from the loss of her lifetime's love and companion. But she recognized that it would be difficult to convince Hilary of that difference. So as they were almost at the Worthington house, Julia limited her response to an admonition to have a warm bath and hot drink right away.

"It's only two weeks to the first performance. Not a good time to be down with a cold."

TWENTY

"I don't think you've been totally honest with us, Dr. Worthington."

Two days later, it was still raining. Even though Inspector Hughes had parked close to the Worthingtons' gate, he was drenched running from the car to the front door. Dr. Worthington had invited the inspector to take off his wet raincoat, but he made no other gesture of hospitality than to usher him into the front parlor. The two men faced each other with weary determination. It was clear from his manner that the vet did not welcome this return visit. For his part, the inspector came straight to the point with his blunt accusation.

"What do you mean?"

The vet's hackles were already beginning to rise. Inspector Hughes affected to look at his notes.

"You alleged that you spent the Friday evening that Brian Dixon was killed having dinner with colleagues, and you referred us to a Dr. Simpson of Totnes to corroborate your statement."

He paused, deliberately.

"Yes."

"Well, Dr. Simpson didn't have quite the same recollection of how you spent the evening. He agrees that you and he and one or two others had a drink or two in the hotel bar between, maybe, five and six o'clock. There was some talk of going into dinner together. But when pressed, he admitted leaving about six for another engagement. He assumed you had dinner with the others but couldn't provide the confirmation we were looking for."

"I suppose I picked the wrong one. I'd forgotten he left early. Let me check with one or two of the others, and I'll let you know when I've talked to them."

"You don't need to bother Dr. Worthington. When your friend, Dr. Simpson, couldn't help, he gave us the names and addresses of three others who were with you that evening."

"Bloody fool!" Dr. Worthington muttered under his breath.

The inspector continued confidently, "There was a Dr. Collins from Exeter. Dr. Collins said he couldn't be sure, but he rather thought you left a few minutes after Dr. Simpson. Two others were subsequently interviewed,"—the inspector made quite a fuss of referring to his notes—"a Dr. Williamson and a Dr. Lovatt, each separately confirmed that impression."

Dr. Worthington turned round to close the parlor door before responding. When he faced the inspector again, he was outwardly calm, but the policeman noticed that he had thrust his hands into his trouser pockets as if to quiet their nervous agitation.

"So what are you saying? Are you insinuating that instead of having dinner, I left the hotel and drove hell for leather back to Hestercombe?"

Inspector Hughes smiled.

"No, I think that's a bit premature. What I would like to know, though, is why you signed the hotel register 'Dr. and Mrs. Worthington.' Your wife is dead, I believe?"

The vet had clearly been anticipating this question. "I wasn't thinking. I sometimes do that automatically."

"You had requested a double room when you made the booking. That too was in the hotel records. That's quite a long memory lapse."

"All right! I had a lady friend with me."

"And she was with you all evening? She spent the night with you?"

"Yes. But what damned business is it of yours?"

It was now the inspector's turn to be angry.

"Because I'm investigating a murder, damn it! And I don't like sending my men off on wild-goose chases, spending public money and wasting their time interviewing people who are no use as witnesses simply because you lied to me."

"I lied to protect a lady."

"That was very stupid. If you'd told me at the beginning that you were merely engaged in a little amorous fling, I wouldn't have had to spend so much time checking up on you."

"How do you know that wasn't a cover? Suppose I did sneak back to Hestercombe with her as my accomplice? How about that one, eh?"

Inspector Hughes had already thought of that possibility. The pathologist had confirmed that the likely time of death was between ten and midnight. If Dr. Worthington had left his veterinary friends around six, he would have had ample time to drive back to the Blymton area before ten and return to the hotel before daybreak. The question was whether the lady friend knew what was going on.

"Somehow I don't think so. But I'll judge that better when I've talked to the lady in question. I'd like her name and address please."

Dr. Worthington stiffened.

"Can't you keep her out of this?"

"I'm afraid not. As I have to keep reminding you, this is a murder investigation."

The vet rubbed his nose and thought for a moment or two, staring hard at the carpet. The inspector, waiting patiently, looked around the dreary room, so hot and stuffy a week earlier and now unpleasantly cold and damp. *These old stone houses. I don't know how people can think they're charming.*

"All right," said the vet finally. "You can talk to her, but first, I must ask her consent to divulge her identity." He glared at the inspector. "I'm not going to tell her what to say. It's a question of honor."

Inspector Hughes stared back undeterred, wondering what the next excuse would be. *Is he afraid she'll ditch him if a policeman shows up on her doorstep without warning? Or perhaps she's married, and we don't want hubby to find out, do we?* Aloud he said, "I'm not worried about you coaching her. I'll know if she's lying, and if she starts lying, you'll really be in trouble. But why don't you phone her now? I would like to get this out of the way."

Dr. Worthington pulled out a small pocket diary and thumbed through it. The inspector stood watchfully in the parlor doorway as the vet went into the hall and dialed a number. The phone appeared to ring for several minutes. Finally, Dr. Worthington put it down.

"No answer. But this is Tuesday, is it not? I rather think Tuesday is her bridge evening."

Inspector Hughes was tempted to force the answer he needed. He knew he could do it. A threat to take the vet to the police station would be enough. Ernest Worthington was a strange man. He couldn't be more than fifty, if that, yet he had this old-fashioned attitude to women. An unlikely murderer. But if he had killed Brian Dixon, he'd be the kind to stand and bluff it out rather than run and hide. No, he wouldn't push it now, but it certainly wouldn't hurt to keep the pressure on.

"Keep trying. I'll expect to hear from you, tomorrow at the latest."

There was a slight noise upstairs as if someone had quietly closed a bedroom door. *Which one is that?* the inspector wondered. *Hilary? Tim? The old lady?* Dr. Worthington appeared not to notice. Inspector Hughes picked up his wet coat and left. The vet watched him scurry through the rain before he closed the door.

Hilary, doing homework by her bedroom window, had seen in the gray evening light the inspector's arrival. She sat very tense and still, unable to concentrate on King Lear, apprehensive about being summoned downstairs. When she could stand it no longer, she opened the door a crack, hoping to hear something. But even when the two men came out into the hall and her father went to the telephone, they kept their voices low, and she couldn't hear what they were saying. In the end, she decided that the inspector wasn't looking for her, and she quietly closed the door.

She returned to King Lear. But it was hard to concentrate on the fortunes of the king and his daughters. The best she could do was speculate on how a father could so misjudge his children. It was strange that siblings, growing up in the same family, could be so different. And yet she and Tim were very different. Their father, like Lear, didn't understand his children, never bothered to listen to them. They were a silent family, each member isolated in his or her life.

By now it was clear that she wasn't going to finish her homework that evening. Her thoughts were taking too many wild flights. Her head was throbbing too. She went in search of aspirin.

The house was very quiet. Tim must be out, as usual. There was no sign of her father. She found her grandmother in the kitchen at the ironing board. The old lady said not a word, didn't even glance at Hilary as she took her oilskin from the peg by the back door, pushed her feet into a pair of green wellington boots, and went out into the rain to shut up the hens for the night.

She sneezed several times as she removed her outdoor gear on her return. That made Mrs. Worthington look up. She noticed now the girl's flushed and drawn face.

"You look ill, child. You should have let me take care of the hens instead of going out in the rain."

"That's all right, Granny. I just have a mild headache. Too much studying tonight, I suppose."

"No, you're sickening for something. You've been sneezing and snuffling for two days now. You go straight to bed, and I'll bring up some hot cocoa for you. And if you're like this in the morning, you had better stay in bed."

Hilary welcomed her grandmother's fussing for once. The hot cocoa was soothing and quickly propelled her to sleep. Next morning, when it was clear that she was worse, she readily agreed to stay in bed. Dr. Worthington stuck his head around the door for a minute but restricted his remarks to advice to keep warm and drink plenty of fluids. He said nothing about his visitor of the previous evening. Mrs. Worthington brought up some tea and toast and a soft-boiled egg. The hens were laying again. Tim went clattering downstairs on his way to school, and then the house resumed its deadly quiet.

Hilary slept awhile then awoke in late morning with a head that was a little clearer but a nose that was running wild. Outside her window was a waterlogged world, the air thick with moisture. Crumpled tissues covered the bedside table and carpet beneath, a sight that distressed her, but she had no energy to pick them up. Only when she had used the last clean tissue could she summon the strength to get out of bed and make her way to the bathroom for a fresh supply.

The telephone in the hall rang as she was on her way back to bed. She knew that her grandmother didn't always hear the phone, especially if she was in the back scullery. She went downstairs to answer it. The caller was her father's receptionist.

"Hello, Hilary. It's Janet. How are you feeling? Your dad said you were under the weather."

Hilary murmured something in response.

"I expect you've got the summer flu everyone's coming down with. At least that's what Dr. Woodhouse calls it. The Parkinsons have it too. That's why I phoned. Dick Parkinson rang this morning with a message that tonight's rehearsal is canceled. I don't know why he rang here instead of ringing you directly. I hope I didn't wake you up."

Hilary reassured her she was wide awake. She liked Janet, a pretty slip of a girl, not much older than herself, but with a tendency to be talkative. Janet rattled on now. "But that's the other reason I rang. Your dad wanted me to tell you that he won't be home for supper. In fact, he may not be home tonight. He got an urgent call to visit a farm, all the way over near Dorchester he said, and it sounded as though it might be a long job."

Janet chattered away, but the rest was inconsequential. Hilary listened amicably for a while and then pleaded faintness and hung up. She relayed her father's message to her grandmother, who scowled and pursed her lips but, for once, made no comment. Hilary went back to bed.

Toward ten o'clock that evening, Mrs. Worthington came upstairs with a mug of hot cocoa.

"I'll see to the hens," she said, setting the mug down and picking up the latest pile of tissue debris. She drew the curtains against the damp night. "Will this rain never stop?"

She came back to the bed and gave Hilary a peck on the forehead.

"Good night, child. I'll pray for your good health to return."

Back in the kitchen, the old woman puttered around for a few minutes before she borrowed Hilary's yellow oilskin and took a flashlight from a shelf by the back door. She strode down the garden path to the back gate and out into the lane that separated the garden from the field where the hens were kept. A figure waiting in the shadows of the garden followed her out into the lane and stepped forward as she pushed against the field gate.

TWENTY-ONE

The telephone woke Julia out of a deep, dreamless sleep. She glanced at the clock as she reached for the phone. *Seven thirty. Who could be ringing at this hour?* It was Hilary, almost hysterical.

"Mrs. Dobson, can you please come over at once. It's Granny—Tim says she's dead—she's out in the lane. Father's not here, and I don't know what to do."

Julia told Hilary to be calm. She'd be there in a few minutes. *What next?* she wondered as she pulled on a blouse and slacks, thrust her feet into sturdy shoes, and, grabbing a cardigan against the cool morning, hurried next door. The rain had stopped, but there was no sign of sun or blue sky. It had all the promise of another dreary day.

She found Hilary huddled in a dressing gown at the kitchen table, red-eyed and sniffling, the cold temporarily eclipsed by grief and fear. The girl clung to her, her body trembling with sobs. Tim, who had let her in, stood to one side, silent but nervous. His eyes glinted with the wariness of a cornered animal.

"Tell me what happened."

As Hilary recounted it, Tim had woken her about half an hour previously to ask where everyone was. He had not been told that this father was likely to be away all night. But his grandmother was nowhere to be seen either. He had looked in her room to see if she had overslept but found not only no grandmother but also a bed that appeared not to have been slept in.

"Where the heck is she?" he had demanded of his sister.

"I haven't seen her since she brought me some cocoa last night. She said she was going to shut up the hens. Oh, Tim, do you think she's had an accident or a heart attack or something? She may be lying out there hurt and can't get up." Hilary was alarmed by now.

"No such luck! She probably got up early and went out on an errand."

"Tim! At this hour of the morning? And her bed already made? That's most unlike her."

Tim shrugged.

"Tim, don't just stand there. Please go and take a look. If you don't, I will."

She leaped out of bed and began to hunt for her dressing gown and slippers, but Tim was already on his way downstairs and out into the garden. Hilary was waiting by the kitchen door when he came running back up the garden path, white-faced.

"You were right. She's lying in the lane by the gate. She looks dead."

"And that's when I phoned you," Hilary finished.

"Put the kettle on, Hilary, and make us all some tea" was Julia's first reaction. "And, Tim, you show me where your grandmother is."

She followed Tim down the garden path. The garden was sodden under the leaden sky. The grass glistened with moisture. Trees dripped in the gray morning light, their leaves hanging down dark and heavy. Pushing through the dank shrubs that crowded the back garden gate, Julia wished she had thought to slip on something more substantial than a cardigan.

Mrs. Worthington was lying in a patch of mud by the field gate. She was, without doubt, dead. Most of her body was shrouded in a yellow oilskin, a garish intrusive element in the muddy scene. Julia could see that the mud had been trampled, as though there had been a struggle. Instinctively, she pulled Tim back.

"I don't think we should get too close. We may destroy important evidence."

"Evidence of what?" Tim looked at her as if she were crazy.

"It doesn't look natural. I think someone may have killed her."

"Killed her!" Tim was even more eager to take a look, but Julia ordered him firmly back to the house.

Hilary had brewed the tea and now stood trembling by the sink. Julia hugged her once again as she broke the news but quickly moved on to the tasks she knew must be done. She phoned first Jessica Woodhouse and then Inspector Hughes. The inspector was not at all happy but promised to get there as soon as he could. She phoned the school to explain why Hilary and Tim would be absent. She poured tea, coaxed Hilary into finding cereal, making toast. The girl moved around the kitchen with automatic motions, weeping quietly all the time.

But though Julia tried to keep busy so she wouldn't have to think, the questions kept coming. Who would want to kill the old lady? She had not been a very pleasant person, but unpleasantness was not usually a reason for murder. And where was Dr. Worthington? Was there a connection with the Hestercombe death? But what could be the link except the Worthington family?

So many questions and no answers. She was glad when the doctor arrived. Jessica came in through the back door, having gone straight to the lane to take a look at the body before coming to the house. She took Julia aside.

"I'm afraid it does look like murder. Marks on the neck suggest strangulation. How sad. I didn't much like her, but that's not a good way to go for anyone."

The inspector arrived a few minutes later. He was not in a good mood. His alarm clock had failed to go off, and he had overslept. The phone was ringing as he opened the office door, but it wasn't, as he hoped, from Wolverhampton.

He'd tried yesterday to call Ruth Matthews, still hoping she'd remember the name of the bed and breakfast in Penzance. At the office where she worked, an irritated Mr. Sparks told him that she had called in sick. But when he dialed her home number, there was no answer. He had called several times but with no response. He finally had to call back Mr. Sparks and leave a message.

This morning's call was not an apologetic Ruth Matthews. Nor was it Dr. Worthington calling belatedly with the name and address of his lady friend, which he'd been asked to provide. It was news of another apparent murder, the last thing he needed to hear, particularly one involving the Worthington family. *Was there a link?* he wondered as he drove through the damp lanes to Blymton. *But what kind of link would it be? Why would the same person want to eliminate both a young man with an eye for girls and a puritanical old woman?*

"Where is your father?" was his first question. Hilary explained about the call to Dorchester. The inspector phoned Janet at the surgery and demanded more specific information. When she claimed to know nothing more, he crossly told her to go through the files, pull out all the ones relating to clients within ten miles of Dorchester, and phone each one to see if the vet was there. "And let me know the minute you find him," he finished.

Next he turned to Hilary and Tim. "You two stay right here. I'll have a lot of questions to ask you, and I don't want you running off. Now if you don't mind, Mrs. Dobson, perhaps you can lead me to the body. Dr.

Woodhouse, I take it you're the Worthingtons' GP. You'd better come along too."

The three trudged down the garden path in silence. The yellow oilskin still looked incongruous against the muddy ground. But this time, a thought that had been germinating in Julia's head since her first sighting suddenly sprouted into a wild but plausible idea. *Wasn't that Hilary's oilskin? Had someone intended to kill Hilary and murdered her grandmother by mistake?* She worked this idea over in her head, while the inspector and the doctor examined the body. *Why would someone want to kill Hilary? Was it the same person who had killed Brian? Did Hilary and Brian know something that made them dangerous? Or were the two deaths coincidental?*

Jessica repeated her verdict, unchanged on a second and closer examination.

"Death by strangulation, I would say, though the autopsy will provide more definite information. It's possible her heart gave out before the killer's grip choked her. Either way, it looks like murder."

The inspector nodded.

"It doesn't look as though she were sexually molested. That's a relief. I'd hate to have one of those maniac killers on the loose. Any estimate of how long she's been there."

"I can't say for sure, but I'd guess about eight to ten hours. She's quite cold, and rigor mortis has begun."

By now a police pathologist had driven up, and an ambulance could be seen a hundred yards away, carefully negotiating the entrance to the narrow lane. The inspector gave out some instructions then turned to the two women.

"That's all I can do here. Let's go inside and start the questions."

Jessica Woodhouse took off to begin her morning rounds, but Julia hesitated.

"Just a minute. Something is bothering me, Inspector. It's the oilskin that Mrs. Worthington is wearing. I believe it belongs to Hilary. Do you suppose that Hilary was the intended victim?"

It sounded crazy, but Julia felt compelled to say it. Inspector Hughes looked back at the body for a minute or two before replying. *Could it be mistaken identity? Damn it, these cases were difficult enough without throwing in another complication.*

"I don't think so. I'll bear that in mind, but I suspect the killer knew he was strangling an old woman, not a young girl."

The inspector marched with determined step past the dripping bushes and up the garden path. *If the murderer of both victims is Dr. Worthington*, he was thinking, *he certainly knew he was killing his mother.* Maybe she had found out about his lady friend and was being difficult. Perhaps she was threatening to tell the lady friend's husband, for the inspector was sure that the vet's fuss about "honor" was his cover for an adulterous relationship. On the other hand, and this was a new thought, if Hilary was guilty of murdering her fiancé—and he hadn't ruled out this possibility yet—perhaps the grandmother had some incriminating evidence that she was threatening to disclose. It was important to keep all options open.

He turned to Julia as they reached the door.

"How did you get into this? Where were you last night?"

"I'm afraid I was at home alone all evening and all night. I was woken by a phone call from Hilary. She was very upset, said Tim had found their grandmother dead and her father wasn't at home. I came over at once."

The inspector merely grunted in response.

Julia followed the inspector inside, seating herself on a stool in a corner of the kitchen. It was a vast, gloomy room, every piece of furniture and object in sight strictly functional, nothing decorative. There was only one window, over the sink, but an overgrown yew tree kept out much of the light. A white globe suspended over the kitchen table cast a circle of light in the center of the room, leaving the corners shrouded in obscurity.

"Any word about your father?" was the inspector's first question. Hilary shook her head. He phoned the surgery again. Janet had turned up nothing.

"Keep going," he barked. "Try everyone in Dorset."

Stupid man, the inspector said to himself as he put down the phone. If he wasn't killing his mother, he was probably off with his woman. His timing was very bad.

"All right. Now let's hear the full story. Who found the body?"

"I did," muttered Tim. "Though Hilary sent me to look."

"I'll talk to her later. First, you tell me what happened. And speak up, young man."

The account Tim gave was essentially the same one that Julia had already heard. Throughout he sat slouched on a kitchen chair, his hands in his pockets, affecting a nonchalant attitude. Julia sensed that he was really very scared.

"Now then," said Inspector Hughes when Tim had finished, "let's go back a bit further. When did you last see your grandmother alive?"

"I suppose it was yesterday evening. She made supper for me."

"Was the whole family having supper together?"

"No, it was just me and Gran."

"Where were the others?"

"Hilary was in bed. Gran took a tray up to her."

"And your father?"

Tim shrugged. "I dunno. Out somewhere."

"Did you ask where he was?"

"No."

"Was there any conversation at all?"

"We didn't talk. I'd pretty much finished by the time she came back downstairs from Hilary."

The inspector waited. "Then what?"

"I went up to my bedroom for a while. Later, I went out."

"What time was that?"

Tim shrugged again. "I dunno. Maybe eight o'clock, half past."

"Did you see your grandmother as you left?"

"She was in the kitchen."

"Did either of you say anything?"

"I didn't. She said something, but I don't remember. I don't usually listen to what she says."

"Where did you go?"

"Out." He would have stopped there, but he saw the mounting anger on the policeman's face and didn't wait for the obvious question. "I went looking for my pals. We hang out around the Market Cross when it's wet."

Inspector Hughes was aware of this and knew that these gatherings sometimes got out of hand. He made a mental note to check last night's police reports to see if any trouble was reported around the Market Cross.

"And how long were you there?"

"I dunno." Tim grinned as though he were about to make a smart remark then thought better of it. "We went over to Billy Harrison's later. His mum works at night, so we often go to his house."

Inspector Hughes knew about that habit too. Neighbors had called police to the house several times, complaining of loud music and other noise late at night. Rosie Harrison, divorced, on the evening shift at the nursing home in the next village, would apologize but seemed incapable of disciplining her teenage son.

"And what time did you leave?"

Tim shook his head.

"I don't pay attention to things like time. I just know I got fed up at some point and left. I didn't even look at the clock when I got in."

"How did you get into the house? Through the front door?"

"Yes. I have a key, remember? You asked me that last time." *Cheeky devil*, the inspector said to himself but let it pass. "I didn't go anywhere near the back if that's what you're wondering."

"Didn't you see lights still burning when you got home?"

"Yes, the kitchen light was on. I turned it out and went to bed."

"You didn't think that was strange?"

Tim shook his head. "Gran often did strange things. It's my opinion she was getting senile."

"There's no need to be disrespectful. Did you look to see if the back door was locked?"

"No. It was closed, I know that. But I didn't know anything was wrong, so I didn't go looking to see if it was locked or not."

"How did you get on with your grandmother? Did you argue a lot? I'm sure you disagreed on most things."

Tim sniggered. "You bet we did. But she'd given up on me, she had. She said so. 'You're doomed,' she'd say. 'Child of Satan,' she'd call me. 'I wash my hands of you,' she said sometime ago, and that was all right with me."

"You hadn't had a row with her recently?"

"No." This was said casually, then Tim suddenly grasped the implication of the question and said fiercely, "No, no! Are you suggesting I'd had a fight with her and killed her? You're out of your mind! I didn't care what she said or did. It didn't make any difference to me. I kept out of her way as much as I could, and that's how she liked it. I had no reason to kill her."

The inspector made no reply. He scribbled intently in his notebook for a few minutes, while Tim folded his arms angrily and, addressing no one in particular, muttered "I didn't kill her" several times.

Julia, watching from her corner, thought how sad and how wrong that no one seemed to care what Tim did. He said he liked it that way, but she suspected that it was a pretense, that he craved attention and affection.

Then it was Hilary's turn. While Tim was being interrogated, she sat slumped at the kitchen table, her head on her arms; but as soon as the inspector addressed her, she sat up and blew her nose vigorously.

"When did you last see your grandmother?"

Hilary explained about being in bed all day with a cold and Granny bringing her a mug of cocoa.

"I suppose it was getting on for ten o'clock because that's when Granny usually goes to bed. I didn't notice the time. She said she'd see to the hens. We have to shut them up at night because there are foxes around. I usually do that, and Granny lets them out in the morning."

"Was it dark, do you remember, when she brought you the cocoa?"

"It was getting dark, but it had been raining all day, so it had seemed darkish all evening."

"Weren't you expecting to hear her come back upstairs after she'd shut up the hens?"

"No. I drank the cocoa very quickly and fell asleep almost at once. I probably wouldn't have heard anything anyway. The walls in this house are very thick, and she walks around very quietly—or at least she did." Hilary's eyes filled with tears. "I can't believe she's gone, just like that, so suddenly. Why?"

"That's what we're trying to find out. Now she was wearing a bright yellow raincoat . . ."

He got no further. Hilary turned immediately toward the back door and gave a loud exclamation. "My oilskin! She was wearing my oilskin! Oh, how awful!"

And with that, she jumped up.

"I haven't seen her. I must go and see her."

"I'm not sure that is wise, is it?" Julia appealed to the inspector, but he offered no objection.

They were only just in time. The police had finished their measuring and photographing and note-taking and were preparing to load the body into the ambulance.

"Why would she be wearing your coat?"

"It always hangs on the back door. She must have borrowed it—I suppose it was still raining last night."

"Did she often borrow it?"

"I don't know. I never saw her wearing it before. But she might have taken it other times when I wasn't around, and she needed a raincoat. I wouldn't have minded."

Confronted with the reality of death, Hilary was calm, letting the tears run silently down her cheeks. She stroked the cold hand that lay awkwardly across the yellow oilskin, and Julia thought she heard her murmur "Good-bye, Gran." She waited until the ambulance doors were closed then walked slowly back to the house.

Inspector Hughes did not resume the questioning. He felt he had the information he needed, for now anyway. It seemed natural for the old woman to borrow a raincoat hanging conveniently by the back door. She was a tall and upright woman, he remembered from his first visit, must be about the same height as her granddaughter, perhaps a bit slighter in build, but that wouldn't matter under a raincoat thrown on for a five-minute trip down the garden at night. And with the hood up, she might well look like Hilary.

He made one last phone call to the surgery before he left. "If and when you hear from your boss, tell him to come to the Taunton police station at once. And when I say at once, that's what I mean—at once. Not when he feels like it."

By now he was convinced that the vet was with his woman, and he cursed his folly in not insisting that the man produce a name and address at their last interview. It would have saved a lot of time and frustration.

There was more frustration when he tried again back at the station to connect with Ruth Matthews. Mr. Sparks had no further word from her, and phone calls to her home produced only the harsh burr of the ringing phone. *If I don't hear soon, I'll have to get the Wolverhampton people to send someone over to her flat,* he told himself. This is not a good time for her whereabouts to be unknown. And yet he was more anxious to know where Dr. Worthington had been last night. He thought briefly about sending a man to wait at the surgery for his arrival, but realized the vet might just as easily go home first or telephone first.

Dr. Worthington's first stop that morning was to his surgery, where a frightened Janet told him of the inspector's rough demands and her own frantic search. She could not give a reason. Inspector Hughes had not explained why he was looking for her employer, and she was too timid to ask. So when, in late morning, an angry Dr. Worthington presented himself at the police station, he had no idea what was in store for him.

"Where the hell have you been?" was the greeting.

"None of your damn business! And what right do you have to terrify my receptionist into telephoning all over Dorset looking for me?"

The inspector paused to enhance the dramatic effect of the news he was about to impart. Then in calm and measured tones he said, "Because I regret to inform you that your mother was murdered last night."

He watched the vet's face closely as he delivered the news. There was no doubt that the shock was genuine. The man's knees appeared to buckle, and he groped for a chair. His normally florid face was ashen-colored.

"I don't believe it. How? Where? At home?" He leaped to his feet. "What about my children? Are they all right? I must get home to them."

"That's all right, Dr. Worthington. They are unharmed, in no danger. Mrs. Dobson from next door is with them. You can certainly go home, but I'd like you to answer one or two questions first. Please sit down."

"Very well, but first, I insist you tell me exactly what happened."

"I'm afraid not. You see, first, I must ask you to account for your movements last night. It is, to say the least, an awkward coincidence that two people have been murdered late at night and on both occasions no one seems to know where you are."

"But this is preposterous! Are you accusing me of murdering my own mother?"

"I'm merely stating the facts as we know them. If we are misguided, you are the only one who can provide a correction. So I repeat, where were you last night, Dr. Worthington?"

The vet had recovered from the initial shock by now. The color was back in his cheeks, and his breathing was more normal, but he still gripped the arms of his chair. He stared hard at the floor for several minutes before he spoke. The inspector waited patiently. His early morning anger was rapidly subsiding now that the man he had been searching for had turned up. The only sign of lingering irritation was the drumming of his fingertips on his desk.

When Dr. Worthington finally spoke, he too had calmed down.

"I did not kill my mother. I spent last night in Dorchester with a friend."

"The same lady friend you say you were with the night Brian Dixon was killed?"

"Yes. Inspector, you had demanded her name and address, and I had promised to tell you. That's why I went to see her yesterday. Look, I might as well tell you the whole story."

"I think that would be wise," the inspector said with a trace of sarcasm in his voice.

"Her name is Pauline Selkirk. I met her a year or so ago when I had a call to a farm the other side of Dorchester. She was there visiting her sister. I gave her a lift back to her house in Dorchester. She's a very attractive woman, intelligent too. I found her company stimulating and restful at the same time. The attraction seemed to be mutual, so I started calling on her whenever I was in the area. We'd have lunch or dinner. Once we met up in London. We talked about marriage, but—"

The inspector couldn't resist the interruption. "I suppose she's already married?"

"Oh no, at least not anymore. When I first met her, she was waiting for her divorce to become final. Her former husband was an airline pilot who ran off with a stewardess. Until the divorce came through, we had to be very discreet. And then I worried about how my family would react if I were to remarry. I knew my mother would object because Pauline is divorced. And I feared that my children wouldn't like anyone taking their mother's place. So we've kept our affair secret. But yesterday, I decided it was absurd to go on like this, and I went to Dorchester not only to tell Pauline that you wanted to speak to her but also to ask her to marry me."

He hesitated for a moment as if deciding whether to edit his story but then continued.

"She was very reluctant. She wasn't sure she could cope with either my mother or the children. I had been using my domestic problems to explain why I wasn't eager to remarry, and now I was trying to persuade her they weren't such formidable barriers. We talked late into the night, but finally she said yes."

So that's what he's been up to, thought Inspector Hughes. *It's a plausible story. But it doesn't necessarily let him off the hook. After all, now that his mother's dead, he doesn't have to face her objections. Isn't that convenient? Too convenient?*

"You were at her house all night then? Can anyone else verify that besides Mrs. Selkirk?"

"I don't think so. We had no visitors. And I put my car in her garage so it wouldn't be seen. That was a habit we'd developed. But, Inspector, you still haven't told me about my mother. What happened?"

The inspector would have preferred not to disclose the details yet in the hope that if the vet were guilty, he might let slip something he shouldn't know. But he clearly couldn't keep him in the dark much longer unless he were going to detain the man, and he didn't have grounds for that. So he explained about the body being found in the lane, Mrs. Worthington apparently strangled as she went out to shut up the hens for the night. He didn't mention the yellow oilskin.

"But what I don't understand is why anyone would want to kill her."

There was genuine bewilderment in Dr. Worthington's voice. Inspector Hughes sighed.

"Why indeed."

TWENTY-TWO

Ernest Worthington's question was asked over and over again in the days following his mother's death, but no one had any answers. At the inquest, the police doctor confirmed that the cause of death was heart failure brought on by attempted strangulation. The verdict was "murder by person or persons unknown."

Julia skipped the inquest but forced herself to go to the funeral.

The funeral service was in Blymton's Methodist chapel, where Mrs. Worthington had been a faithful worshiper. It was a gray service in a gray building on a gray day. Mrs. Worthington's last social occasion was as bleak and comfortless as the rest of her life had been. It was also sparsely attended. Dr. Worthington and his children were the only family members present. Another son, who had emigrated to New Zealand years before, did not return. The only other mourners were a handful of elderly men and women from the congregation. They whispered and shook their heads as they creaked into the chapel. A strange man, manifestly a plainclothes policeman, sat off to one side. He tried hard to look inconspicuous, but his presence was distressful to several of the ancient mourners. Hilary too gave nervous glances over her shoulder from time to time.

Julia sat at the back with Joan Croft, who crept in surreptitiously as the service was beginning.

"I thought the Worthingtons deserved some moral support," Joan whispered. "And I'm now repenting my joke that no one would be surprised if Dr. Worthington were to kill his mother. Not that I think he did. Probably some prowler."

"I suppose I came for the same reason," said Julia. "I also wish we hadn't discussed her as a potential killer. But I'm regretting too that I didn't try to get to know her. She must have been lonely by herself in that gloomy house all day."

"Not necessarily. She didn't have to stay at home. There were plenty of things she could have done in the village if she wanted company.

I think she preferred to be alone. I save my sympathy for her son and grandchildren whose lives have been blighted for the last several years."

In the week or two after the second murder, the pace picked up sharply, reducing discrete events to a confused blur. Newspaper and television reporters converged on Blymton, exciting the children and those villagers who saw a chance for a moment of fleeting fame. Others like Julia hid indoors until the novelty had worn off and the reporters had moved on to the next news story.

Somewhere in the middle of it all, Nigel phoned to say he wouldn't be calling on her on his way back to London as he had hoped to do. He was being recalled early because of an emergency. He didn't offer any explanation, and Julia was too well-schooled in diplomacy to ask.

"Any progress with the investigation into the Hestercombe death?" he asked.

"Not that I know of. I'm afraid the trail is pretty cold. But you must have heard of the latest development? Hilary's grandmother was found murdered the other day."

"I did hear something on the radio, though I try to stay away from the news when I'm on holiday. It's quite a coincidence. Is it definitely murder this time?"

"No doubt about it," and she described what had happened, ending up with the worrisome fact that the old lady was wearing Hilary's oilskin.

"I'm sure the murderer thought that he was killing Hilary. I'm frightened that whoever it is will try again."

"It depends what the reason was. The girl could be vulnerable if she knows something that could be vital to identification of her fiancé's killer, even if she's not aware that she has such information. Have you said anything to Jack Shaw?"

"No. I did mention it to the inspector who's investigating both murders, but he didn't seem to take it seriously. I understand your need to get back to London quickly, but I'm disappointed you won't have time to stop."

"I'm sorry too, but you should talk to Jack. You can trust him, you know. And he's more familiar with the case and the people than I am."

That was true, and with that, Julia had to be content. Nigel added that he would try to get down for a weekend sometime soon, perhaps for the play. "And if you have any reason to come up to London, let me know. I might be able to sneak away for lunch."

Julia telephoned Jack, who said her suspicions were plausible, and he'd consider stationing a man on guard at the Worthington house.

"The trouble is that I can't keep someone there indefinitely. If she was the intended target and it's important that she be silenced before she reveals something, then the killer may try again very soon. But if that's not the reason, if the motive is revenge for instance, he or she may be content to wait until everyone's guard is relaxed before striking again. I don't want to scare the girl, but if you could impress on her the importance of behaving cautiously, it would help. And if she does know something, then she ought to tell us at once."

Julia also voiced her concern to Sergeant Nelson. He appeared on her doorstep to take a formal statement. She invited him into her sitting room and explained once again that she hadn't heard a thing.

"I was at home alone. I spent most of the evening here in this room, reading, with music playing most of the time. And since this room is at the front of the house, I would be unlikely to hear anything happening back in the lane. It was after eleven when I went up to bed, and by then, I understand Mrs. Worthington was already dead."

Sergeant Nelson looked around the white-walled sitting room with its floor-to-ceiling book-filled shelves flanking the fireplace. All those books! How could anyone spend an entire evening reading? And she probably wasn't listening to decent music. Even before he asked the perfunctory question, the routine way of checking her veracity, he knew what kind of answer he would get.

"Some Mozart piano concertos. And then some dreamy Delius to put me in the mood for sleep."

"You say you were alone all evening. No visitors, no phone calls?"

"My daughter phoned, quite late because she'd been out at a meeting that evening, probably around ten."

He doesn't expect to learn anything from me, Julia told herself. *It's a total waste of time, just something to put down in their records. Checked all possible witnesses, etc. He's still young,* she observed. *What can he know of life, even if he is a policeman? He wants a simple case, and he isn't interested in considering complicating possibilities.* But she was determined to push her theory about Hilary as the intended victim at every opportunity, and she offered it now to Sergeant Nelson.

"That yellow oilskin is a very distinctive garment. We've had a lot of rain lately, and I expect Hilary has been seen wearing it on several occasions. I do think you should seriously consider the possibility that she was the intended victim. And that, having failed this time, the killer could strike again."

"We'll take that into account, Mrs. Dobson. We are looking at this case from every possible angle. Did the killer know the victim? Is there a connection to the Hestercombe murder? Et cetera. You can be sure we are following up every possibility."

He rose to leave. At the door, he asked, "I wonder who would have a reason to kill Hilary Worthington."

"Who would have a reason to kill her grandmother?"

Sergeant Nelson did not answer.

Despite the sergeant's obvious skepticism, Julia took seriously Jack's advice to warn Hilary, though she hoped to do it without unduly frightening the girl. She was still pondering this late one afternoon when she was discussing a possible redesign for the front garden with the church verger who had offered to help.

"You're on the right track there, Mrs. Dobson," he said when she had described her idea for paving the entire front area with large flagstones, leaving just a few spaces for small clumps of flowers here and there. "I know where I can find you some nice flags. I'll have to bring you some of my compost too. This soil has no nourishment."

They were busy marking out where small flower beds would go and measuring the area to be paved when Hilary came along the street, a laden shopping basket in each hand. She paused at the gate.

"Thank you for coming to Granny's funeral. That was kind of you."

"It was the least I could do. How are things going?"

"We manage." She rested her baskets on the wall. "Tim and I have been upset by more than just Granny's death," she volunteered and broke the news that their father was contemplating remarriage. "We haven't met her yet. Maybe she'll be all right."

And with that, she hurried on.

"Looks like Dr. Worthington's troubles aren't over yet," the verger remarked.

Julia was sure that Hilary had deliberately chosen to deliver her bulletin when she knew that a prolonged conversation would be unlikely.

It suggested that either she was more distressed than she appeared to be or that she hadn't decided what she felt about having a stepmother. Julia decided that the time had come to force a conversation. She made a meat-and-potato pie and a rich chocolate cake, put them in a basket, and in the evening, when she thought Hilary would be at home, she took them over to the Worthingtons' house.

To her dismay, it was the vet who opened the door.

"I'm sure this is a difficult time for you. I've brought some food. I thought it would help Hilary with a meal. It's a lot of responsibility for her to take on."

There was no telling how he would react. He might think she was interfering again or patronizing them. But to her surprise, he smiled shyly and held out his hand for the basket.

"That's very kind of you. It is hard to manage. Hilary does her best, but she has her school work too. I've just packed her off to the library to do her homework because here she keeps breaking off to make me some tea or iron a shirt."

Julia was disappointed that Hilary was out, but encouraged by the marked change in the man's disposition, she decided to deliver the warning to him. When she asked if he would have a few minutes to talk, he ushered her into the house and offered her tea or sherry.

The somber parlor was as uninviting as ever, slightly stuffy and chilled at the same time. A stiff spray of gladiolus in a plain glass vase on a low table near a window only enhanced the funereal atmosphere. But there was warmth in Ernest Worthington's manner as he produced glasses and a bottle from the depths of a large mahogany cabinet.

"I reproach myself for being away the other night," he confessed as he poured sherry. "If I had been at home, my good mother would be alive today."

"It's possible. But you can't be sure. You shouldn't dwell on it. Guilt is poor nourishment for the soul." He shook his head but made no response. Emboldened, Julia continued, "In my first days of grief, I used to blame myself for not going with my husband on that last trip. The plane would still have crashed, killing me too, but all the same, I felt guilty. But life is full of decision points, paths not taken. Some consequences are more important than others. And we can never know with certainty which was the pivotal one. I think we owe it to those we have loved and lost, as well as to the people we love and still have, to stop worrying about where the error lay, put guilt and regrets behind us, and go on living the best way we know."

I can't believe I'm talking like this, she said to herself. *I don't follow my own advice.* She put down her glass. "Forgive me for babbling on like this, talking in clichés."

"But clichés are what we need at times like these. There's too much to comprehend for original thought. Action helps too." He was twiddling the glass in his fingers, staring at the pale amber liquid, then abruptly he said, "I am going to remarry. I hope we can arrange that fairly soon, restore some normality to the household. And I have to start paying more attention to my children. What alarms me most about the horrible events of last week is the thought that my children might have been in danger too."

Julia seized the opening.

"That's what I wanted to talk to you about. I think Hilary was, and is, in danger. Did you know that Mrs. Worthington was wearing Hilary's very distinctive yellow oilskin?" He nodded. "I think Hilary was the intended victim, not her grandmother. And if that's so, the killer could try again."

"That thought had occurred to me. And I think Hilary realizes it too, though I don't know why anyone should have reason to kill her. We haven't talked about it. When she told me about my mother wearing her coat, she was very distressed. I think she suspected the killer was after her. But she didn't seem to want to talk about it, and I'm not very good at having frank conversations with either her or Tim. I let it pass."

"I don't know either why someone would want to kill her, unless she knows something connected to Brian's death. But she should be warned, even though I realize you may not want to alarm her."

"But she should be alarmed. I can't watch over her night and day. She has to be on her guard. She's not a child. She's seventeen. That's old enough to leave school, to drive, almost old enough to drink. She's probably engaged in other adult pleasures too. She was talking about getting married. I can't hope to protect her from the evil in the world. Yes, I should talk to her."

"You say she's at the library this evening. I worry about her being out in the village alone after dark."

"She'll be home before dark. The library closes at nine. But if it makes you feel better, I'll walk up the street to meet her. And now may I pour you another glass of sherry?"

TWENTY-THREE

The killer seemed to be in no hurry to strike again. As each day passed without any further incident, Julia began to relax. But tensions in the village remained high. Tempers were short; minor incidents turned into crises. Rumor and speculation were rampant, yet at the same time people seemed to be avoiding one another.

The police questioning was incessant but seemed to go nowhere. Inspector Hughes confessed himself baffled during one difficult meeting with the superintendent.

"I thought you'd pretty much decided that Dr. Worthington was your man," Jack Shaw said testily after the inspector had spent half an hour ruling out one villager after another.

"I haven't totally given up on him. But it does rather look as though his suspicious behavior was nothing more than a misguided effort to cover up an affair with a woman. After his mother's death, he finally gave me her name and address, and she has essentially confirmed his account of where he was on the occasion of both murders."

"She could be covering for him."

"Right. And that's why I haven't finally ruled him out. But for now it's not a strong case."

"What about the son?"

"That's a tricky one. I hauled him in to the local station the other day, thought the experience might cool him down a bit. The lad's going to get himself in real trouble one day if someone doesn't take him in hand. He runs around with a gang of louts who engage in more than your routine teenage rowdy behavior. We've had reports of vandalism, petty thievery, maiming and killing of animals, though it's been difficult to pin anything on them. When I pressed him about this the other day, he brazenly denied doing anything illegal, but when I got specific, like accusing him of killing a cat belonging to an old woman in Blymton and nailing the carcass on her door, his denial was a lot less convincing. I could seriously consider him a prime suspect in the death of his grandmother. I gather she made some pretty strong statements about his behavior. She might have gone one step too far and triggered an angry attack that turned murderous."

"I thought we were assuming that there's a link between the two murders? Tim Worthington may be a likely suspect in the murder of the old lady, but I don't see him as the Hestercombe killer."

"I agree. I see him as an impulsive actor, someone who could kill in a fit of anger. Or he might take part in a gang murder, especially if, as I suspect, some of his friends dabble in cannabis. But I don't see either scenario being acted out at Hestercombe. As long as we work on the assumption that the same person did both jobs, then the young man can't be high on the list of suspects. But if they're not connected—"

"What about the daughter?"

"Hilary Worthington? A similar problem. I could see her as the killer of her fiancé because she thinks he's going to drop her for an old girlfriend. But I don't see her killing her grandmother."

"But suppose the old woman knew something that led her to suspect the girl's complicity in the Dixon murder? Suppose she had heard her leave the house the night Dixon was killed and come back very late? Suppose she was threatening to report this?"

The inspector pondered that one.

"I did consider that possibility. But if Mrs. Worthington had heard something that night, I believe she would have spoken out at the time. I didn't know her, but from what I've heard, it would be contrary to her moral code to shield someone, even her own granddaughter, if she were accused of murder. And how would the girl get out to Hestercombe and back? It must be at least five or six miles across the fields, longer by road."

"She could have gone over there with Dixon. We have only her word for it that she did no more than phone him that evening. She could also have gone to his lodging and then with him to Hestercombe. Perhaps she walked back. Don't you think she could have managed that?"

"Perhaps," Hughes conceded. "She's an athletic kind of girl."

"We know someone probably visited him that evening because of the cigarette stubs. Does she smoke?"

"I asked her that. She said no."

"Have you tried to find anyone who saw a car outside Dixon's lodging that evening? Have you tried to find anyone who saw a girl walking along the roads between Hestercombe and Blymton late that night? Show me some hard evidence."

"We have been asking if anyone saw a strange car on Berry Lane that evening, but so far we've had no luck."

"Luck isn't going to get you your murderer," Shaw snapped.

"We have been doing the legwork. But the trail was pretty cold when we started."

"Sorry, sir." A young constable stuck his head around the door. "A phone call I think you want to take. On drugs."

Jack Shaw grunted but picked up the phone. The inspector, welcoming the interruption, chatted with the young man for a minute or two about the forthcoming annual cricket match between the Somerset constabulary and their counterparts in Dorset. The constable slipped away as the chief put down the phone.

"Some things are going our way. There's a promising lead on the drug ring we've been trying to crack. It looks as though we may be able to close in before too long. About time. It's been a long haul." He shuffled the papers on his desk, signaling that the meeting was over. The drug ring was a national case, being handled on a need-to-know basis, and not one to discuss with his subordinate. But the inspector had one more piece of information to impart.

"There is one other possible lead. We've been doing some checking up on the Matthews woman. You know we never did find the Penzance bed and breakfast where she claimed to be that night."

"You considered her a suspect because you thought he might have rejected her and she killed him in anger?"

"Yes."

"But why would she have killed Mrs. Worthington?"

"Mistaken identity. She thought it was the girl. The final act of revenge."

"Very dramatic. But will it fly? Isn't she back in Wolverhampton?"

"That's another curious thing. I wanted to arrange for her to go down to Penzance and try to retrace her steps for us so we could settle the matter once and for all. It so happened I was trying to get hold of her the day the old woman was killed. I phoned the office where she works but was told she was at home, sick. I phoned her home, but there was no answer. I tried several times and again the next day, but still no answer."

The inspector paused for maximum dramatic effect, but his boss sat impassively, waiting for him to continue.

"I called Wolverhampton and asked them to send someone over. It was afternoon before they went. They found her at home all right. Her story was that she'd collapsed with the flu and had slept for two days, ignoring the phone. She'd asked Dixon's mother to take care of the child."

He paused again.

"So?"

"So while everyone assumed her to be at home in bed, it's technically possible that she could have popped over to Blymton to knock off Hilary Worthington and caught her grandmother by mistake." He caught the fleeting look of annoyance that crossed the chief's face but pressed on regardless. "It's a long shot, I know. But until we've found that bed and breakfast in Penzance, I don't think we should rule her out completely, at least not for the Hestercombe case."

"Well, you can keep looking, but I think we'll find our murderer much closer to Blymton."

People in Blymton clearly shared this view, and the prospect that one of the villagers was a murderer was very unsettling. The cast and crew of the Players were particularly edgy. Dick Parkinson was in a perpetual state of agitation. Both he and Molly were irritated by the implications of questions that Inspector Hughes put to them that Hilary had something to do with one or both murders. He complained about this to Julia, adding, "They're also making everyone in the Players feel as though they are hiding something. It's having a terrible effect on the cast."

With less than two weeks to performance, the play was far from polished. Dick was heard wishing that the police would halt their investigation until the play was over. Molly's observation that most people probably found the real-life drama of mystery and murder more exciting than any play was no solace.

To avoid the tension, Julia deliberately missed a couple of rehearsals. Her work was essentially done anyway now that Bottom's head was finished. But then Molly phoned to ask if she would be willing to come to the Saturday afternoon rehearsal to take care of her little boy. "Dick wants to go straight through the play without a break, and my mind will be much easier if there's one person I can rely on to watch him all afternoon. He seems to behave so well for you. But if you think I'm imposing on you, do say so. I wouldn't want to do that."

It is a bit of an imposition, thought Julia, but she didn't have anything special to do that Saturday afternoon, and she was curious to see the play come together.

Much to everyone's relief, the run-through was a success. There were few flubbed lines, hardly any missed cues. Julia, sitting to one side of the auditorium with one eye on the stage and the other on the Parkinson child, was impressed by the high standard of acting for an amateur troupe. Toward the end, some of the crew began to wander in, and they too were caught up in the spirit of the play. There was little of the whispering and scuffling that often disturbed rehearsals. Mike Hatfield slipped in just in time to witness Pyramus's glorious death. He was dressed more smartly than the other young men, Julia noticed, with a navy blazer and crisp white open-necked shirt. On his way out for the evening, she decided.

After Puck had made his closing appeal for applause, Dick jumped up onto the stage with a loud cry of "Well done, everyone! Let's adjourn to The Feathers for a well-deserved drink and a little critique."

He offered to buy Julia a drink in gratitude for her valuable child-minding, but she declined gracefully. She had been invited to a dinner party at Blymton Manor and didn't want to get a head start on the evening's drinking.

She was preparing to leave when Mike sauntered by, heading for the stage where the cast still congregated.

"Leaving already?" he asked. "Don't you want to join in the postmortem?"

There was a sardonic tone to his voice that displeased Julia. "I should hope not," she countered. "I think Dick sees it more as a celebration. We've all been through so much the last few weeks. But perhaps it's different for you. You're a relative newcomer to the group. You weren't touched by the death of Brian Dixon as the rest of us were. Am I right?"

It all came out so quickly that Julia barely registered what she was saying. Mike offered no answer to her question, just shrugged and moved on. Julia felt she had touched a nerve but was more concerned at what had led her to sound off like that. What was it about the young man that always seemed to irk her? She watched him now, up on the stage, talking to Hilary, who appeared to be listening attentively to whatever he was saying. Perhaps she was misjudging him. Perhaps he was just what Hilary needed at this time.

As she approached the Worthingtons' house, she noticed a car parked off the road. The driver appeared to be sorting some papers, but Julia noticed that he gave her a short, sharp glance as she walked by. *So Jack has put a watch on the Worthington house*, she concluded. It also occurred to her that the man would be better employed watching Hilary rather than the house. But at least it was something.

TWENTY-FOUR

"The first body was found in a Lutyens garden? How bizarre!"

"Julia was the one who found it."

"Incredible! Do tell!"

Richard DeVere, having set Julia up to tell her story, moved away from the group of guests having predinner drinks on the terrace at Blymton Manor. It was a mild, calm evening. The sun was hanging low over the shrubbery, making long shadows across the terrace. The air was thick with the scent of lilies raising their noble heads, dark red and creamy white, from two huge tubs at the top of the terrace steps. With some reluctance and with minimum detail, Julia did what was expected of her. She was beginning to wish she had not accepted Bridget's invitation, although at the time she had been excited at the prospect of a social evening, the first party since her return to England.

"It's just a smallish gathering," Bridget had said when she phoned the invitation. "Once a year, Richard invites his London solicitor and wife down for the weekend, and we usually have a few friends in for dinner while they're here. Gerry, that's the solicitor, seems to run through wives as fast as my son outgrows his jeans. I haven't met the latest one, but they seem to get younger every time, so she's probably barely into her twenties. It should be interesting."

The new wife turned out to be closer to thirty, but she had the exuberance of a teenager. "That's Holli with an *i*," she said with a giggle when Bridget introduced her to Julia. She described herself as a journalist but subsequent questioning revealed that she was an editorial assistant at a magazine for teenagers. She wore both her hair and her skirt extremely short; her bright magenta jacket was almost as long as the slick black skirt. Long and intricate silver earrings jangled as she swung her head to emphasize every phrase. Julia took an instant dislike to her. It was she who had demanded that Julia tell how she found the body.

"And now you have another murder, though in some scruffy back lane instead of in a gorgeous garden. Most peculiar!"

Holli's interest waned as Richard moved away from the group and into the house. She turned her attention to the male guests, but it was evident that such Blymton worthies as the rector and the bank manager did not have the same appeal as the lord of the manor. Her husband watched all this with amusement. He stood to one side, leaning against the balustrade, a man with the beginnings of a paunch and an aura of world-weariness.

Richard's reappearance with two new guests was a merciful diversion. A tall sandy-haired man with a freckled face who bore a close resemblance to Bridget was introduced as her brother, Ben Russell. His companion, Giles Hamilton, was a shy, pale wisp of a man whose graying hair and sagging skin suggested he was several years older than Ben.

"What did I tell you?" murmured a voice in Julia's ear. It was Jessica Woodhouse who, until now, had been hovering on the edge of the group, taking no part in the conversation. Jessica, hearing that Julia had been invited to the dinner party, had volunteered to drive her over to Blymton Manor. On the way she had speculated who the other guests might be.

"I expect it will be the usual crowd. Richard's solicitor and his wife. The rector and Joan. The bank manager and his wife. I wonder who the two single men will be."

Julia looked puzzled.

"If you and I are included, Bridget's bound to have asked two unattached males so that we're all neatly arranged in pairs. Then we can go into dinner in twos, just like Noah's ark."

"That happens on the diplomatic circuit, but surely not in Blymton?"

"Indeed it does. I think hostesses here see single women as predators, out to snatch their husbands. I know I never get invited to a party unless there's a spare man available to chaperon me."

Jessica turned into the gates of Blymton Manor with a screech of tires and roared up the drive as though chasing a demon.

"Who will be protecting the married men of Blymton tonight?"

She swung the car expertly into line with others already parked by the front entrance. She pulled off the sandals she had been wearing to drive and thrust her feet into a pair of dressier shoes that she pulled out from a pile of assorted items littering the backseat.

"My first guess would be wicked Ben, Bridget's brother. He lives a wild life, according to most of his family. Bridget's about the only one who accepts him as he is. I think Richard is a bit cool toward him. I like him. He's usually bloody good company. He has a live-in boyfriend whose name I forget and who usually tags along. By inviting Ben, Bridget would get her two extra men."

Julia decided that she too like wicked Ben. He had a sharp wit and an infectious laugh and soon had the measure of the giddy editorial assistant. He seemed not at all interested in the local murders and quickly steered the conversation into other, and to Julia, more interesting quarters. An architect by profession, in no time at all, he was chiding Richard for not doing more to improve the estate.

"It's so deadly boring, nothing but grass from here to the horizon. And the horizon is nothing more than a line of totally predictable trees. You should introduce some excitement into the landscape. Plant a maze. Build a folly."

Richard, who had clearly heard all this before, listened patiently until Bridget interrupted with a summons to dinner.

The dining room was just what Julia would have expected, a large and handsome room where mahogany and silver gleamed in the candlelight. Family portraits on all four walls stared solemnly as the guest distributed themselves around an exceedingly long table. Bowls of pink bourbon roses on the table and sideboards softened the formality. To her relief, Julia found herself well down the table from Holli, who had a place of honor next to the host. Instead, she was flanked by the shy Giles and a man who introduced himself as the local estate agent. As they spooned their chilled watercress soup, the estate agent tried to interest her in selling Flora Cottage. Julia listened politely but was glad when Mrs. Mudge, coming round to remove the soup dishes, caused a natural break in the conversation. Leaning over to pick up Julia's dish, Mrs. Mudge whispered, "It's a nice crown roast of lamb we've got for you tonight. I'll see you get a good piece."

As she tucked into her good piece of lamb, Julia found herself talking to her other neighbor. She soon perceived that he was not shy but reserved, deliberately withholding himself. Nevertheless, she persisted. She had just learned that he was a furniture designer when Ben, who was sitting opposite, leaned across the bourbon roses with a joke.

It was a slightly off-color joke, and he spoke loudly enough to attract the attention of the whole table. Holli gave a loud guffaw and followed up with a worse joke. Even Gerry looked embarrassed. The rector suddenly developed an intense interest in his piece of lamb. Richard tried to take charge by rushing around refilling glasses and chattering furiously about the wine and its vintage, but he was only fueling the merriment of Ben and Holli. They continued to challenge each other for dominance of the conversation, though by the time Mrs. Mudge had cleared away the meat plates and served everyone with strawberries and cream, they had run out of jokes and had switched to exchanges of salacious gossip.

When the party adjourned to the drawing room for coffee, Ben subsided. He went at once to the grand piano in the corner and began to play, skillfully but softly as if he were playing only for his own ears. Holli and Jessica and some of the men moved through the drawing room to the billiards room beyond, and a hilarious game was soon under way.

Like the dining room, the drawing room was large with venerable paintings on the walls, but it was furnished more informally with plump sofas and deep armchairs in soft shades of lemon and rose. It was a congenial room for quiet conversation, and Julia hoped that the billiards game would last all evening. She took her coffee over to join Giles, who was sitting by himself near the piano. She wanted to hear more about his furniture design, but he was determined to talk about murder.

"It seems incredible to me that no one from Hestercombe was involved in that first murder," he began.

"That was my first thought too. But the police say they have cleared everybody."

"I suppose all the young man's friends in Blymton have been grilled by the police too."

"Indeed they have. They complain about it all the time. In fact, I believe one or two of them don't have good alibis. But then nobody could think of a motive for any of these young men."

"None of them was lusting after his fiancée?" asked Ben, who by now had stopped playing and was listening.

"No. Mike Hatfield seems to be pursuing her now, but I don't think he knew her before Brian was killed."

"Mike Hatfield? I hope that's not the Mike Hatfield I know," said Ben, suddenly serious.

"I don't know much about him. I believe he runs his own business, but I don't know where he lives."

"What does he look like?"

"Well-built, fairly tall, dark curly hair, quite good-looking, pleasant manner. I'd say he's in his late twenties, possibly thirty."

"Would the words 'suave' and 'charming' describe him?"

"Yes, that's exactly how I'd characterize him."

Ben shook his head. "It sounds awfully like the Mike Hatfield I know, and that's not good news. Mike appears suave and charming, but underneath he's seething with rage. He has a grudge against the world."

"But it's not necessarily the same person, is it? Couldn't there be two people with the same name?"

"Possibly. The Mike I know also has his own business. Lives in Taunton. Runs a little operation selling fire extinguishers, at least that's his legal business. But he also has a nice little sideline in cocaine."

"That's a rather startling accusation to make. How do you know?"

"I'd rather not say, if you don't mind. Let's just say I know he handles the stuff. But he's definitely a nasty piece of work and not one that any nice young lady should get mixed up with."

"Could he be a murderer?"

"I don't like to malign anyone, but yes, if you told me he'd killed someone, I could believe it."

Julia was shaken. It was unnerving to think that someone might be able to dissemble so well. She realized that she had been thinking of him as a pleasant distraction for Hilary, perhaps one day a replacement for Brian. But it could all be coincidence. After all, why would Mike want to kill Brian? Had Brian somehow got mixed up in drugs? That seemed unlikely, but then if Mike's charm was only skin-deep, perhaps Brian's apparent solidity was just a facade too. And where did old Mrs. Worthington fit into this? Her head began to spin.

Jessica, bored with billiards, came back to the drawing room, intent on talking to Ben and Giles. Holli was close behind her. Julia, unable to cope with Holli at that moment, escaped through the open French window to the terrace.

The moon was up, a full moon that bathed the broad lawn in its ghostly glow. The trees at the far side of the lawn rose dark and mysterious against the sky. The lilies breathed their perfume extravagantly into the night. It was easy to push aside nasty thoughts about charming men who might be killers when confronted with such serene splendor.

Richard DeVere and Peter Croft were leaning against the balustrade.

"Isn't it beautiful!" Julia said.

Richard shook his head. "I agree with Ben. The garden is boring. But I don't want him messing it up with his wild fancies. He'd ruin it—and me too, probably."

"Mrs. Dobson is a keen gardener," the rector noted. "You should put her to work on it."

"Not a bad idea," said Richard, turning to Julia. She was intrigued. They talked animatedly about paths and pools and old-fashioned roses until the rector interrupted them.

"I don't want to break up the party, but I have early service in the morning, so I'd better be off to bed," he fussed, shaking hands vigorously. "Thank you so much. A delightful evening! And a beautiful night! 'The Moon of Heaven is rising once again.' *The Rubaiyat*, you know." He winked at Julia and was gone.

Julia and Jessica took their leave shortly before midnight. Julia was in a philosophical mood.

"Isn't it fascinating how easily one can form an opinion of someone from first impressions only to learn something totally unexpected about them. For instance, I'd no idea our rector could quote *The Rubaiyat* of Omar Khayyam so readily."

"The reverend Dr. Croft is a deep, deep well full of surprises. He's a keen Arabist. I'm told he's been known to quote the Koran in his sermons though I've never heard him do it."

"Then there's the young man from the Players who's been hanging around Hilary Worthington recently—Mike Hatfield. Do you know him?"

"Dark curly hair, looks like a rugby player except he doesn't have a broken nose, and talks like a real charmer? Is that the one?"

"That's the one."

"He was after her again this evening."

"What do you mean?"

"I saw them outside The Feathers. I was on my way home to get ready for Bridget's bash, and they were standing outside the pub. There were a few others around. I suppose they'd just come from rehearsal. But these two were to one side, by a car. It looked as though he was trying to persuade Hilary to do something, go into the pub, go for a ride in his car. Anyway, she didn't want to do whatever it was. I only saw them for a minute, you realize, as I was driving by, but during that minute, she was shaking her head and moving away, and he was putting out a hand to restrain her. Not very bright, if you ask me, to be wooing a young woman so soon after she's lost her lover."

They had reached the gate of Flora Cottage. As Julia was about to get out of the car, Jessica asked, "So what surprising thing have you learned about Mike Hatfield?"

"Ben mentioned tonight that he knows a Mike Hatfield who, as he described him, sounds just like the one we know. But Ben says he's a dangerous character, boiling with rage underneath all that charm. He also hinted that Mike deals in drugs. If they are one and the same, he's not the right person for Hilary at any time."

"I wouldn't worry about it. I'm sure young Miss Worthington can take care of herself."

But Julia had a hard time putting Mike Hatfield out of her mind. In bed, she tossed and turned for what seemed like an eternity, alternating short drifts into sleep with long wakeful periods. Finally, sometime after three in the morning, she fell into a deep, dreamless sleep.

When she woke, it was already well past eight o'clock. She hadn't slept that late in years. She felt surprisingly refreshed, as though sleep had dissolved all her anxieties. Last night's fretting about Mike and Hilary seemed fanciful in the clear light of day.

It was a glorious morning. A light breeze was fluttering the curtains, but it promised to be a hot day. The garden beckoned. She would not go to church but instead have a leisurely breakfast outdoors. It would be wonderful to indulge in reading the fat Sunday newspaper all morning.

She was sitting under the old apple tree, the remnants of breakfast on a small table beside her, her head deep in the newspaper, when she heard Hilary calling out to her. The girl was leaning from an upstairs window, near enough to be seen but too far away for Julia to hear well what she was saying. She waved and called, "Come over."

A few minutes later, Hilary came running round the side of Flora Cottage in a state of deep distress. She was trembling and near to tears.

"Hilary! Whatever's the matter?"

"Oh, Mrs. Dobson, something's happened to Tim, I know it has. He's disappeared! There's no sign of him anywhere. And Father's not at home, and I don't know what to do."

TWENTY-FIVE

"Something terrible has happened to him! I know it has."

Julia calmed down the hysterical girl and took her into the kitchen to make fresh coffee. Hilary stopped sobbing, but her hands shook as she took the mug of coffee. She sat down at the kitchen table, hair straggling untidily over her shoulders and repeating, like a mantra, "Something has happened." Julia leaned against the kitchen sink, feeling weary of it all.

"You say your father isn't at home?"

"He went to Dorchester after breakfast to fetch his—his lady friend. He's bringing her home to meet us."

"Perhaps Tim doesn't want to meet her. He may have run away instead."

"I don't particularly want to meet her, but I haven't run away."

"Tell me what you actually know. When did you last see Tim?"

"I'm not sure. Sometime yesterday. I think he went out as usual in the evening, but he didn't come back. His bed hasn't been slept in."

"Didn't your father realize Tim didn't come home last night?"

"He made a comment about Tim being out late again last night and sleeping late this morning and almost went upstairs to scold him. But then he looked at his watch and said he'd better be off. As he left, he said he'd be back by teatime, and he wanted us both here. He told me to wake Tim up and make sure both he and his bedroom were presentable."

"And when you went to wake him up, he wasn't there."

"That's right. I didn't go up right away. The house was so peaceful without him around. But when I did look for him, the room was empty."

"You'd better get hold of your father."

"I don't know where he is, not exactly. I don't know where she lives in Dorchester, but anyway, they were going to have lunch somewhere and then come back here for tea. I said I'd make a cake."

Julia was angry. *He's still neglecting his children. He wasn't aware that his son was out all night, left without seeing him. He's gone off for the day, leaving them to wait apprehensively for him to return hours from now, bringing their new mother. No wonder Tim ran away. That must be what happened. He'll come home tonight or tomorrow morning, when she's safely back in Dorchester.*

She said none of this aloud, except to reiterate that the boy must have run away.

"No, he's been murdered too."

"Now, Hilary, that's nonsense. If I thought that, I'd have phoned the police at once. But I'm sure he's hiding somewhere, and he'll be back as soon as the coast is clear."

"I hope you're right. I'm so afraid. Gran used to say that accidents and other bad things always happen in threes. Tim may be the third victim."

"Why would anyone want to murder Tim?"

"Why did someone murder Gran?"

Julia seized the opening to warn Hilary. The child—and she was behaving like a child rather than a sensible young woman going on eighteen—was being remarkably obtuse in not sensing her own danger.

"If the killer is going to strike a third time, I think you are a more likely victim. I'm sure whoever killed your grandmother thought it was you."

"She was wearing my oilskin."

"Exactly. You are much more vulnerable than Tim. You should be very cautious about where you go and who with, especially in the evening."

"But why me? What have I done?"

"I don't know. I asked Jack Shaw that question, and he thought that if Brian's killer also tried to murder you, it might be because he suspected you knew something that could get him in trouble."

Hilary did not reply but sat staring at her empty mug. Julia refilled it and then, with a barely suppressed sigh of impatience, tried again.

"Is there anything you can think of that would provide a clue? Something Brian might have said?"

"I wish I could. So much of those last few weeks seems to have been blotted out."

There was one other question that Julia wanted to ask. There seemed no easy way to introduce the topic, so she asked abruptly. "How is your friendship with Mike Hatfield going?"

Hilary looked surprised. "It's not going anywhere, not if I can help it. He keeps pestering me to go out with him, but I don't want to go out with anyone, not for a long time. Please don't start imagining things between us."

"I won't do that. In fact, I'm relieved to hear you aren't encouraging him. I've heard things about him that suggest he may not be a very nice person. I don't think he'd be suitable for you."

"Suitable or not, it doesn't matter. I'm not interested in him. Thank you for the coffee. I'd better go now and make the cake." She stopped at the door. "Are you sure Tim's all right?"

"I think he'll turn up very much alive. But perhaps not before tomorrow."

"Father will be furious. But that's too bad."

"Hilary," Julia called to her as she went out into the garden. "Don't judge the woman your father is bringing home before you even meet her. Wait and see what she's like. She's probably just as apprehensive about this meeting as you are. And remember that you'll be leaving home before too long, and Tim too in another few years. Your father will need someone. Give her a chance."

Hilary nodded but left without another word. *I hope the stepmother works out,* Julia thought, *so that I can hand Hilary over to her and get on with my own life.* She remembered now, with wry amusement, Hilary's odd comment at Hestercombe about plants having uncomplicated lives. When all this was over, it would be refreshing to concentrate on garden design where the most daunting problem would be shrubs that failed to thrive or frost in May.

She went back outside to resume her idle Sunday morning, but the spell was broken. She picked up the paper and began to turn the pages over, looking for some diversion, but saw only reports of scandal and tragedy and distress. And so many involved children. Four children abandoned by their parents in an empty house, sick and hungry. A small boy kidnapped by his divorced father. Two teenagers who committed suicide.

Could Tim have been so unhappy at the prospect of a stepmother that he killed himself? That was something neither she nor Hilary had considered. But she quickly dismissed it as most unlikely. Despite all his posing, Tim struck her as all bluster like his father.

Thoroughly depressed by now, she abandoned the paper and sought distraction in gardening. The herbaceous bed along the wall was showing signs of neglect, and she was soon busy pulling up weeds and dead-heading spent flowers. *I will definitely make changes here this autumn,* she decided. *I wish I knew more about garden design. I was talking off the top of my head to Richard last night, but garden design is probably the best idea I've had about what to do with my life.*

Nevertheless, try hard as she would to think about gardening rather than disappearing youths, her thoughts kept returning to Tim. What had that silly boy done? And when was all this going to end? She needed to talk to someone. Not Jack Shaw, who would be reassuring but not very satisfying. Someone like Nigel. Talking to him would be like slipping on a familiar garment. She had received a note from him to say that he hoped to come down next weekend for the play, bringing Chip and Diana with him. But that was a whole week away.

Then, as she clipped and forked, an idea took shape. The previous day, she had received a letter from her solicitor asking if she would be coming up to London anytime soon. There were some papers that needed her signature. Perhaps she could combine a visit to the lawyer with a call on Nigel.

She pocketed her secateurs and went into the house to telephone. *I expect he's out on this fine Sunday,* she told herself as the phone purred away, but after several rings, he answered a little out of breath.

"I was just leaving, on my way to the pub for a bite to eat, when I heard the phone. How nice that it's you and not a call from the Yard."

"I won't keep you from lunch. I'm still counting on you for next weekend, but I'd like a chance to talk before then, if that's possible." And she explained her need for a trip up to town in the next few days. "If I picked the right day, would you be able to get away for lunch?"

"What about Tuesday? That would be the best day for me. I think I could manage an hour or so. What's happening? Any new developments?"

She told him about Tim and her assumption that no foul play was involved.

"I agree. He's probably just run away. A plea for attention or avoidance of his intended stepmother. At least I hope that's what it is and not something even more foolish."

"You mean killed himself?"

"It's possible."

Nigel's haste in suggesting this possibility was alarming. But he was always blunt, Julia remembered. And that was what she wanted, to talk to someone who wouldn't dance around.

"But I think it's unlikely," Nigel went on. "He'd be more likely to do that at home where it would create maximum effect."

"Hilary fears he's the third murder victim."

"I doubt it, but I suppose one shouldn't rule it out. Have you reported him missing?"

"No. I thought the police didn't pay attention to missing person reports until they've been gone for at least twenty-four hours."

"Normally, yes. But given what's been happening to the Worthington family recently, you should tell Jack Shaw right away."

She phoned Jack's home, but the Shaws were out enjoying the pleasant weather. She left a message on the answering machine.

The Shaws had gone to the annual cricket match with the Dorset police, which, to Jack's satisfaction, Somerset won. Jim Nelson did a splendid job, surviving some fast-paced bowling long enough to score a respectable eighty-six runs before being caught out. Tom Hughes took his partner off to the pub afterward to celebrate.

"That wasn't bad, my lad," he said warmly as they sat with their beer in the mellow evening sunlight of the pub garden. "You stood up to that bowling very well."

"That was a stupid mistake, being caught out like that. I should have pulled it round more. I knew it was a bad stroke as I was hitting it."

"Don't fret over it. Anyone can be caught out. What matters was not letting him bowl you out. Now if we could only come out on top with some of our cases, I could sleep well at night. Have another?"

Nelson drained his glass, wiped his mouth, and held out the empty vessel to the barmaid who came over at his boss's command.

"There are some things you can't win no matter how hard you try."

"Now, now, Nelson, that's defeatist talk, and I won't have that in my department. Especially after we've just won the Dorset match for the first time in four years. Take it as an omen."

"You mean we'll now have a breakthrough in the Blymton murders?"

Hughes sighed. He took a large slurp of ale and stared up toward the sinking sun for a minute or two before replying.

"I think on that one we're going to have to come up with some original idea to break the case."

"How about starting with no murder?"

The inspector raised his eyebrows. He'd tossed this one round himself. He was curious to hear the young man's opinion.

"Keep going," he said.

"Maybe the reason we're not getting anywhere is because there's nowhere to get. Perhaps we're just chasing one of those—what do you call them, those mythical monsters?"

"Chimera."

"That's right. Suppose the coroner was right after all. I know they say the man was left-handed, and yet the gun was in his right hand. It could have been an accident, couldn't it? He was holding the gun in his right hand, just holding it, not intending to shoot or anything, and the thing went off by mistake."

"It sounds reasonable to me, but the chief isn't buying. That Mrs. Dobson has some hold over him. We can't go in and tell him that there was no murder. He'll be down on us like a ton of bricks. Even if we never find a killer, he'll refuse to accept that it was an accident. There's the old woman's death too, whether or not there's a connection. We've got to keep plugging away."

"I'd better get home, or I'll be in trouble." Nelson finished his beer and stood up. "You said you could give me a lift?"

Hughes didn't speak as they drove off. It was one thing to preach patience to his zealous subordinate. Nelson didn't have the chief on his back, demanding results. Yet everywhere he turned there seemed to be nothing but frustration. When was all the legwork going to pay off? If the killer was Hilary Worthington, why hadn't their inquiries turned up evidence of a girl thumbing a lift back to Blymton that night? If Dixon had a visitor at his digs that night, why hadn't someone noticed the arrival or departure of the visitor or even a strange car parked outside? Neighbors were usually nosy enough to spot things like that. Was there a connection between the two murders, or was it coincidence? Should he stop focusing on the Worthington family and take a harder look at the young men who worked with Dixon in the theatrical group? Some of them had weak alibis. Perhaps they should be questioned once more. That would be a good way to absorb some of Nelson's energy. And he still hadn't given up on the young woman from Wolverhampton. He remembered now that she was supposed to be down in Penzance this weekend, trying to retrace her steps to the place she said she'd stayed the night of the first murder.

"Let's stop at the station to see if there's any news," he said.

He wasn't really expecting anything, but they arrived at the station just after Jack Shaw's phone call. He was reporting the message found on his answering machine. Tim Worthington had disappeared.

"Oh my God," said the sergeant. "Not a third murder!"

TWENTY-SIX

Later that evening, Julia received a phone call from Hilary in another high state of excitement.

"Has Tim come home?" asked Julia hopefully.

"No. The police were here earlier asking for particulars. Did you report him missing?"

"I didn't make an official report, but I did leave a message on the superintendent's answering machine at home. I thought he ought to know. Was your father upset by the police visit?"

"Not really. He's much more angry with Tim. Like you, he thinks Tim has run away and done it to annoy him. It's a shame because Pauline was also upset, and she's a nice person. I think I approve of her. I'm glad you cautioned me to wait and see."

"It sounds as though you got off to a good start then," said Julia, very relieved.

"But that's not why I'm phoning. I've got something to show you. Father left about an hour ago to take Pauline home. After they'd gone, I began thinking about what you said this morning—was there anything that might provide a clue? And I remembered a packet of things that Mrs. Dixon sent me, mementos of Brian. It arrived the day Gran was killed, and I didn't feel like opening it then. It's mostly photos and postcards, but there are a couple of newspaper clippings that are curious and possibly significant. Shall I bring them over for you to see?"

"I'll come over to your house if you don't mind." Julia's protective instincts were at work again. No need to have Hilary out at night unnecessarily.

Hilary had the contents of a large manila envelope spread out across the kitchen table. The two newspaper clippings, yellow and beginning to crumble at the edges, were opened up. Large sections were underlined, with notes scribbled in the margin.

"That's Brian's writing," said Hilary. "But I don't understand what he's saying."

Julia sat down and studied the clippings. They were from the local paper three years ago, one dated two weeks after the other. The earlier one was a long account of a fire in a village outside Taunton. A picture showed firemen carrying an old woman out of a burning house. They were not identified in the caption, but someone had drawn a line from one burly fireman to the margin and written there the letter M. A second line had been drawn from another fireman, partly hidden by his colleagues, and to this was added the letter B, followed by a question mark.

"I suppose that B is Brian," said Hilary, "though it's hard to see any of their faces with those huge helmets."

According to the report, the house had been owned and occupied by an eighty-year-old woman. She was asleep in bed when the fire broke out around midnight. Firemen had to find their way through thick smoke to find her. She was alive when they brought her out, and she kept saying something about a box. But outside, among the lights and hoses, with the men in their clumsy uniforms running back and forth, she had a heart attack and was declared dead on arrival at the hospital.

Much seemed to be made of a rumor that the old woman who had been something of a recluse, had kept a lot of money in the house, and yet none had been found in the burned-out shell. It was suspected that her hoard, if it existed, had gone up in flames along with the rest of her worldly goods. This section of the report was heavily underlined, and in the margin was written: "What happened to the box? Was this the origin?"

What caught Julia's interest, however, was a reference to the fireman who had been first into the burning house and had begun the rescue operation. His name was Michael Hatfield. She looked back at the picture.

"M must be Mike Hatfield."

Other firemen had been quick to give Mike the major credit. "Mike was the one who found her," said one. "We were only just in the nick of time. Another minute, and we couldn't have got to her." This whole section was heavily underlined. Mike's name had a box around it, and in the margin were three exclamation marks. One of the firemen had been killed when the burning house collapsed on him.

The second clipping was a much shorter report, following up the earlier one. The woman's doctor had publicly repeated the rumor of a box full of banknotes, hinting that he had once caught a glimpse of it. But no trace of box or money had been found, though the debris had been carefully searched. Since the woman had left no relatives, no heirs, no one seemed to be upset by this news, just curious. This clipping had some underlining but no notations.

"Why did he keep these?" asked Hilary. "What does he mean about 'the origin'?"

"I don't know," said Julia slowly. "If it wasn't for his notes, one would think it just a souvenir, a record for the scrapbook. But I think it could be significant."

Julia reread the reports carefully. A day or two earlier, she might not have taken them seriously. But what Ben had said about Mike last night seemed, in some unknown way, to have relevance to these reports. All she said to Hilary, however, was "I think Jack Shaw should see them. If you'll lend them to me, I'll take them to him tomorrow."

Julia phoned the Taunton police station first thing the next morning. Jack was in a meeting, but she made an appointment to see him right after lunch, mentioning that she had some possible evidence to discuss.

On impulse, she then rang Helen Shaw to see if she would be free for lunch. Tim's disappearance still nagged her. She needed reassurance from a professional in the field that for him to run away would be a fairly normal reaction for an adolescent boy to the prospect of an unwelcome stepmother. Helen responded in her usual brisk manner by suggesting a time and place to meet.

The restaurant was the one where Julia had lunched with Hilary and Myra Dixon after the inquest. It was still filled with gray-haired ladies in cardigans talking in modulated tones. They talked about gardens for some time, comparing notes on black spot, mildew, and other malign influences. Then, abruptly, Helen asked if there was any news about Tim.

"No news. I tried to inquire before I left this morning, but there was no answer at the house, and at Dr. Worthington's surgery, the receptionist said he was out doing his rounds. As far as she knew, the boy had not come home."

Julia then related what had happened, from Ernest Worthington's plans to remarry, to the initial reaction of his children, Tim's disappearance, and Hilary's fears about murder. Helen listened attentively.

"His disappearance at that particular moment must be more than just coincidence," she said when Julia had finished. "There has to be a connection with the imminent arrival of a stepmother. It's a classic bid for attention that, I suspect, he wasn't getting from his father."

"But could he have done more than just run away? Could he have killed himself?"

"How long has he been missing? It's been more than twenty-four hours, hasn't it? No, I think suicide is unlikely now. When teenagers commit suicide, it's usually done very openly. There would be a body by now."

"That's what Nigel said."

"We are seeing more of this desperate behavior by young people these days. Even running away is a desperate response to an unbearable situation. What's particularly worrisome is that in some cases, the unhappiness isn't manifest for years. The young person may appear totally normal, be outwardly pleasant, and yet underneath be boiling with anger. Then one day, without warning, something triggers an explosion."

Not exactly a description of Tim, Julia thought. His anger has been very manifest. But it was similar to Ben Russell's description of Mike.

Jack greeted her warmly and apologized immediately for not responding to her personally after he received her phone message about Tim.

"I gather Hilary's very upset by the boy's disappearance," he continued. "Her father is more angry than worried. Seems to think the boy is trying to make him look foolish in front of his intended wife."

"So you're not taking it seriously?"

"Not unless he stays away too long. We're keeping our eyes open, of course. I expect someone will run across him before too long. Until we've settled these wretched murders, we have to know what all the Worthingtons are up to."

"You haven't made any further progress then?"

Jack picked up a paper from his desk.

"Only to eliminate a possible suspect, though I never thought she was a serious one. I've had a report this morning from Penzance. One of my women officers took Ruth Matthews down there this weekend to find the place where she claimed to be the night Brian Dixon was murdered. She remembered the direction she took when she left the station, and they finally found the house. The landlady was able to identify her. I don't think it was a setup."

Julia looked puzzled.

"It occurred to me that she would have had enough time to arrange something. She might have had a friend in Penzance who, with a little warning and preparation, could have pretended to run a bed and breakfast and agreed to corroborate her stay on the crucial night. But my woman verified that it was a legitimate operation and saw the register that Ruth Matthews signed that night. But I was told you were bringing in some possible new evidence," he added.

Julia was carrying the clippings in a large envelope. She explained how Hilary came to have the clippings then turned them over to Jack.

"I'm not sure how relevant this information is, but I have a hunch that there is some connection. I would hate to put someone under suspicion unfairly." *It's easy*, she thought, *to want to suspect Mike because I've heard bad things about him. But just because he's a drug dealer doesn't mean he's also a murderer. And I'm not even positive that Ben's Mike Hatfield is the one we know.*

He studied them for some time, his face registering no emotion. Then he picked up his pipe, took a pouch of tobacco from a drawer, and went over to the window. He filled and tamped the pipe for a minute or two before lighting it. That done, he puffed and stared out of the window.

"I remember that fire," he said finally. "We were sure there had been a strongbox with a considerable amount of money in the house. It should have survived the fire. Our only guess was that someone did find it and kept it, but we couldn't trace it to anyone. I didn't realize that both Dixon and Hatfield had been at that fire."

"Does the fact that Brian kept those newspaper reports and the comments he made suggest that he suspected Mike of stealing the money?" ventured Julia. "I'm not sure exactly what he means by 'the origin—question mark' unless he is speculating that this money was what enabled Mike to start his business."

"Possibly."

He said nothing further for a few minutes, apparently deep in thought.

"I'm not sure how much to tell you," he said at last. "Enough to keep you alert, I suppose, though I don't want to put you in danger." He turned round to face Julia but stayed at the window, leaning against the sill. "We've had our eye on Hatfield for some time. I'd rather not go into details, but we think he's operating on the wrong side of the law. Nothing to do with these murders. We've never heard anything to link him with Brian Dixon. On the other matter, we would have pulled him in months ago, except we hope that if we're patient, he'll lead us to the big fish."

Julia felt a tremor down her spine. It was one thing to hear from Ben about an unsavory character called Mike Hatfield who might or might not be the person she knew. It was something else to have the superintendent confirm that identity.

"But was he ever questioned about the murders?"

"Yes. And he couldn't fully account for his movements either night. Talked about going to the cinema by himself, spending some time in pubs. But the pubs he named were large crowded ones where no one pays attention to who's there and who's not. A couple of fellows he named as companions for part of the time are the sort who'd commit perjury without blinking. But you can't charge someone with murder just because they can't prove where they were when the murder took place, unless they have a strong motive and have clearly benefitted from the death. One or two others in that theatre group had similar difficulties in accounting for their movements at critical times. Since Hatfield had joined the group after Dixon's death, we didn't press him very hard. As I said, we didn't see a connection."

He came back to the desk and read through the clippings again.

"This morning, I went back to the files on these two murder cases and reread everything we've got. Hilary made a remark at the inquest that no one paid much attention to at the time. She said that, a few days before his death, Brian had talked excitedly about possibly going into business with a friend. He hadn't mentioned the friend's name or what was involved. I'm wondering now if the friend was Hatfield, trying to recruit Dixon into his little game."

"I think it was. I overheard Mike introducing himself to Hilary at the Blymton fete a couple of weeks ago. He said then that he and Brian had been talking about going into business together. It was odd. He'd sent her a note of condolence and a plant after Brian's death, but she hadn't a clue who he was. Brian had never mentioned his name to her."

A new thought suddenly struck her.

"But Mike doesn't necessarily know that. He's been trying hard to befriend her these last few weeks. If he did kill Brian, he might be anxious to find out how much she does know. And as I've thought all along, he meant to kill her, to silence her, when he killed her grandmother by mistake."

Julia was excited now, carried along by what seemed to her an inexorable logic. It made sense. Except that it didn't explain why Mike had killed Brian in the first place.

Jack continued to frown at the clippings in his hand.

"Could blackmail be involved?" Julia asked.

"Possibly. Look, I can't say more now, except to assure you that we will follow this up. Perhaps we can move a bit faster on our other case too. Be on your guard" were his parting words. "Hatfield could be dangerous."

TWENTY-SEVEN

"Now I know you want to talk about those awful murders, but first, I want to talk about you. How are you doing, Julia, honestly?"

Julia and Nigel were at a table in a quiet corner of the Savoy Grill. It promised to be a wonderful respite from what, so far, had been a very annoying day.

The first annoyance was remembering, as she was getting dressed, that she had forgotten to fill up the car on the way home from Taunton the previous day. She thought the car might have enough petrol to get her to the station, but she wasn't sure. It was doubtful that she'd have time to stop on the way if she wanted to get the early train. She held her breath all the way to the station but made it without mishap, just in time to catch the train. However, the train was crowded, and the coffee, when she found the buffet car, was lukewarm. The only food available was a dispirited ham sandwich or a packet of soggy potato crisps. When she reached London at last, the traffic was appalling. Even though the taxi driver spun off into empty side streets at every opportunity to avoid the worst of the jams, she still arrived almost half an hour late at the solicitor's office.

Now in the hushed splendor of this restaurant, she could put all that frustration behind her. She had been surprised and delighted, on phoning Nigel from the solicitor's office on completion of her business, to hear that he planned to take her to the Savoy. She had expected no more than a simple pub lunch and said so.

"It's not every day I have the opportunity to lunch with an attractive woman," he replied gallantly, "so I want to make the most of it—impress any of my acquaintances who may be present."

"I'm glad I wore my best bib and tucker," she countered. "I only wanted a quiet chat."

Nigel had secured a secluded table that offered the right atmosphere for a quiet chat. *Luxury has its charms*, Julia decided, leaning back into the soft banquette and reveling in the fine linens and silver, the sparkling crystal, and the fresh flowers. It seemed a long time since she had felt so spoiled, and she welcomed it. Nigel ordered a bottle of Pouilly Fuisse to go with their grilled sole and asparagus.

"I'm fine, really." It didn't sound very convincing, so she went on. "Things could be worse. I don't have to worry about money. I'm in good health. I seem to find plenty of things to do. I'm making new friends. But . . . but . . . at times I feel incredibly lonely."

She drank some of the wine and made an effort to pull herself together.

"Don't worry, Nigel. I won't let you down. I'm not going to burst into tears or create a scene. I can control it in public. But on my own, in private, especially in the evening . . ."

Nigel reached out to touch her fingers lingering on the stem of her glass.

"That's all right. I didn't mean to upset you. But you should let your old friends help you through this as much as we can."

"Thank you, Nigel. You are one of the few old friends I can actually talk to. Most of our friends are scattered around the globe. I've come to realize that I have no real roots, not in Blymton or London or England or anywhere. So when I most need an anchor, I don't have one." She gave a fragile laugh. "I'm mixing metaphors, I know. But I don't feel I have any purpose in life."

"That's not so. You are doing very useful things right now in Blymton from what I hear. You have taken a motherless girl under your wing. You are very busy trying to put the local police to shame by solving murders for them."

Julia laughed, more heartily this time. "Has Jack been complaining?"

"Of course not. But he has expressed concern for your safety. We seem to be dealing with a fairly intelligent murderer, someone smart enough to try to make a murder look like a suicide."

"But stupid enough to kill an old woman whom he mistakes for a young girl."

"Assuming it was mistaken identity and not someone out to get rid of an old windbag. There are times when I think the girl's father is the most likely culprit. He was known to be hot-tempered, he thoroughly disapproved of the young man his daughter was proposing to marry, and his mother must have been a pain in the neck. The discovery of his secret mistress to some extent reinforces such a theory."

"But she has provided him alibis for both murders," protested Julia.

"She could be conspiring with him. I'm sure she didn't want the mother-in-law around, preaching fire and brimstone every five minutes. And perhaps she wanted someone better than a fireman for a son-in-law."

"Could conspiracy be proved?"

"Probably not. We'd have to wait for one of them to make a slip."

"Not a nice prospect for Hilary, living with a father who has perhaps killed her fiancé and his own mother."

"I keep reminding you, Julia, that the world is not a pretty place. The only viable alternative may be Hilary herself, though I know you don't want to hear me say that. The third strong candidate, the former girlfriend, has been exonerated, according to Jack."

"You've talked to Jack then. Since my visit to him yesterday?"

"No, he phoned me yesterday morning about something else. But he told me then about the clearance on the Matthews woman. He also mentioned that you were coming in to see him with some new evidence. By the way, did the young runaway turn up?"

"Not yet. But he will. I can't imagine anyone wanting to kill him. Or that he'd kill himself, though at times he is pretty bizarre. But a new line of thinking has opened up, a new suspect too."

She told him about the newspaper reports and Jack's response. "So blackmail may have been the motive," she concluded. "It's the first suggestion of a motive apart from the Worthington family's opposition to Hilary's engagement."

Nigel turned to look her straight in the eye.

"I really don't want to say more about this Hatfield fellow than Jack has already told you, except to confirm that he is mixed up in some bad business. If he—"

"It's drugs, isn't it?" Julia interrupted.

"All right. That's the trouble with you intelligent women. You're always one step ahead. But seriously, if he's involved, you could be in real danger."

"Then I need to know what's going on."

Nigel put down his knife and fork. He stared down at his hands for what seemed like ages, but Julia waited patiently. At last, after a quick look around the room, he turned to her and, in a low voice, said, "It's cocaine, the latest upper-middle class form of recreation. We know there's a ring smuggling it into the country, but so far we've only put our fingers on a number of the distributors, small fry for the most part. Hatfield is one we have evidence on, but as Jack told you, we haven't closed in on him because we hope that he can lead us to some of the men at the top. In fact, I rushed home from my holiday a couple of weeks ago because the Yard thought we were about to have a breakthrough. But our source disappeared at the last minute, leaving us high and dry. I think they know we are on their tracks. That's why it's so dangerous. They're likely to be desperate men. And if one of them has already committed murder twice, then he has nothing to lose and probably everything to gain by killing again."

This was a new dimension to the case. It was imperative that she warn Hilary as soon as possible. She voiced this concern to Nigel.

"Definitely. His attentions to her suggest to me that he's worried about her rather than wooing her. If he tried once to get rid of her, he could well try again. He made a stupid blunder that time, and this may have shaken him into lying low for a while. But he won't wait too long, particularly if he hears we're closing in on him. If he believes Hilary knows something that could lead to murder charges as well as drug charges, he'll want her out of the way. And if he perceives that you have been meddling too, you may also be a target. Both of you should watch what you do and where you go, especially in the next week or two. With luck, we can pull him in before the end of the month.

"And now let's talk about more pleasant things."

Through strawberries and cream, they talked about Nigel's sailing holiday and Julia's gardening. Julia reminded him about his promise to come down to Blymton for the play, and he declared that not only would he be down on Saturday morning, but he would bring Chip and Diana with him. It was all arranged, rooms booked at the local inn for Saturday night.

When coffee came, Nigel brought her up to date on the London scene—concerts, plays, exhibitions, and a little gossip too. There was an exhibition Julia had hoped to visit after lunch, but she was now having second thoughts.

"I ought to take the next train back to Taunton so I can make sure Hilary is all right."

"I don't think you need to rush back. Hilary's at school, isn't she? She should be all right there. I only wanted you to be on your guard. I'm not advising you to lock yourselves up. You can go to the exhibition and get a late afternoon train and be home in time to warn her before it gets dark."

He walked with her along the Embankment so that she could take the tube at Charing Cross. "Much faster than taxis in this infernal traffic," he promised. Julia walked with a light step, abandoning herself to the pleasure of being back in London with an old friend, away from Blymton and its concerns.

She found the exhibition entrancing and left reluctantly to catch the four thirty-five train. The exhilaration lasted through the crowded, hot underground ride to Paddington. But as the express train lumbered through London's western suburbs on its way to Taunton, the glow began to fade. When the tea trolley came round, she bought tea and biscuits; but the tea was so strong as to be bitter, and the biscuits were stale. The journey had never seemed so long.

At last, the train pulled into the Taunton station. She rushed for the exit, only to be pulled up by someone calling her name. It was Molly Parkinson, standing by her car in a five-minute waiting zone.

"Hello, Molly. I've just been up to London for the day. Don't say Dick was on that train too?"

"No, but his mother was. Dick's gone to meet her. She's coming to stay for a week so she can babysit for us during the dress rehearsal and performances. It will be such a relief. And here she is."

Dick approached, carrying a small suitcase and accompanied by a pleasant-faced woman, probably in her late fifties, who had a very excited Parkinson child by the hand. Introductions were made, and Julia inquired about the progress of the play.

"I think it will all come together by the first night. We're going to work on a couple of rough scenes tomorrow night, dress rehearsal Thursday night, and then we're on." He chuckled. "This will be my last restful evening this week, so let's go and enjoy it. Can we give you a lift home?"

Julia thanked him but declined and hurried off to her car. She remembered to get petrol, which delayed her slightly, but she felt the delay was better than the risk of being stranded on some quiet country road.

A note was waiting for her when she arrived home. It had been pushed through the letter slot and lay on the hall carpet.

Dear Mrs. Dobson,

I got a message from Dick Parkinson about a meeting this evening to plan a cast party. He'd like both of us to be on the committee, so come along if you don't get back too late. 7 o'clock at the Village Hall.

Hilary

Julia looked at her watch. Twenty past seven. She had just missed Hilary. The silly girl must have misunderstood the message. Dick had said he was looking forward to a restful evening. It must be at some other time. But it was strange that Dick hadn't mentioned a cast party, especially if he wanted to Julia to help plan it.

She stood in the hall transfixed as the light slowly dawned. Dick hadn't said anything because he wasn't planning anything. It was a trap. She and Hilary were being lured to the Village Hall on a pretext. And Hilary had already gone.

TWENTY-EIGHT

While Julia's train was rumbling out of Paddington station, Hilary was on her way home from school. She ran eagerly up the front path. Tim would surely be back home, sitting at the kitchen table or up in his room. She took a deep breath and opened the door.

The house was cold and silent. Instinctively, Hilary knew it was empty; but all the same she went round the house, looking in every room, even into her grandmother's bedroom. It looked exactly as the old lady had left it, Bible by the bedside, hairbrush and a box of hairpins resting forlornly on the dresser. There was no sign of Tim, not even any indication that he might have returned home for food or a change of clothing and left again.

It's odd, she thought as she looked round her brother's room, *Tim has been perfectly beastly to me the last year or so, and with his guns and his Nazi-worship, he's become a generally obnoxious creature. But he is my brother. We had some wonderful times together as children, when Mother was alive.*

Back in the kitchen, she made tea and then phoned her father's surgery. Janet answered. No, her father hadn't heard anything about Tim. He was out now, on a call, and wanted Hilary to know that he could be late for supper so she should keep it warm for him.

"I have another message for you," she added. "From Dick Parkinson."

"Yes?"

"He said to tell you that there's to be a meeting tonight for a few people to plan a cast party for the Players. He wants you to be on the planning committee. You should go to the Village Hall for a meeting at seven o'clock."

"Seven o'clock, tonight, Village Hall. Yes, I can do that."

"There was one other thing," Janet added. "Mr. Parkinson was very particular about this. He said you should bring Mrs. Dobson with you. Said he'd tried to phone her, but there was no answer. He particularly wants both of you on the planning committee."

Hilary knew that Julia was going to London for the day, so wasn't surprised that she'd been asked to relay the message. She could leave a note at Flora Cottage if Julia wasn't back by seven.

She finished the tea, made herself a sandwich, and settled down to do her homework. As the clock neared seven, she put some cold ham and tomatoes on a plate, put out the bread and butter and some soup in a pan, and covered it all with a clean dish towel. She scribbled a couple of notes and propped up the one for her father against the cloth. When Julia didn't answer her knock at Flora Cottage, she pushed the second note through the letter slot.

The Village Hall was only a few minutes' walk away. It was set back slightly from the main street, across from The Feathers. A row of shops stood to one side, and a detached house, shrouded in shrubs, flanked it on the other side. The car park between the hall and the shops contained one or two cars, but none that Hilary recognized. It was strange that the Parkinsons' car wasn't among them. They must be running late.

She pushed open the huge wooden door of the hall. Windows high up in the walls of the main chamber let in ample light, though a thick stand of oaks near the west wall shaded out the evening sun. Her nostrils caught the aroma of damp wood found in old village churches. The hall itself was somewhat ecclesiastical with its lofty windows and rows of chairs facing the stage. The set was already in place for Thursday's dress rehearsal.

Today the air was also redolent with the sweet scent of new-mown hay. Bales of hay were stacked at the rear of the hall, awaiting movement to the wings from where they could be shunted onto the stage for the woodland scenes. *I hope we can perform at the Manor*, Hilary said to herself as she threaded her way through the chairs to the doorway on the far side of the chamber. *The play is so perfect for outdoors. It won't be half as dramatic in here, though the hay will help.*

Light and a noise from below suggested that the Green Room was the meeting place, though it was odd that she could hear no voices. *I must be one of the first to arrive*, she thought.

She descended the open stairway to find an empty room.

"Hello," she called. "Anyone here?"

Props were laid out on the table, Bottom's head the most conspicuous. Costumes hung on a rack to one side, a little forlorn, like sale garments. But there was no jacket, no handbag, not even a notebook.

She began to feel uneasy. She didn't know why, except that the place seemed to be too quiet. She had never been alone in this building before. It was eerie.

Then there was a rustling sound from the small storage room at the far end of the Green Room. The door was slightly open, and now she noticed the light was on there too. That was it. One or two of the cast had arrived ahead of her and were hiding in there to tease her.

"Hello you lot. I know you're in there. Come on out."

Silence.

Boldly she strode over to the door, flung it wide open, and marched in. The next instant, someone grabbed her from behind, and a blow on her head sent her flying. The world went black.

When she came to, she was sitting on an old, upright wooden chair, and someone was tying her hands behind its back. Turning her heard—painfully, as something throbbed inside her skull—she saw that it was Mike.

"Mike Hatfield! What on earth are you doing? Let me go!"

"Where's that nosy Mrs. Dobson? I thought she was coming with you?"

"She went to London for the day. I left her a note in case she gets back in time. What's going on? Is this a joke?"

"You could call it that."

Mike, having secured her hands and arms, now began to tie her legs to the chair. Hilary struggled, trying in vain to kick his hands away. He didn't speak until he had finished his task even though Hilary persisted with her questions, growing more angry with each one.

"Where are the Parkinsons? What about the meeting for the cast party? Was it you who left the message for me? You're hurting me. Do you realize you could be arrested for this? I could have you prosecuted for assault!"

"Not so loud, or I'll have to gag you."

"But why, why, why? What is all this about?"

Mike stared at her then laughed harshly.

"Don't play the innocent with me, you silly bitch. You know what's been going on. He told you, didn't he?"

"Know what?" she asked, beginning to feel desperate.

Mike lit a cigarette and blew the smoke in her face. *Of course she knows. She's just shamming. How much should I say?* he asked himself. *How long should I wait for that other stupid woman to arrive? No, not stupid. She's smart, but she's too nosy for her own good. This girl will have talked to her. I must get rid of them both. If she doesn't come, dammit, I'll have to think of some other way to dispose of her.*

Hilary was silent now but visibly trembling. He could see the fear in her eyes. He savored the power he held over her, feeling the urge to inflict pain that can accompany absolute power.

"Did Brian Dixon tell you he was going to marry the other woman? Is that why you killed him?"

"What do you mean? I didn't kill him!"

"But I saw you. I was at Hestercombe that evening, and I saw you there."

"But I didn't kill him! I just tried to stop him firing that bloody gun."

"You killed him, and then you ran away. I came along behind you and tried to cover up for you by making it look like a suicide, but you had to spoil it all by claiming it was a murder, and then you tried to pin the murder on me! You are a damn silly fool, Hilary Worthington, but you are also a dangerous young woman, and that's why I can't afford to have you around anymore."

Hilary stared at him, openmouthed but speechless, as the import of his words sank in. The nightmare that she had suppressed the past few weeks rose up to haunt her again. The struggle in the garden at Hestercombe, her hands on the gun trying desperately to wrest it from him, the loud retort as it fired, Brian falling heavily into the flowerbed, the gun dropping from her hands. She had almost convinced herself that this was just a nightmare, that she hadn't been at Hestercombe that night, that someone else had been there, had deliberately killed Brian and had then faked a suicide. Now here was this interfering, obnoxious person rearranging her story. And what was he going to do to her? She let out a loud wail.

"You beast! You rotten, nasty, murdering . . . !"

She got no further, Mike had snatched a cloth and stuffed it into her mouth. He was just in time. As he secured it with a knot behind her head, he heard a noise upstairs.

It was the creak of the heavy wooden door being slowly opened. Mike stubbed out his cigarette, tiptoed to the stairs, and cocked his head to listen. He could hear nothing at first, but then a scuffling sound followed by whispering. It was clearly not Julia Dobson. It sounded more like children, but even children would interfere with his plan.

Glancing quickly round the Green Room, he spotted the huge ass's head. With a chuckle, he pulled it over his head and cautiously crept up the stairs.

Half a dozen boys were spread out around the rear half of the hall. They had pulled apart one of the bales of hay and were strewing it over the rows of chairs. Mike watched them, unobserved, for a minute or two. In one way they were helping his plan. Reports of youths vandalizing the Village Hall would complicate investigations into what he was about to do. But he needed them out of the way before the Dobson woman showed up.

He gave his best impression of a braying donkey, a loud nasal whinny that echoed to the rafters as he leaped forward from the doorway. The effect on the boys was electric. They stood stock still for an instant, then one of them let out a scream and rushed for the door. The others fled after him.

There's a risk they might tell someone, Mike realized. But he felt it was a slight risk. They would have to explain why they were in the hall, and the hay would be incriminating.

He went back downstairs to his prisoner.

"So why did you kill your boyfriend?" he taunted. His voice sounded hollow inside the head, unnatural. It would be easy to believe that what he was saying was also unreal, but Hilary knew it was close to the truth. That was what was so painful. Indirectly, unintentionally, she had killed him.

"He wasn't going to marry you. He told me so that evening. Yes, I was with him when you phoned. We'd been talking about him joining me in the business. He wasn't being very smart about it, tried to blackmail me."

He paused to remove Bottom's head and light another cigarette. Hilary was crying now, tears spilling down her cheeks and dampening the cloth. She made moaning sounds, trying to speak, but Mike ignored her. He was wound up, eager to justify himself.

"You didn't know your nice boyfriend was a blackmailer, did you? I wanted to talk terms with him, but instead he kept asking where the money to start the business came from. 'I told you,' I said, 'from my aunt who died.' Then he came right out and said it. 'You stole it from the house that burned, the one where we rescued the old woman, but she died.' That really got my goat. I don't like the word 'stole.' And it was me who rescued her, I pointed out, not we. He was safely outside while I went in. I was the one that risked my life, so why shouldn't I get a reward?

"'But how did you do it?' he asked in that dumb way he had. So I told him. It was Jake who brought out the box. I saw him dump it by the bush and run back into the house. The old lady was crying for her dog as well as her box. And then the house fell in, and Jake was killed. No one else had seen him with the box. I pushed it well under the bush, out of sight, and then went back later in the night and retrieved it. The funny thing was, the dog was outside all the time. It was the barking dog that woke up the neighbors who called us out. If it wasn't for that dog, you and I wouldn't be here today!"

Mike laughed, a demonic laugh.

"Why am I telling you all this? You knew it anyway. He said he'd told you about his suspicions. And you knew I was there when you phoned that evening. That's why you've tried to implicate me in his death."

Hilary shook her head vigorously.

He looked at her closely, trying to tell from her eyes whether she was telling the truth. He couldn't be certain. "Well, it's too late now. You'll still have to go. You've set the police on my tail with your insinuations that I killed your boyfriend, and you'll have to pay for that. But I have to get that Mrs. Dobson too. She knows more than she lets on. Are you sure she's coming?"

Hilary just glared at him.

"Come on, you can at least move your head. Are you sure she's coming? Nod if you are."

Hilary nodded. She didn't want to lead Julia Dobson into trouble, but at this point, her friend seemed to be her only hope. Mike seemed determined to kill her, though she couldn't imagine how, nor why he hadn't already done it. If Julia guessed that the note about a meeting was a trick, she might send for help. She just had to keep Mike from killing her until that help arrived.

"All right. We'll wait. And while we're waiting, I'll tell you what really happened that night.

"As I said, he was interested in coming into business with me, but he was also trying to blackmail me. He ended the discussion by saying that he'd left his wallet at Hestercombe and had to go back there to get it. He also said, and this will interest you, that before he made up his mind about my offer, he had to settle with his women. 'I'm probably going to go with the mother of my son' was what he said, 'but I have to deal with Hilary first.' So there, you see, he was never going to marry you, and when you turned up as he was getting in his car and jumped in beside him, I bet he told you."

I don't believe a word of it, Hilary thought. Brian didn't say anything of the sort. Her arms were beginning to ache from being pinioned behind her. Her head throbbed. More critically, it was becoming difficult to breathe. Her nose was increasingly stuffed up with so much crying, but the gag prevented her from breathing through her mouth. *I shall suffocate soon if he doesn't take this off,* she thought and began to moan in an effort to make Mile realize this. But he interpreted it differently.

"You don't like what I'm telling you, do you? Because you have a distorted idea of what real life is like. You're just like all these village women around here. You want everything to be neat and tidy, everybody behaving nicely, no one doing mean or nasty things. Well, let me tell you—"

But at that moment, he heard a noise from above. This time, it had to be Julia Dobson.

"Hello," he heard her call out. "Hilary, are you here?"

With a grin, Mike picked up Bottom's head and put it on Hilary.

"There," he whispered, "wait until she sees that!"

And he took up his position behind the storage room door, waiting for Julia.

TWENTY-NINE

Tim Worthington was bored. Running away had been fun for a while. He was sure he'd got everyone upset about his disappearance. The police had come to Billy's house, of course. It was the first thing they'd think of, ask his friends where he was. Tim had prepared them.

"After my gran copped it, that stupid inspector kept on at me with his questions about what we'd done and where we'd been, but he didn't get anything out of me," he bragged. "He even dragged me into the police station, thought that would scare me. But it's easy to put them off. You just keep saying you don't know what they're talking about."

So Billy and everyone else had lied gamely, although they all knew he was hiding under Billy's bed.

Billy's mother, working until midnight, usually slept late and then went out. She rarely ventured into Billy's bedroom. Tim stayed hidden there, sleeping himself or, when he knew the coast was clear, playing Billy's radio quietly. Billy had been able to smuggle food up to him. It seemed as though he could stay hidden there forever.

But, he began to wonder by Tuesday, why would he? Why had he done this? To shock his father. Frighten away his would-be stepmother? But what next? He hadn't thought that far ahead. Should he just saunter back home? It was important to wait long enough so that his father would be more worried than angry. But how long was long enough?

Confinement in Billy's bedroom was becoming tedious. The first couple of evenings, while Billy's mother was at work, all the gang had been at the house, and he had been downstairs with them, talking, playing cards, horsing around. But this evening, they'd been too restless to stay indoors and had gone out, leaving him alone in the house. He helped himself to some biscuits and pop and settled down to watch television. Mrs. Harrison wouldn't be back from work until late, so he reckoned he was safe anywhere in the house as long as he kept back from the windows.

But Rosie Harrison was not feeling well that day. She'd hurt her back the previous evening, lifting an overweight patient. She'd gone into work, but her back was so bad there was little she could do; and after a few hours, she was sent home.

So Rosie Harrison walked into her living room shortly before seven o'clock that evening and found Tim Worthington on her sofa with the television going full blast.

"What are you doing here?"

Tim leaped to his feet at once but then was uncertain what to do next.

"Everyone is looking for you. We thought you'd been murdered. Have you been home?"

Tim didn't answer.

"Does Billy know you're here? Where is he, anyway?"

Tim remained silent. *That boy of mine has been up to his tricks again,* thought Rosie.

"What's your phone number? I'm going to ring your father and tell him you're safe."

Tim knew he didn't want to be handed over like that. If he was going back, it would be in a manner of his own choosing. So he stared at Rosie but said nothing.

"All right, if you won't tell me, I'll ring the police."

Being handed over to the police would be even more ignominious. While she was dialing, Tim slipped out of the house.

The Harrison house was one of a row on the outskirts of the village, across from a large pasture. Tim ran across the road, climbed the gate into the field, and ducked behind the hedge. Bent low, he skirted the field to a copse on the far side. There he stopped to collect his thoughts. *I might as well go back,* he decided, *now they know I'm alive and well. But I'm going to walk in by myself, in my own time, preferably late when they've all gone to bed.*

In the meantime, he would go in search of the gang. If they were lounging around the Market Cross, he would be out of luck. That place was too public. But they might be over in Blymton Manor wood. That was on the other side of the village, but he would work his way over there through the fields and lanes.

He crossed another large pasture where black and white cows stared at him with mournful faces and then a field where wheat was beginning to ripen. Next he came to a narrow lane where he took a chance and ran a few hundred yards in the direction of Blymton before ducking behind another hedge. *This is easy*, he thought. He trotted across another field or two before coming to one of the main roads leading out of the village. This road was well-traveled, and he had to wait behind the hedge for a few minutes until it was safe to cross. The land here was rising slightly, providing a view of the red-tiled village roofs.

As he surveyed the road from the safety of the hedge, he caught a glimpse of familiar figures in a lay-by at the bottom of the hill. He couldn't see clearly what they were doing. They were too far away to hear him shout. It would be quickest but too risky to run down the road. Instead, it took him several minutes to work his way down the hill through the fields. He hoped they wouldn't ride off before he came within hailing distance. But they were still standing astride their bikes, showing no signs of moving on, when he burst through the hedge at the end of the lay-by.

"What are you doing here?" was their first reaction. Tim explained. Billy groaned. "She'll be after me for this."

"What's happening?" Tim asked.

"We just saw a monster in the Village Hall!" This came from the youngest member of the gang, a ten-year-old who was easily frightened. But as the others clamored to explain, they all sounded pretty scared by what they had seen.

"We were down by the hall—"

"Your sister went in first—"

"So we knew the door was unlocked—"

"There didn't seem to be anyone else around—"

"So we went in too, and there was a lot of hay, and we were messing it around all over the place and—"

The clamor subsided. There seemed to be a reluctance to describe what happened next, except for the ten-year-old who repeated, "And then the monster appeared."

"What monster?"

"It had a huge head, and it shrieked—"

"There's no such thing as monsters," Tim scoffed. "Not these days, anyway." The older boys were shuffling their feet, trying to dissociate themselves from the youngster's panicky reaction.

"Go see for yourself then."

"All right, I will."

"You can't go into the village without being seen," someone pointed out. "They'll be looking for you now."

Tim was always ready for a challenge. "Yes, I can. I got here from Billy's house without being seen. I bet I can get over and into the Village Hall without anyone seeing me."

He pushed through the hedge into the adjacent field and headed off toward the village. The hall was on this side of the village's main street, so he didn't have to worry about crossing a heavily traveled road. And there were fields immediately behind the hall, so he could work his way over there under cover. It would be a cinch.

As he approached the hall, however, he realized that one hazard lay ahead. The hall had been built with its entrance at the side but close to the main street. The parking area was a large and open swath of gravel that he would have to cross to reach the door. There were only two cars, both close to the street. At this point too, he had pedestrians to worry about as well as people in cars. A few people passed by, walking their dogs or on their way to the pub across the street. And if the interfering Mrs. Harrison had called the police, they would now be out looking for him.

As he watched, assessing the risk, he saw Julia Dobson hurrying, almost running, across the road. She looked around the parking area, staring so hard in Tim's direction that he was afraid she had spotted him. But without breaking her stride, she went straight to the door and entered the building.

Tim waited to see if she would emerge screaming, scared off by the "monster," but nothing happened. A car pulled into the parking lot, but its occupants went straight across the road to the pub. Even more convinced that there was nothing frightening inside the hall, Tim decided to take a chance. He crawled through a hole in the hedge and ran across the parking area. The door was slightly open, leaving a gap just large enough for him to slip through.

That same evening, the young police constable assigned to watch the Worthington house was also bored. This really was a valuable waste of police time, sitting in a parked car in a quiet village street on the off chance that someone might come along and try to murder one of the occupants of the house. The daughter had come safely home from school and was now inside, presumably eating her supper and watching television, while he sat here twiddling his thumbs.

So he was greatly relieved when the radio crackled and he learned he was needed for a more urgent task. The missing Tim Worthington had reportedly turned up in a council house at the other end of Blymton. "Get over there and get a statement from the woman who found him" were the instructions. "We don't have anyone else to send. And keep your eyes open for the lad. He's on the run." The constable took off at once before anyone could have second thoughts. And that's why, a few minutes later, when Hilary left the house and headed for the Village Hall, no one saw her go.

THIRTY

Julia's first instinct on reading Hilary's note had been to rush off to the Village Hall. But a moment's reflection persuaded her that though that might be heroic, it probably wasn't the most practical response. Instead, she looked for the police car that usually sat outside the Worthington house, but it was not there. She would have to try to reach someone by phone.

She phoned the Worthington house first but got no answer. Next she phoned Jack Shaw's house, but all she got was the answering machine. Finally, beginning to feel that she'd have to be heroic after all, she phoned the local police station. She tried to explain to an obviously young recruit what had happened. He listened earnestly and began to ask questions since he wasn't at all sure what she was going on about. He was familiar with the two local murder cases, but he didn't understand what a meeting at the Village Hall for people involved with the Players had to do with murder. In desperation, Julia told him to get a message to either Superintendent Shaw or Inspector Hughes and hung up.

The Village Hall was only five minutes away, but Julia made it in less. She opened the door as quietly as she could, but it creaked nonetheless. She deliberately left it slightly ajar in case she needed to make a quick exit. She thought she heard a slight scuffling sound coming from the vicinity of the Green Room, but though she froze and listened carefully, she heard nothing further. After a moment's hesitation, she decided to call out. She was sure she was walking into a trap, but she was also sure that whoever might be lying in wait for her had heard the creaking door and would know of her presence.

"Hello," she called out. "Hilary, are you here?"

Her voice echoed in the huge chamber, but there was no response.

It's possible, she told herself, that Hilary isn't here. *But I believe she is, and I think someone else is here too. The silence is oppressive.*

She moved slowly across the chamber, puzzled by the hay strewn over the seats and aisles. Something was definitely wrong. The hay gave off its sweet scent as she brushed against it. Its warm outdoorsy smell was incongruous in the menacing atmosphere of the hall.

She crept cautiously down the stairway to the Green Room. Nothing seemed to be amiss. The door into the storage room was ajar, and she could see a light inside. Quietly, she made her way across the room and pushed against the door. As it swung freely back, she caught sight of a figure wearing Bottom's head and bound to a chair. She could see at once it was Hilary. Without a second thought, she rushed forward. At the same instant, someone leaped out from behind the door and grabbed hold of her.

Mike pinioned her arms and twisted a piece of cord around her wrists. Then he pushed her to the floor and swiftly tied her ankles together.

"What the hell do you think you are doing?

Julia was very angry, angry at herself for walking into the trap but even more angry at what he had done to Hilary. She could hear the girl moaning under the huge mask.

"Take that head off her, you brute," she demanded. She didn't really expect him to comply, but he pulled it off at once—roughly, causing Hilary to groan. He threw it on the ground and trampled on it, smashing it to pieces.

Julia was too incensed at the sight of Hilary gagged and trembling with fear to care about the destruction of her handiwork.

"And take out that gag!"

"Any more of that, lady, and I'll have to gag you too. All in good time. I have other things to do first."

"No, first, you can tell me what is the meaning of this. What have we done to you?"

"Ask your young friend there. She's the one to blame, though if you hadn't stuck your big nose into things that were none of your business, I wouldn't have had to deal with you. Yes, I know she can't talk now, but when I've finished, you'll have a few minutes to catch up on the story. But you'll have to talk fast because you won't have long."

He left the little room, lighting a cigarette as he went, and they heard him go up the stairs. Several minutes of odd noises followed. He was clearly going up and down the stairs and seemed to be carrying something that bumped on the steps. Julia managed to roll over far enough so that she could see out of the door. The table in the center of the Green Room blocked most of her line of sight to the stairs, but it looked as though Mike were bringing some of the bales of hay downstairs.

He returned to the storage room, looking very pleased with himself. He noticed that Julia had moved and nudged her back with his foot.

"Too late to crawl out," he said. He deliberately flicked ash from his cigarette over her.

"You'd better be careful with your cigarette around all that hay," Julia warned.

Mike laughed. "But careless is just what I intend to be."

"You killed Brian Dixon, didn't you?" Julia charged. "And old Mrs. Worthington too."

"No, I didn't. She killed her boyfriend, not me. As for the old lady, I don't know who killed her, but it wasn't me."

He must be crazy, Julia told herself. *He's certainly high on something. Of course he killed them. And it looks now as though he intends to kill both Hilary and me. Our only hope is to stall for time, long enough for help to arrive. Thank goodness I phoned someone. I just hope that young policeman got hold of someone who would understand my message. I must try to keep Mike talking.*

"But if you didn't kill them, why kill us?" she asked. "What have we done to you?"

"I told you, you'll have to ask her," gesturing toward Hilary. "I don't have time. I have to get out of here."

"What are you going to do with us? Are you going to take us with you?"

"No, you stay here. It's a shame to lose such a fine old building, but this old barn is going to burn down. You, alas, will be trapped inside."

He was actually smiling as he said this. *It would be funny*, Julia thought, *if it weren't so frighteningly real*. She suspected that he was under the influence of some drug.

"But when they find us trussed up like this, they'll know it was no accident, and when they catch you—and they will catch you—you'll have four murders to account for."

"Not four. I told you, I didn't kill the other two. Anyway, I don't intend to be caught. I'll be far away. But you won't be tied up because you will have untied yourselves. I'll loosen your wrists just a little, enough so that you can work them free. Then you can undo the other ropes. But by then the fire will be going strong, and you won't be able to get out."

In a few swift moves, he loosened Julia's wrist bonds, turned out the light, and shut the door behind him. She heard him turn the key in the lock and remove it. She couldn't hear but could guess what he did next. He put the key in his pocket, flicked his cigarette lighter, and applied it to the hay that he had dumped at the foot of the stairs. Then he ran upstairs and set fire to three or four of the large bales at the back of the hall. The hay was slow to catch fire, but as soon as he was satisfied that it would burn, he left the building, locking it behind him, and drove off at high speed.

Despite the dark, Julia managed to pull her hands free and undo the cords around her ankles. She felt her way across the floor to the door and the handle, not really expecting it to open and yet disappointed when it didn't. She felt for the light switch before remembering that it was on the outside. Disappointed again, she groped her way over to Hilary. The first thing she did was to remove the gag.

"Don't worry, Hilary, we'll find a way out."

They were brave words, but she didn't know how they could get out. As she fumbled to undo Hilary's bonds, reassuring her that all would be well, she tried desperately to think of what they might do. Even in the dark, she could tell that Hilary was in a state of collapse. After the girl was freed, she remained slumped on the chair, shaking and crying. Julia put her arms around her, trying to rouse her to action, but she appeared to have given up. Julia, though terrified that they were both going to die, was determined not to give up without a fight.

As her eyes grew accustomed to the dark, she was aware of a gap under the door that let in a chink of light. Soon it would let smoke in too. She could smell it already. The hay had looked rather green, and it might not blaze easily; but it could certainly smolder, and smoke was as deadly as flame. One thing they could do was shout for help so that if someone came to the hall, alerted either by her message or by the sight of smoke, they would know that people were trapped downstairs. She made her way back to the door and began banging on it with her fists and shouting for help at the top of her voice.

When Tim slipped through the door into the hall, he could hear voices down below. They were faint and indistinct, but they sounded normal, nothing supernatural. The place was eerie, with its lofty roof and high windows, all this hay at the back and the shadowy stage at the far end. But having made it so far undetected gave him confidence to determine what it was that made his friends run. As long as he didn't disturb the people downstairs, he could have a good look round. The stage would be a likely place to start.

He crept down to the front of the hall. A short flight of steps to one side led up onto the stage. Beyond the big blue curtains, the scenery was in place for the start of the play, two large pillars flanking a throne. He was about to go over and sit on the throne, just for the fun of it, when he heard someone running up the stairs from the Green Room.

Peering cautiously round the curtains, he saw a man emerge from the stairway. The man picked up one of the bales of hay and half carried, half dragged it down the stairs. He repeated this a couple of times and then stayed downstairs. Tim waited, uncertain. Some instinct told him that he had better stay out of this. He was still trying to decide whether to stay put and wait for whoever it was to leave or to sneak out while things seemed quiet down below when he heard a door bang and the man came running back upstairs. He bent over to do something at the back of the hall then left the building slamming the door behind him.

Tim waited for a minute or two then decided that he'd better make a run for it. But as he made his way down the stage steps, he saw, to his horror, smoke rising from the hay at the back of the hall. More smoke was coming from the doorway that led downstairs. Then he heard banging from below and a woman's voice shouting for help.

His first thought was to get out as fast as he could. But he remembered one of the boys saying that he had seen Hilary going into the hall. Was that Hilary he could hear? It was hard to tell, but it was definitely a woman. And he had seen Mrs. Dobson coming into the building.

He fumbled for a light switch at the top of the stairs but even before the light clicked on, he could see smoke rising from below. He took a deep breath, clapped a hand over his face, and plunged down the stairs. The cries for help came from the far end of the room. The first task, however, was to put out the fire. There was no sign of water in the room, nothing liquid. But the costumes hanging on the rack might do the trick. He grabbed a couple of heavy cloaks and smothered a few flames beginning to flicker on the surface of the hay. He kicked and stamped at the smoldering hay until he was satisfied that the fire would not take hold, at least for a few minutes.

The banging and shouting were becoming more urgent now. But the door was locked, and there was no key in the lock. Recalling what he had seen on television dramas, Tim began to kick at the door but without much effect. He seized a chair and tried to use that as a battering ram, but the solid wooden door withstood the blows without a mark. He could hear someone trying to break down the door from the other side, but still the door would not yield. He was looking around desperately for something heavier than a chair when he heard the woman shout, "Get the key!"

"There isn't a key."

"Try the box! On the shelf!"

The smoke was beginning to thicken again, but he could see easily enough a shelf near the door, which held some books and a shoe box. The box was full of odds and ends, among them several keys. Some were obviously unsuitable, and Tim tried a couple of possible ones before he found one that miraculously fitted the lock. He pushed open the door, knocking Julia, who was behind it, to the floor.

Hilary, who had been unable to muster the energy to shout for help, sprang to life now on seeing her brother.

"Tim, you're alive!"

"We'll all be dead in a few minutes if we don't get out of here quickly," said Julia sharply. She didn't know what Tim was doing here or what providence had brought him to their rescue, but she wasn't about to waste precious time finding out now.

Smoke was filling the room. Julia snatched some of the silky garments she had spent so much time sewing and ordered her companions to cover their noses and mouths.

"I wish we had some way of dampening them, but they'll be better than nothing. Crouch down and stay as close to the ground as you can."

Tim kicked the smoldering hay bales away from the stairs, and choking and spluttering, they made their way up. The hall was also filling with smoke. More ominously, the hay at the back had burst into flames. The fire was blocking their way to the door.

"This way," said Julia, heading for the stage. "Let's try to make it backstage. There's another door there."

Hilary, over the first delight at seeing her brother, was weakening again. Julia and Tim had to half carry, half drag her down the chamber. At one point, Julia wasn't sure they would make it. Her lungs were about to burst, and her eyes were smarting so much that she could hardly see. It had been a long day. She seemed to have no reserves of energy left. But somehow they reached the stage and pulled Hilary through to the backstage area. The air here was smoky, but it was less dense.

They were in a narrow corridor behind the stage, naturally dark because it had no windows, but even murkier because of the smoke. Julia, fumbling along the wall, found a light switch that worked. The light revealed a door at one end, the emergency exit that Julia had remembered. But to her dismay, it refused to open.

"I think it's bolted," said Tim. "Look, up at the top."

That's surely illegal, thought Julia, but aloud she tried to be encouraging.

"I'm not sure that I'm strong enough to boost you up there, but if you could give me a leg up, perhaps I could reach it," she suggested.

Tim bent his knee, and with one hand on his shoulder and with his hands at her waist to steady her, she stretched her arm and found she could just reach the bolt. At first, it wouldn't budge; but after a few hefty swipes, it gradually slid back. Julia jumped down, coughing.

"Thank goodness. This smoke is about to get us."

But still the door wouldn't open. Tim banged it angrily.

"Someone has locked it and taken away the key," he said. "Why would they do that?"

Why indeed, thought Julia. *Just the thoughtless kind of thing you and your friends do all the time. But there was no time to waste on recriminations. The smoke was chokingly thick now.* "Get down on the ground," she gasped, "as low as you can." As she crouched down, she realized Hilary was trying to say something.

"The loo, the loo has a window."

"Bless you, Hilary," said Julia. "Of course. Why didn't I think of that?"

The corridor they were in divided the stage from a row of small rooms, mostly windowless dressing rooms; but at each end, there was a toilet. She knew that the ladies' toilet had a window. The door was just a few feet away. Bent low, they found the door, which, to their relief, was not locked. They crawled into the little room, Julia pushing the door shut as fast as she could in an effort to keep out the deadly smoke, though she knew it was only a matter of time before it seeped through the cracks.

The toilet was large for the purpose, dimly lit by a small window of frosted glass six feet above the floor. In addition to the toilet stool itself, behind a half partition, there was a large sink and beside it an old wooden chair. Tim dragged the chair under the window and climbed up to see if he could open it. It hadn't been opened in years and seemed to be stuck fast. He banged on it with his fist.

"Don't do that," said Julia. "You'll cut yourself, and then you'll bleed to death."

"Bleed, choke, or burn, what's the difference?"

"It's too small for any of us to get through, even if he does open it," Hilary whimpered.

"But we could at least get some fresh air, and that may enable us to hang on until we're rescued," said Julia. "Surely someone has seen by now that the hall is on fire and has called the fire brigade."

Looking around for something to help Tim open the window, she found a canister of toilet cleaner under the sink. She passed it to Tim, who, with one strong blow, dislodged the window catch and pushed it open. He leaned out and gasped the fresh air greedily.

"Help!" he screamed. "Help! Help! Help!"

THIRTY-ONE

Inspector Hughes and Sergeant Nelson were not at the station to take Julia's urgent call because they were in a nearby village interviewing a young woman about a car. They had interviewed all Mrs. Beldington's neighbors in the hope of finding someone who had seen a strange car or person outside her house on the night of the Hestercombe murder but had turned up no solid leads. A request for information had even been broadcast on regional television. Then, late this afternoon, a call had come in that sounded promising. Shelley Cox lived in a village five miles from Blymton, but on the night in question, she had been visiting her aunt in Blymton. The two men left at once to interview her.

Shelley Cox was an engaging young woman with polished nails, a pert nose, and an eye for the sergeant.

"You say that you saw a car outside Mrs. Beldington's house on the night of June third," the inspector began. "That was over a month ago. How can you be sure of the date?"

"Well, I know it was June third because I went off to Spain the next day for my holidays. I'd booked it last Christmas, and I'd been counting the weeks and days ever since, so I it had to be June third because I was flying off on the fourth. And I went over to Blymton the night before to see my aunty Meg. I'd lost my camera, and she said she'd lend me hers. I didn't want to go away without one. I might meet a sharp-looking Spaniard and want to take his picture."

She paused to wink at the sergeant, giving the inspector the opportunity to interrupt. "And you saw a car on Berry Lane?"

"Yes. My aunt lives on Berry Lane. There are always cars parked along the road there, but this one was different, a dashing sports car. I parked right behind it."

"What kind of car? A convertible?"

"No, but it was a real flash job, shiny black, low slung—you know how those sporty cars are," and she waved her tanned arm in an appropriately curving gesture. "A foreign car perhaps? I don't know much about cars except that there are some I like to ride in. That was definitely one," and the sergeant got another wink.

"I don't suppose you noticed its number?" he asked.

"No."

"What time was this?"

"Perhaps about nine o'clock. I know I was running late, still had packing to do, but I did want the camera. I didn't stay long, but the car was gone when I left. I even wondered if I'd dreamed it."

"Why have you taken so long to come forward with this information?"

"I told you, I left for Spain the next day. I was there for three weeks. I wanted to make sure I got some sun this summer," and she stretched out her bare arms and legs to show off her tan. Sergeant Nelson tried not to look impressed. "I didn't really know about it until I went to see my aunt again last night to take the camera back and show her my pictures. She was telling me about the murders here, and then I remembered the car. She said I ought to tell you."

They tried to get a better description of the car, but the more she tried to remember, the less reliable her answers seemed.

Back in the car, Inspector Hughes radioed in to the station.

"A black sports car, perhaps Japanese or Italian, probably only a year or two old, registration number unknown. Seen on Berry Lane where Dixon lodged about nine o'clock on the night of his murder. It's a long shot, but see if anyone we're keeping an eye on, for any reason, drives such a car."

And in return, the duty constable relayed Julia Dobson's message. The inspector muttered something under his breath about "that woman" but turned the car around and headed toward Blymton.

Billy Harrison and the rest of the gang had watched Tim scurry off across the field before mounting their bikes for a direct approach to the village. On reaching the Village Hall, they first went across the street to hide their bikes behind the pub. Then they crouched down behind a row of cars in the pub forecourt. "The cops'll be out looking for us as well as Tim if Billy's mum has squealed," warned the gang leader.

It seemed like a long wait to the restless boys, but it was no more than a few minutes before one of them spotted Tim peering through the hedge behind the hall. One or two pedestrians went by, including a woman who crossed the street and went into the hall.

"You see," said Billy, "She's gone in. I bet what we saw was just someone dressed up for one of those stupid plays."

"Let's go over and see," suggested the ten-year-old, half rising. The leader quickly suppressed that idea.

"No, Tim hasn't won the bet yet. He has to get inside the hall. Let's wait."

They ducked again as a car swung into the hall parking area, keeping well out of sight as four men emerged and crossed the road to the pub. After another minute or two, Tim made his move and disappeared into the hall. "Now?" someone asked, but their leader still held back, reluctant to concede defeat. "Wait till he comes out." But the waiting was tedious, and the boys grew restless. Eventually, he yielded. "All right. But let's be careful. If there's something going on in there and they've nabbed Tim, we don't all want to go barging in, or they'll grab us too and accuse us of helping Tim run away."

"There's the hay too," observed the ten-year-old.

"Right. So let's play safe. Just one of us go and have a look."

"I'll go," volunteered Billy, anxious to make up for his mother's squeal. "I'll wave if everything's OK."

But he had barely moved out from behind the parked cars when a man emerged from the hall, locked the door behind him, and jumped into a car. The gravel crunched under his tires as he backed out and drove off at high speed.

"Blimey," said Billy, "is Tim locked in?"

Caution was thrown to the winds as the boys raced across the street. The door was indeed locked. They called out Tim's name, but there was no response. They rattled the handle and kicked at the door, but these were merely gestures of frustration. They knew there was no possibility of breaking down that solid oak.

"Now what do we do?" one of them asked.

"We can't leave him locked in there."

"He'll starve to death."

"We ought to tell someone."

"Oh yes? And who?" sneered their leader. "Are you going to march into the police station and tell them you know where Tim Worthington is?"

"There might be a reward," someone suggested.

This was greeted with derision. "Not for us."

"They'd just find a way to blame us for him being locked in."

"Who was that man anyway?"

"Perhaps he was a plainclothes detective. He's captured Tim and gone off to get reinforcements."

"But what do we do?"

No one answered. They were standing there nonplussed when a passing police car braked sharply and pulled into the car park. The constable who had been interviewing Mrs. Harrison was returning to his watch at the Worthington house but keeping a sharp eye open for the missing boy. Spotting the gang that the boy often traveled with, he instinctively knew they could tell him something.

"What's going on here?" he asked. There was a lot of feet-shuffling and turning of heads, but no one spoke.

"Have you seen Tim Worthington today?"

Again, the embarrassed silence. The constable knew he was on to something.

"Is he in the hall?"

This time, he didn't wait for an answer but went straight over to the hall door. He was sure now that the boys knew that Tim was inside. But the door was locked. He shook the handle, but it was definitely locked. He was turning away when he suddenly stopped and sniffed. He seemed to smell smoke.

"What have you been up to? Have you been inside there?"

There was a lot of head shaking, a little too vigorous, and one or two half-hearted nos. He sniffed again. He could definitely smell smoke, and it seemed to be coming from inside the building. He stepped back and looked at the windows. They were too high up to see into, but he thought he could see smoke rising to the roof inside.

"I think the hall is on fire. Are you sure there's no one inside?"

"We did see some people go in," confessed Billy, becoming frightened now. The constable ran back to his car and radioed for help.

"Get the fire brigade here too," he added. "There's a fire inside the building."

"Inspector Hughes and Sergeant Nelson are already on the way over to you" was the reply. "We had a message about some odd things going on at the Blymton Village Hall. The fire brigade should be right behind them."

The other two policemen pulled up as the constable was getting out of the car. Inspector Hughes immediately took charge. After a quick briefing from the constable, he sent his two subordinates to reconnoiter the building and turned his attention to the boys.

"All right, I want it straight, no lies, no omissions. People's lives may be at stake here. Who did you see go into the building?"

"There was a woman," began the gang leader.

"And Tim," interrupted Billy, having decided to err on the side of preserving life rather than loyalty to his leader.

"And Tim's sister too," added the ten-year-old. "Remember when we were here at first—"

He broke off, having caught a warning glance from the leader who was beginning to worry about the hay and their potential culpability for the fire.

"There was a man here too," he said quickly. "A strange man, no one I know. He left the hall a few minutes ago. He was the one that locked the door."

"What did he look like? Where did he go? What kind of car was it?"

The answers to the first two questions were not very helpful, but between them, the boys could accurately describe the car. Sporty but not a convertible, low-slung, shiny black. One sharp-eyed youngster even had a stab at the number. Inspector Hughes barked a command into his car radio.

Sergeant Nelson now came running from the back of the building to report that there was only one other door to the hall, and that too was locked.

"It's another heavy oak door. Won't be easy to break down. But we can hear someone inside there."

"How many? One? Two? More?"

"Can't tell. We've been calling to them, but we're not sure they can hear."

"These windows are too damn high. Isn't there a window at the back too, one that's lower than these?" the inspector asked, and hearing that there was, though a small one, he sent the sergeant over to the pub to look for a ladder.

He strode to the back to see the small window for himself. It was about six feet off the ground, a frosted-glass filled aperture too small for anyone bigger than a child to crawl through. The constable greeted him excitedly.

"Someone's banging on the window from the inside."

"Don't just stand there, man. Find something to break the glass. Dammit, that fire engine had better get here soon!"

The words were hardly out of his mouth when he heard its siren. It was the most welcome sound he'd heard in a long time. And almost simultaneously, the window sprang open, and Tim was heard, shouting for help.

When Mike Hatfield left the hall, he drove off at a furious pace through the village. Once at a safe distance, however, he slowed down. This was not the time to be stopped for speeding. He didn't intend to be stopped for anything.

His escape plan was simple. Simple and as foolproof as his murder plan had been. That had nearly been foiled by Julia Dobson's late arrival and by the unwelcome appearance of a pack of boys. But he congratulated himself that he had handled them well. The hay was a bonus. He'd thought of bringing along a can of petrol to help get the fire going, but smoke would do the job just as well, perhaps better. They'd both be dead long before anyone noticed the fire. Flames might have attracted attention prematurely, and traces of petrol in the hall would have complicated the investigation into these "accidental" deaths.

He patted his pocket where the keys to the hall doors lay. Even when people did realize the hall was on fire, they'd waste time breaking in. He'd checked the back door, the one that was used as an emergency exit. It was locked and bolted. The District Council was quite keen on the exit being accessible when people were in the building, so Dick Parkinson always made a fuss about opening that back door when he arrived for rehearsals. But he always locked it at the end, again at the District Council's instructions, as a safeguard against vandalism. Mike had needed a key to get into the hall this evening. But that hadn't been difficult. He had simply pocketed the front door key, always left in the open door so it wouldn't get lost during last Saturday's run-through. There had been plenty of time to have a copy made and return the original before the end of the rehearsal. No one had noticed.

Yes, he'd thought of everything, everything that mattered. Now all he had to do was to keep his head and follow through with the rest of his plan.

He glanced at his watch. He was running a bit late. He was heading for Weymouth to catch the night ferry to Jersey. If by some remote chance the police did connect him with the fire in the hall and the two dead bodies inside, he knew their first move would be to put a watch at Heathrow and Gatwick airports and perhaps at the major Channel ports. They'd never expect him to head for the Channel Isles. From Jersey, he could cross quickly to France tomorrow, and then he'd be on his way to Spain and points south. He would buy a dinky Renault in France, an anonymous set of wheels to take him to a new life, at which point he could acquire a really top-notch sports car, like a Ferrari or even a Maserati. He chuckled with satisfaction at the prospect.

So he had reason to be pleased with himself. He felt no remorse. *Nobody cares about me*, he had realized long ago, *so it's up to me to look out for myself.* He had set himself a goal: to make lots of money fast—legally or illegally, he had no scruples. He could have made a lot more if it hadn't been for those two women. Another twelve months would have done it, especially if Dixon had come in to help him. Dixon would have kept the legitimate business running, while Mike concentrated on the more lucrative drug deals. He reckoned he could have strung an assistant along for about a year before he began to suspect that there was more going on than simply selling firefighting equipment. But then the women interfered.

If I made a mistake, he told himself, *it was helping Hilary Worthington cover up what she did. Whatever she says, I'm sure it was no accident.* He had seen her get into Dixon's car, and worried that the young man might have talked about his blackmailing attempts, he trailed them to Hestercombe. He'd had to park outside the large gates that Dixon had locked behind him and trek on foot up the long drive to where their car was parked.

There was no sign of the couple, and he was wondering whether it was worth waiting for them to return when he heard the gunshot. He ran as quietly as he could in the direction of the sound. The girl came stumbling down some steps some distance ahead, far enough away for him to duck behind some shrubs before she came running past. Although it was dark and there was a low cloud cover, his eyes were sufficiently adjusted to recognize her. She ran silently, like someone in a trance. He was sure she hadn't seen him.

He soon found the body, lying in a flower bed below a wall, still warm but with life clearly gone. He had to search for the gun, eventually finding it on the edge of the wall. Had Hilary shot him? That's what it looked like. Why else would she run? Could he make use of this? Suppose he made it look like a suicide. Hilary would get away with murder, but he would have something to hold over her if she should attempt to carry on the blackmail. It was worth a try. He wiped the gun clean before putting into the dead man's hand. So what if it was the wrong hand? Why did she and that friend of hers have to start shouting murder? And why did Hilary kill her grandmother? Did the old woman know she was out of the house that night?

He'd done nothing but wait and watch until the second murder. But that was when the police started asking too many questions prompted, he knew, by those women. Some of his contacts hinted that the police were closing in on their activities too, so he didn't want to make himself conspicuous by offering information about what he'd seen at Hestercombe, let alone what he'd done. He began to make plans for departure. Getting rid of the two women was part of the plan. It was partly to make sure they couldn't try to pin both murders on him, but it was partly also revenge.

His drug contacts would miss him, of course. He didn't owe anything, so he didn't think they'd try to find him. All the money he had was rightfully his, what he had made from the highly profitable deals that had been sent his way. He had enough to be comfortable for a while. All tucked away in the glove compartment. A cold thought suddenly struck him. Suppose those boys hanging around the pub had tampered with the car while he was inside the hall? He'd had to leave it unlocked so that he could get away quickly. The packets of cash were too bulky to stow in his pockets. He'd had to leave them in the car. He leaned over to reach the latch of the glove compartment. It was still locked. But the maneuver had briefly deflected his attention from the road. As he straightened up, he heard a blaring horn. He caught a glimpse of the huge lorry that came round a bend in the road too fast and too wide before it rode over his car and carried him to oblivion.

THIRTY-TWO

"She lied to me," said Julia bitterly. "I believed her, but she was lying."

Jack Shaw nodded. "She lied to all of us." He was tempted to add that he had warned Julia that Hilary might be implicated, but he bit his tongue.

It was the day after the fire and the dramatic rescue. All three of those who were trapped had inhaled a considerable amount of smoke, but Julia had apparently not suffered any serious physical harm. The hospital had kept her overnight as a precaution, but now she was home and awaiting the arrival of Emma, who had insisted on coming down from Yorkshire to take care of her mother. But Julia was emotionally scarred. She lay on the sofa all day, drained of energy. Her eyes were dull, her demeanor listless.

Jack had confirmed what she thought she had heard in her brief conversation with Mike in the basement of the Village Hall. Hilary had been at Hestercombe with Brian on that fatal night. Jack had come from the hospital where Hilary, who had suffered the worst from the experience, was still under observation. She had given him a statement. He had not pressed for it, seeing her condition, but the doctor gave the go-ahead, saying that it might speed her recovery if she could get it off her chest.

She had been given a private room, but it was still a clinically bare hospital room, not a friendly environment for a chat. Hilary smiled bravely when he sat down beside her, but he could see the tension in her face.

"When Brian hung up on me that Friday evening, I was sure his old girlfriend was with him," she said. "Since I hadn't seen or heard from him all week, and I knew she was around, I was afraid he was going to throw me over for her. I decided to go over and have it out with him.

"It was easy to slip out of the house without anyone seeing or hearing me. I've done it several times. When I reached the street where Brian lived, I saw him about to get into his car. He was alone, but I still thought he was on his way to see her. He said he was going to Hestercombe to look for his wallet that he thought he'd lost there. But he didn't want me to go with him. Of course, I thought he was lying. Before he could stop me, I'd jumped into the car beside him. We did drive to Hestercombe, and he did find his wallet on the grass where he thought it might be. Then . . ."

She paused here and blew her nose violently. This recollection was clearly painful for her, but Jack made no attempt to intervene. After a minute or two, she continued.

"Then he said he was going to test his bloody gun. He said the bottom of the garden would be a good place to do it and set off in that direction. I followed, trying desperately to convince him that this was a bad idea. I said someone would surely hear, but he said not. He had only a couple of bullets, and even if anyone did hear, they'd think it was a car backfiring. He even laughed that he might hit a cow, but he'd take his chances.

"I followed him down the path through the rose garden to the pergola. There he stopped and pulled the gun out of his pocket. I tried to grab it, but as we struggled over it . . . it went off. He made no sound, just fell over and toppled into the flower bed below the pergola. I . . . I . . ."

She covered her face with her hands. Jack waited patiently.

"It looked as though he were dead. I couldn't believe it."

Another long pause. "And what did you do then?" Jack prompted.

"I ran away."

Jack stared at her in disbelief.

"I know I shouldn't have, but I did. I was scared. No, I was panicked! I didn't know what to do except get away as fast as I could. So I ran home. You're wondering why no one saw me. It was late, there was little traffic, and I stuck to the lanes. When I heard or saw a car coming, I crouched in the ditch or behind a hedge. No one saw me. I ran most of the way, and I was exhausted when I finally got home. I fell into bed and asleep at once, and when I woke the next morning, I was convinced it had all been a bad dream."

"But it wasn't a dream."

"No. And yesterday, at the Village Hall, it turned into a real nightmare. Mike Hatfield told me that he had followed us to Hestercombe. He was the one visiting Brian that evening, and he saw me get into Brian's car. He says he heard the shot and saw me running away, and then he accused me of murder. He even said he tried to cover up for me by putting the gun in Brian's hand so that it would look like suicide. But I didn't kill Brian! I know I didn't touch the trigger. It was an accident. You have to believe that!"

"So why did you insist it was murder?" Jack had to ask that question.

"I don't know. I don't know. I don't know."

And that was all she would say.

"But what about Mrs. Worthington's death?" asked Julia when Jack reported this to her. "Mike Hatfield was emphatic that he did not kill her."

"That's a mystery. Hilary is also emphatic that she did not do it. Although they're both liars, I'm inclined to believe Hilary rather than Hatfield. Since he's now dead, I expect we'll end up concluding that he is the most likely suspect and close the case."

"What happens next?" asked Julia. "Will she be prosecuted?"

"Probably not for murder. We've no way of proving that it was anything other than an accident. But we'll have to charge her with leaving the scene of a fatal accident and with perjury at the inquest. A lot of people will be very angry with her when the full story is known. She has wasted a lot of valuable police time and energy on a false hunt for a murderer. But I doubt she'll be sent to prison. Her youth and previous good behavior will help. I expect she'll get a suspended sentence with mandatory counseling and be on probation for a while."

"What a sad way for a bright young girl to start off in life. How could she be so stupid?"

"Helen's explanation is that it's a classic case of extreme denial, suppression of a very painful memory. When she woke up the next morning, she convinced herself it was just a nightmare. That's why she was so tense the next day at the garden party. She was half-expecting Brian to show up but at the same time half-fearful that he would not. She was perhaps also afraid to tell the truth lest she be accused of murder. She says she learned only yesterday when he was holding her prisoner that Hatfield had seen her running away, but he may have been dropping hints before that."

"Do you believe her when she says it was an accident?" asked Julia.

"Do you?"

"I'd like to think so, but I don't know what to believe anymore. And I'm not sure I care."

Emma arrived later that day. Julia was glad to have her there to keep other people at bay. The toll had been greater on her spirit than on her body. She had emerged from the fire gripped by a dark melancholy, akin to that of the days following Frank's funeral. It was not something she felt inclined to talk about, and she told Emma she wanted to be left alone.

The only visitor to gain admission was Jack Shaw. He came back with a bunch of flowers and a further report about Mike Hatfield.

"Hatfield may have been afraid that we were closing in on him. He was using his business as a front for drug dealing. He imported fire extinguishers from Germany and sold them to retailers and small businessmen. It was legitimate at first, but somehow he got involved with drugs and began smuggling cocaine into England in the fire extinguishers. He wasn't a principal in the business, but his role was a critical one. I expect he was paid handsomely for it. We were hoping Hatfield could lead us to the people who supplied him on the continent."

"What was the connection with Brian?" asked Julia. "Was he also selling drugs?"

"We haven't seen any evidence of that. We think the trouble between them goes back to when they were both in the fire brigade. After you gave me the newspaper clippings that suggested Hatfield might have stolen money from the fire, I ordered an investigation into his business. It turns out that he opened a bank account just six months after the fire with a sum of money that was close to what was believed to be missing. He had a plausible tale about where he had obtained so much cash, and an inexperienced bank manager didn't inquire further. According to Hilary, Hatfield told her while he had her trussed, that Dixon was trying to blackmail him, presumably about this questionable acquisition of so much money."

"So Brian's suspicions were probably correct," said Julia. "Hilary said the first she knew anything was when Mrs. Dixon sent her the newspaper clippings. But I don't know whether that was true or another lie. I remember that at one point she was talking as though she knew what was behind Brian's death and that may have been enough to frighten Mike. That must be why he wanted to get rid of us." To herself Julia added, *I wish he had succeeded.*

She was preoccupied with her own inner turmoil. In the basement storeroom she had been sure she was going to die and had desperately wanted to live. The urge to survive had been paramount. Yet now it seemed a betrayal of Frank. Several months ago she had mourned not only the loss of Frank but also her own survival. She was tormented by the conflict between this fervent desire to live and renewed guilt at surviving Frank's death.

She slept uneasily for about forty-eight hours, alternating between periods of sleep and wakefulness that took no account of night and day. Her sleep was troubled with more vivid, often violent dreams. Jessica, calling on her during a wakeful spell on the second day, chastised her for being so guilt-ridden and gave her a sedative.

When she awoke the next morning after a long night of dreamless sleep, Julia felt much better. Her body appeared to be restored, and her spirits were refreshed. Her survival still seemed a burden to be carried, but it no longer seemed quite so heavy.

Reluctantly, she asked Emma to inquire about Hilary and Tim. Tim, it turned out, had rebounded quickly from the ordeal. Dr. Worthington, with some prodding from Pauline, treated him as a heroic rescuer rather than as a runaway and lavished attention on him for a few days. Pauline was diplomatic enough to let father and son spend time alone together while still conveying to the boy that his welfare was important to her. Tim accepted the overture at its face value and suspended judgment. He was trying to work out the significance of his experience. He suspected that it was a turning point in his life but wasn't sure what to do about it.

Hilary recovered physically in a few days but became totally withdrawn, refusing to go back to school.

"She would like to see you," Emma suggested. "I believe she thinks she owes you an apology."

"She certainly does. I'm not sure I want to hear it, but I suppose I should."

Julia waited another day and then walked over to the house next door. She noticed immediately a marked change in the Worthington household, cheerful flowers in the parlor and a fire that had been thoughtfully lit on a cool, damp July day. Pauline's influence was already leaving its mark. But when Hilary appeared in the doorway, she was pale and trembling.

"I'm so sorry," she said, her voice little more than a whisper. "Can you forgive me?"

Julia hesitated for a moment then went forward and put her arms around the girl. She hugged her for a minute or two then stepped back, still holding onto the girl's shoulders. She looked Hilary directly in the face.

"You'll have to earn the forgiveness. No more lies. I have two questions for you, and I want straight answers."

Hilary nodded.

"First question. Was Brian's death really an accident? No evasions, fudging. I want the full truth, whatever it is."

"Oh yes, yes, yes, it was! I was angry with him, but I wouldn't have done anything to harm him. You have to believe me, you do—"

Julia interrupted her with a shake of her shoulders and a stern voice.

"No, Hilary, no histrionics. Just the plain simple facts. So that death was a genuine accident. What about your grandmother? Did you kill her?"

Hilary held Julia's eyes in a steady, clear gaze.

"No. I did not kill Gran."

Julia stared back at Hilary, searching for any hint of prevarication.

"All right," she said finally.

"I couldn't kill anyone. I don't like any kind of violence. That's why I didn't want Brian to mess around with that bloody gun."

Hilary was calm now. Julia released her grip on the girl's shoulders.

"I'll forgive you, but I can't forget. You'll have to earn back my trust, as I expect you will with everyone else you know. You've really messed things up for yourself. It's going to be a rough passage for a while, but I think you have guts, and as long as you stop trying to manipulate other people and don't tell any more lies, you'll make it."

And there, she told herself, *ends my sermon.*

Nigel phoned that weekend. Julia could hear the concern in his voice as he inquired about her recovery.

"I feel some responsibility for your ordeal since I encouraged you to linger in town last week when you were anxious to get back to warn Hilary. I'm very relieved it wasn't a fatal mistake."

"It's not your fault. You did warn me, and so did Jack, that I could be heading for trouble. And I was a little rash in my haste to rescue Hilary."

"One thing I learned quite early in my profession was that danger often lies where you least expect it. But you mustn't brood about what you did or didn't do. When I come down for the play, I hope you will have put all this behind you."

"I'll try," promised Julia but wondered how easy it would be.

THIRTY-THREE

Somerset police have announced that they are closing the books on the two Somerset deaths they have been investigating in recent weeks. At a press conference yesterday, Chief Superintendent Jack Shaw said that Hilary Worthington, fiancée of Brian Dixon, the first person to die mysteriously, had confessed to being with him at Hestercombe on the night he died. He had been intending to see if his father's gun still worked, and when she tried to stop him, the gun fired accidentally, killing him instantly. The case had been investigated as a possible murder. Charges may be filed against Hilary Worthington for false statements she made at the inquest and in subsequent police inquiries.

Police confirmed, however, that the death of Mrs. Margaret Worthington, Hilary Worthington's grandmother, was murder. "We believe," said Shaw, "that she was murdered by Michael Hatfield, who mistakenly thought that he was killing her granddaughter. We are now closing the case." Hatfield was killed in a car accident two weeks ago after locking Hilary Worthington and Mrs. Julia Dobson in the Blymton Village Hall and setting fire to the building, with the intent of killing the two women inside.

Ruth, sitting at the kitchen table late at night, read the first two paragraphs of the newspaper article for the umpteenth time. She put down the newspaper and laid her head on the table. Everything was going to be all right.

She had known instinctively that Hilary was somehow responsible for Brian's death, though her interpretation had been that Hilary had driven him to suicide. That was why she had wanted to punish the girl. Now that she knew Hilary was at Hestercombe that evening and was asserting that she struggled with Brian for possession of the gun, Ruth was even more convinced that it was no accident. Hilary had actually killed him. Justice would have been served if it Hilary had gone to her death in the yellow oilskin.

She hadn't gone to Blymton with the intention of actually killing Hilary, but she had been determined to do her harm. In conceiving this act of vengeance and during the journey to Somerset, she had no clear idea what she would do but knew that somehow she would find Hilary and punish her for causing Brian's death. It had been a very risky adventure but in actuality very simple. The rain had helped. No one had paid attention to a nondescript woman in jeans and dark windcheater with its hood pulled down over her face traveling cross-country on a series of trains and buses. She had not slept or eaten during the whole twenty-four-hour excursion, so there was no one to remember her ordering a meal or asking for a room. She had no desire for food or rest but was driven by a pure and burning lust for vengeance, her final gift to Brian.

It was dark when she arrived in Blymton. At this point, she realized that she didn't know where Hilary lived. She was reluctant to ask for direction; but even if she risked it, on this wet night, the village was deserted. She wandered along the main street, looking carefully at each house though she didn't know what she was looking for. It was sheer luck that she found the right one. A shingle on the gate of an old house carried the name Worthington. This had to be Hilary's home. It was an appropriately ugly house, unadorned, unwelcoming, no lights in the windows. She opened the gate and crept round to the back, where a broad shaft of light from a downstairs window illuminated a small stretch of lawn bisected by a stone path.

While she stood there, wondering what to do next, wondering too, if this was a fruitless errand after all, a door opened and someone emerged to walk briskly down the path. The person was wearing a bright yellow slicker, its hood drawn up over the head. Some instinct told her that this must be Hilary. Everything fell into place. She had come here, not knowing how she would find the girl or what she would do, but this sighting was a clear indication that she was doing the right thing, that her purpose was valid. Justice would be served. She quietly stepped down the path behind the yellow-coated figure, through a gate, and out into the lane, and then things had gone terribly wrong.

The scarf that she flung round the woman's neck and pulled tight had been quickly removed once she saw that it was not Hilary, but it was too late. The woman had keeled over, a gurgling sound coming from her throat. The scarf was still in a drawer, but she would get rid of it one day. She could never wear it again.

The area by the gate had been muddy, and she must have left footprints. That was surely the only thing that could link her to the scene. She had worn ordinary cheap trainers that she scrubbed clean on her return and later tossed into a litter bin on the other side of Wolverhampton.

When she realized the mistake she had made, Ruth was horrified. She briefly contemplated confession and then suicide. But either would create yet another victim: Adam. She must live and must keep her secret for his sake. It was bad enough that he had lost his father. He shouldn't also lose his mother.

To have the police come looking for her shortly after she returned was cause for alarm. But they were only trying to verify her movements the night Brian was killed. Her pallor and trembling could be attributed to her illness because she had genuinely been ill. The whole excursion to Blymton had happened in a delirium. But in the weeks that followed, she had been living in fear that there would be another knock at the door and questions asked that she couldn't find a plausible answer for. Now for the first time she felt safe.

Hilary was still alive, but Ruth's passion was now spent. Hilary would not escape punishment, though it would be a slap on the wrist compared to what she deserved. Ruth would have to live with her dark secret, at least until Adam was grown, perhaps forever. She thought she could do this. She would certainly try.

She folded up the newspaper, turned out the kitchen light, and went to bed.

THIRTY-FOUR

A Midsummer Night's Dream had to be postponed because of the serious damage to the Village Hall. The flames had not reached the roof or the stage and backstage apartments, but many of the chairs had been burnt, and the inside of the heavy oak door was charred. The stout stone walls were blackened but intact. Smoke and water from the hoses had caused most of the damage. The hall would be repaired and restored, but it would be months before it could be used again.

Dick Parkinson, after consultation with the DeVeres, boldly set a new date for opening night at the Manor in two weeks' time. This interval, he hoped, would be short enough to keep up the momentum and yet would allow time for replacing items lost in the fire. People rallied around, sewed costumes, created new props, and donated items.

As the day drew near for the rescheduled opening night, the weather, for once, cooperated. The native spirits that assure rain for important picnics and cricket matches must have been asleep. The sun shone brightly but not too warmly for the entire weekend.

Crowds turned up to see the play for each of the three performances. Those who hadn't reserved seats in advance brought folding chairs or blankets and spread out over the lawn. Some came for the vicarious thrill of seeing Hilary or Julia or other principals in the real-life drama. Some were attracted by rumors that television cameras might be there. Many felt that it was the fashionable thing to do so that as long as people talked about the Hestercombe murder and its sequel, they could say that they saw the play associated with the dramatic events.

Nigel came down for the Saturday evening performance, bringing Chip and Diana, a postponement of the visit planned for the original date. Emma came back too for the weekend. Seats had been reserved for them toward the front of the formal rows of chairs. A blast of trumpets from some hidden source hushed the chattering audience and sent stragglers scurrying to their places. Theseus and his Amazonian bride strode onto the terrace and the enchantment began.

Despite the delay, the Players were at their peak. It didn't matter that some of the costumes were makeshift and theatrical scenery was nonexistent. The Elizabethan terrace was a splendid backdrop for the court scenes, and the terrace steps provided opportunities for a little slapstick as the Athenian workmen rehearsed their play. A bird singing somewhere in the shrubbery added the perfect note of verisimilitude for the woodland scenes.

It was fitting that, after an evening with Shakespeare's dream fantasy, Julia should have a satisfying night's sleep and wake, feeling better than she had in months. In a moment of inspiration, she suggested a visit to Hestercombe before her visitors had to return to London. After a hearty lunch at The Feathers, steak and chips and homemade apple pie washed down with mugs of beer and cider, they crowded into Nigel's car and headed toward Hestercombe.

The garden was placid under a lavender blue sky where fluffy white clouds idled in the warmth of the sun. Julia led her friends along the now-familiar route down the steps into the rose garden and from there to The Grey Walk. The Great Plat below and the flower beds atop the enclosing walls were bright with color, punctuated by the cool green of the grass borders and the warm pink-gray stone paths. Emma now took the lead, springing up the flaking stone steps to the lily pool in The Rotunda.

"Isn't it wonderful," she exclaimed, stooping to examine a clump of tiny pink-tipped white daisies," how these small plants grow in the crevices of the stonework so that they almost carpet the steps and the walls!"

"Some aren't so small," murmured Nigel, brushing past a large white cistus that straddled across his path.

Julia paused on the small terrace between The Grey Walk and The Rotunda. "This is what I am planning to do in my front garden. Pave it with flagstones interspersed with plantings of soft gray and white and blue. Scented flowers like lilac and lilies and nicotiana."

"Thymes that give off their scent as you walk on them," suggested Nigel.

"Exactly."

By now Julia and Nigel were lagging behind the others. Emma and the two young Americans had struck up an easy friendship almost at once. They bounded ahead to the Orangery and then across the broad sweep of lawn below. But when they beckoned from the east end of the pergola to the other two, still absorbed in planning the new garden for Flora Cottage, Julia shook her head.

"I'm beginning to feel a bit tired. I'll go back to the bench in the rose garden and wait for you there."

Nigel insisted on accompanying her. Julia didn't resist, realizing that this was a chance to talk to Nigel alone for a few minutes. Nigel was the one person with whom she could share what had been troubling her. He listened without interruption while she recounted how guilty she had felt, not so much at being a survivor for the second time but at realizing how much she wanted to survive.

"But that's healthy, Julia," he said when she had finished. "For some, it happens sooner than others, but that's a blessing. The sooner you can get on with the rest of your life, the better. That's not to deny your loss, but you have to learn to absorb it and derive new energy from it." There was a pause, and then he resumed, "I do know what you are talking about. Years ago, I had a very similar experience. It took me far too long to pull through to the point where I could begin to enjoy living again."

Julia looked at him in surprise.

"I didn't know—" she began.

"No, no one did. That was, no doubt, one reason why my recovery was so slow." He put his hand briefly on Julia's arm. "I'll tell you one day, Julia, but not now. As T. S. Eliot says, 'Humankind cannot bear very much reality.'" Then, as if to cut off further conversation along this line, he said quickly, "This is a lovely garden. I can see why you are attracted to it. I hope this death hasn't spoiled it for you."

"No. I don't think bad memories linger in a garden. It's odd that you should have quoted that line from Burnt Norton because that poem was also running through my head. I suppose the rose garden evoked it. There's such wonderful garden imagery in the poem."

"'The door we never opened into the rose garden.' Very apt. I believe children today aren't made to memorize poetry as we did at school. I'm glad we did. It adds perspective to life."

"As do gardens. They can be neglected and die, and yet there's something about a garden that seems eternal. I suppose it's the natural succession of life and death, next spring's buds on a tree behind the autumn berries. Plants lose their leaves or disappear into the earth, but spring always returns, bringing new life. Hestercombe brought death and disruption into our lives, but I believe it will also bring renewal."

Nigel stretched out his legs in the sun and took Julia's hand. "I believe it's already restoring you to life," he said gravely.

"Yes," said Julia. "I believe it is."

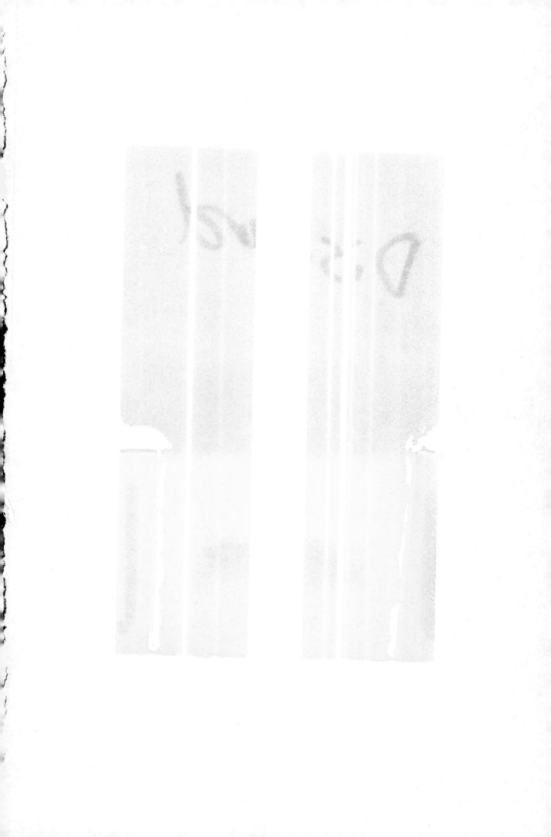

Fiction Vincent

Discard

Printed in the United States
By Bookmasters